Books by John D. MacDonald

The Travis McGee Series

THE
LONELY
SILVER
RAIN

John D. MacDonald

ALFRED A. KNOPF

New York   1985

THE
LONELY
SILVER
RAIN

THIS IS A BORZOI BOOK
PUBLISHED BY ALFRED A. KNOPF, INC.

Copyright © 1985 by John D. MacDonald Publishing, Inc.

Library of Congress Cataloging in Publication Data
MacDonald, John D. (John Dann), [date]
The lonely silver rain.
(The Travis McGee series)
I. Title. II. Series: MacDonald, John D.
(John Dann), [date]   . Travis McGee series.
PS3563.A28L6   1985   813'.54   84-23373
ISBN 0-394-53899-4

Manufactured in the United States of America
First Edition

THE
LONELY
SILVER
RAIN

For Jean and Walter Shine

Every extreme attitude is a flight
from the self – – – the passionate
state of mind is an expression of
inner dissatisfaction.

ERIC HOFFER

Without a family, man, alone in the
world, trembles with the cold.

ANDRÉ MAUROIS

THE
LONELY
SILVER
RAIN

1

Once upon a time I was very lucky and located a sixty-five-foot hijacked motor sailer in a matter of days, after the authorities had been looking for months. When I heard through the grapevine that Billy Ingraham wanted to see me, it was easy to guess he hoped I could work the same miracle with his stolen *Sundowner*, a custom cruiser he'd had built in a Jacksonville yard. It had been missing for three months.

When I heard he was looking for me, I phoned him and he said he would appreciate it if I could come right over. Billy had come down to the lower east coast early and put himself deeply in hock to buy hundreds of acres of flatland too sorry to even run beef on. After he put up the first shopping mall, he went even deeper into hock. He and Sadie were living aboard a junker with a trawler hull at Bahia Mar, living small while he made his big gambles. He was betting that the inland would have to build up to support the big beach population, and he kept right on pyramiding his bet until all of a sudden it turned around, and he became F. William Ingraham, owner of shopping malls, automobile agencies, marinas, a yacht brokerage agency, and a director of one of the banks which had been tightening the screws on him a few years earlier.

He bought waterfront residential land and one day when the house they had planned together, he and Sadie, was half built, she was there one morning looking at tile samples for the master bathrooms when she gave the young subcontractor a strange look, dropped the tile she was looking at and toppled into the framed area where the shower was going to be. She was two and a half weeks in intensive care before everything finally stopped.

They'd been married twenty-eight years and had no kids. He sank into guilt, telling anybody who'd listen that if he hadn't been so greedy he could have cashed in earlier and smaller, with more than enough to last them the rest of their lives, and she would have had a few years in the house she wanted so badly. Everybody who knew him tried to help, but we couldn't do much. He went into that kind of decline which meant he was going to follow her to wherever she had gone as soon as he was able.

But a woman half his age named Millis Hoover pulled him out of it. It took her the best part of a year. She had been working for him. Sadie's house had been finished and sold. And he had sold off everything else, paid his debts and resigned from all boards and committees, and put the money into insured municipal bond funds. He lost all interest in making money, in wheeling, dealing and guessing the future.

It was Millis who worked him around to buying a penthouse duplex in the new Dias del Sol condo, three twenty-story towers about eight miles north of Fort Lauderdale. It has indoor and outdoor pools, health clubs, a beach, boat slips on the Waterway, a security staff, a good restaurant, room service, maid service and a concierge to help with special problems. It cost him one point two five million to buy it and, with Millis' help, to furnish it. One room was set up as a small office, because it was more efficient to have her working there. Then she moved in, because that was more convenient too. She nagged him into using the body-building equipment, into sunning himself, into doing laps in the pool every day, into eating sensibly and even into giving up his smuggled Cuban cigars and his half bottle of bourbon a day.

After he began to take pride in how he looked and how he felt, he began to take more of an interest in how Millis looked and, in time, how Millis felt. And that did not surprise anyone who had been following the woman's reconstruction of Billy Ingraham.

Anyway, I was given the expected security check in the small lobby of Tower Alpha at Dias del Sol at a little after ten in the morning on October 3, a Wednesday, and after Mr. Ingraham had confirmed to them that I was indeed expected, they aimed me toward the elevator at the end of the row.

Billy let me in. He has a big head, big thick features, a white brush cut and little brown eyes. He is instantly likable. In that sense, he has always reminded me of Meyer. Both of them treat you as if you are one of the high points of their day. Both of them listen. Both of them seem genuinely concerned about you.

"Hey, Trav! You look like you been adrift on a raft. You look damn near scrawny. What's going on? Where were you?"

"Bringing that old sloop of Hubie Harris' back from Marigot Bay at St. Lucia."

"Hope nothing happened to Hube."

"Nothing permanent. He fell and broke up his knee. Those two kids of his, twelve and thirteen, wanted to try to bring it back by themselves, but he didn't want them to try. I'm not much for sloops, or any kind of sailing, so the kids were useful. What took so long was dodging here and there, trying to stay away from a tropical storm that was trying to be a hurricane but couldn't decide which way to travel. Got in and they told me you wanted to talk."

"Come on upstairs and we'll have some coffee."

We went up an open iron circular staircase and through a doorway that opened onto a wide patio garden overlooking the sea. The view was spectacular. I could see the deeper blue of the Stream way out. A tanker, deeply laden, was riding the Stream north, and closer, this side of the Stream, a pair of container ships were working south. Small boats danced in the glare and dazzle of the morning sun.

Millis was grubbing at a flower bed. She wore a wide straw hat, a black string bikini and red sandals. She was sitting on her heels. She turned and stood up and dropped her cotton gloves and grubbing tool by the flowers and came toward us, cool and elegant and remote inside her coffee-cream tan, her slenderness, looking out at us through the guarded green lenses of her tilted eyes, smiling a three-millimeter smile.

"Travis, you know my wife, Millis? You know we got married last June?"

"William darling, Mr. McGee was at the wedding!"

"Oh, hell. Sure. I'm sorry. I wasn't tracking real good that day."

We sat on white iron chairs at a round white table and Millis brought us coffee and went back to her flower chores. "I guess you heard about our new boat getting stole."

"I heard it was taken, but I didn't hear any details."

He got up and went away and came back in a few minutes with some eight-by-ten color shots of the *Sundowner*, some of them taken from a helicopter.

"Very pretty," I said, studying them.

"A real gem. Fifty-four feet. Big diesels. Solid as a rock.

What scalds me, Trav, was the timing of it. We wanted to take our honeymoon trip in it right after the wedding, but there'd been a delay in getting it outfitted just the way we wanted it. Well, sir, by the fourth of July I had it all equipped and provisioned, and ready for a test run. We went north up the coast, with me running it fast and running it slow, checking out the radar, Loran, recording fathometer, digital log, ship-to-shore, Hewlett-Packard 41-C with the Nav-Pac for this area. We checked out the stereo system, television reception, AC and DC, the generators, autopilot, battery feed, navigational lights, cold locker, stove, every damn thing. It all worked just fine, but you know me, Trav. I've owned enough boats for enough years to know that when you really go cruising, the things you need most are the things that quit first. She was all provisioned too, even to two cases of that Perrier champagne Millis likes.

"The sea held calm and a little after noon I came to a little inlet I've been through before, but the chart showed just enough water for me to ease through on a high tide and we were a couple of hours shy of the high, so I moved around to the lee of a big sandbar island, worked in close, threw the hook and let it slide on back to deeper water. We were planning to take our trip up the Waterway to New England, and start in a day or two, and I felt we had the right boat for it and I felt good about making that trip. I'd always wanted to do that. We had lunch and some of that good wine out in the hot sunshine and the summer breeze. I dropped off and when I woke up Millis had swum and waded over to the sandbar island."

He stopped and looked to see where she was. She was over at the far corner of the big terrace, working the flower beds. The breeze was from the sea, so his chance of being overheard was very slight. But he lowered his voice so that I had to lean toward him to hear. "After the way Sadie was," he said, "I have one hell of a time getting used to Millis' ways. She was over there shelling, naked as an egg. She's big on nature things, Trav. Jogging and roughage and workouts and so on. The few houses I could see were far away and there were a couple of boats way out, so I climbed down to the rear platform there and eased into the water in my trunks and went ashore to where she was shelling, knowing she would have something to say about people being too modest for their own good. But damn it, Trav, being outdoors naked makes me walk kind of hunched over. I keep waiting for a wasp to come along, or an airgun pellet or a thorn bush. And I don't like being naked in the water either. Crabs, stingrays, jellyfish.

"She showed me the stuff she'd been picking up. She had some little purple shells and she wanted me to help find her enough more so she could string a necklace. So all of a sudden I heard the *Sundowner* kick over. She caught right away. The way I figured it, the damn bastards had come out of that inlet in an outboard skiff, seen us hunting shells, seen my cruiser, then circled out around so they could come up on it on the blind side, where they boarded her, snuck forward and cut the anchor line, then started her up. They didn't start her from the fly bridge where I could have seen them, but from the pilothouse. All I ever saw was the beat-up old aluminum boat they had in tow, with the motor tilted up. It had a milky look the way old aluminum gets in salt water. He took off, swinging way out and heading north, keeping it slow and steady so as not to swamp his skiff. Know what the insurance son of a bitch said to me? He said leaving the keys in the panel was contributory negligence. My God, it was sitting there in front of us! What kind of idiot would have locked it up?"

Billy and Millis swam to the beach on the narrow spit that

lies east of the Waterway. He parked her in some scraggly brush, walked down to where some people were picnicking, told his sad story and traded his gold seal ring for a red and white poolside cover-up for Millis. Her gold bracelet guaranteed the taxi ride back to the Dias del Sol, where the resident manager let them into their penthouse.

"I'm still damned mad," Billy said. "Millis and me, we put a lot of thought and love into that boat, getting it just like we wanted it. Shit, I can afford more boats, but it won't be the same. And I was humiliated, standing there watching some young punk go grinning off with the boat, cash, wine, food, credit cards, car keys and boat keys and house keys, and some of the finest boat rods made. Nobody has done a damn thing. And I've been told you can do things when the law gives up."

"I've been known to strike out."

"You want to take a shot at it? You get thirty big ones cash in hand the day I set foot on her again."

"Lots of pleasure boats have been disappearing these last few years, Billy. And very few have ever been recovered. I don't work on a fee basis. Anything I can recover, I keep half, or half the value."

His thick gray eyebrows went halfway up his red forehead. "Isn't that a little heavy, McGee? I put seven hundred and twenty into that sucker."

"It isn't heavy because I'm talking about the value of what I recover. That sucker isn't a seven-hundred-and-twenty-thousand-dollar boat anymore, not after three months. Also, stolen cruisers usually end up in the drug business, where people don't play pat ball. Also, I swallow my own expenses, win or lose. And it gives me a lot of incentive to look for something that's half mine. I find it in fair shape and it will pay for another piece of the retirement I keep taking now and then. Or, look at it this way. Let's say the odds against any recovery are about five hundred to one. A flat fee would start me out pretty listless."

"If you get it back, how do we put a value on it?"

"Get it surveyed as is by a licensed marine appraiser."

He frowned, and then stuck his beefy paw out. We shook hands and he said, "Done. Tell you a secret. I'd almost give you full value just to get one back at the scum that took it away and left me nothing but a hundred-and-ninety-dollar Danforth anchor and ten feet of rubber-coated chain."

Millis had finished gardening. She hosed off her tools and shut them up in a little blue locker and then came and sat with us. "Billy told me you did find a boat for someone, Mr. McGee."

"Years ago," I told her. "Five at least. It belonged to one of the Cuban buddies of Batista who got out just before Castro removed his head. And he bought a house, a motor sailer and the good life with money he'd squirreled away in Chase Manhattan while he was still a Cuban politico. Those particular immigrants aren't my favorite people. Anyway, he used a Cuban crew, and the wrong batch of Cubans took it right out of its slip at a Miami yacht club and sailed it away. There was joy and rejoicing in the Cuban community."

"How did you get it back?" she asked.

The question was mild, but it had a contentious sound. Just a little too much emphasis on the "you." How could *you* do anything so difficult? And a faint expression of disdain, a challenge in her flat stare. New wife in the long, dogged process of detaching her husband from all prior friendships.

"Somebody told me where I could find the *Aliciente*. She'd been renamed the *Priscilla*. Two months after Calderone got her back, she blew up one night twenty miles off Key West with him aboard."

"Somebody just happened to tell you where to find it?"

She wore an expression of vivid disbelief. "Why would anyone do that?"

"If you've got about a day and a half to spare, Millis, we could sit around and I could try to explain what I've learned about Cuban refugee politics in Miami."

"I'm sure you have better things to do."

"I'd guess we both do."

"What's with you two?" Billy asked angrily. "How'd you both get off on the wrong foot so fast?"

She stood up. "Sorry, Billy. I guess I'm just fascinated by people who can accomplish impossible things." She headed for the doorway into the apartment and turned and said, "What does *Aliciente* mean, Mr. McGee?"

"Temptation," I told her. She nodded, without surprise, as if she had known the meaning of the name and wondered if I did. I saw something in the back of her eyes, something that moved and challenged, creating awareness. We were in a silent communication inaccessible to the husband sitting heavily beside me.

When she was gone, Billy said, "Sorry about that. She always tries to keep me from being taken by some con artist. She thinks I'm too trusting. Hell, I've followed my instinct all my life and it hasn't hurt me more than three or four times. You're giving me a proposition where I can't lose. I pay you nothing, or I buy my boat back for half its market value."

2

On that Wednesday afternoon I drove on up to where the cruiser had been stolen. The town inside the inlet and on the far side of the bridge over the Waterway was named Citrina. New condos and malls were being built at all four corners of it, and parking was a serious problem. The police chief was a happy fat man with several fingers missing from each hand.

I gave him one of my Casualty-Indemnity cards and said it looked as if we were going to have to pay off on the *Sundowner* that got stolen out there at the inlet last fourth of July, and I didn't want to take up his time but just needed to find out if they'd made any progress at all since we last checked with him. Because if there was any progress at all that meant a chance of recovery, and—winking at him—the longer we hold the money, the more money the money makes.

He beamed and told me I was in a rotten line of work, and he lumbered over and got the folder and brought it back.

"Nothing to add," he said. "We got the same two missing persons as before, with no way of knowing if they'd anything to do with it. They were going together and they could have just run off elsewhere." He laid the two glossies in front of me. Even in black and white I could tell that the boy was a buck-tooth redhead. He had a long neck, a prominent Adam's apple and a squint. The girl was cuddly blonde, with an imitation show biz smirk and some acne pits. They were posed pictures.

"High school yearbook," he said, "from two years back. Howard Cannon and Karen McBride. He's a bad kid, comes from trashy stock—drunks and wife beaters. Lots of trouble with the law. She's a dentist's daughter. Her people tried hard to break it up. Too hard. Sometimes you let it go on, and it wears itself out. They sent her off to an aunt in Wisconsin and she hitched all the way back. I've distributed copies to all the interested parties. Got some extras here if you want a set. Physical description and history on the back of each one. Nobody has heard from either of them. Friends or families. Got everybody alerted to get in touch first thing if they hear anything."

"Is it likely they could have done it?"

"Possible. Howie did fool things on impulse. He was with the McBride girl that day. His tin skiff is missing. They had the feeling the whole world was against them. Howie's spent most of his life on the water. He worked at Tyler Marina and she wouldn't let them send her off to school, and she worked at the K-Mart. Maybe he just swung around close to look at that new boat. Climbed aboard and found it was empty. Saw the keys, checked the fuel, talked her into it. Tied the skiff off, cut the anchor line and left. Could have been that way. Could just as easy been some other way too."

"They probably went right on over to the islands," I said. "Safer for dockage and fuel over there."

"Owner left over nine hundred dollars aboard, and it was all provisioned for a long cruise. Nice honeymoon for those kids. Find themselves some little cove down in the Exumas. All fine until the day you have to pay for your fun."

Meyer came over to my houseboat, the *Busted Flush*, that warm October evening to find out how things had gone with old Billy. We sat in the lounge and I told him, and spread the photographs of the boat and the suspects out on the tabletop.

"I think I was working my way around to changing my mind and telling Billy it would be a waste of time, but that bride of his rubbed me the wrong way. So I am stuck with taking some kind of a shot at it. Chances vary from very slim to none. Where *did* he find that Millis?"

"She was working for him."

"I know that. She went to work for him, what was it, two years or three years before Sadie died."

"From what you say about the way he looks and acts, Travis, she's good for him. So why care about her prior activities?"

"Something just a little out of focus there, Meyer. She's a beautiful woman. She's living well. But she has her guard up."

He examined the color shots of the *Sundowner*. "Distinctive. Certainly no mistaking it for a production boat. Beamy. Lots of range. Displacement hull?"

"Yes. Twelve knots top cruising. Fifteen-hundred-mile range."

"Probably been repainted by now. Not too useful for the drug trade. Too small to lay around offshore as a mother ship, and too slow to make night runs to the beaches. All in all, a little too conspicuous to be useful."

I opened a pair of beers and took them back to the table. "Humpf!" said Meyer.

It is his declaration of surprise and satisfaction. It is what he would have said were he to have discovered the theory of relativity.

"What's with the humpf?"

"I was looking for a recognition factor which would probably remain the same. Take a look."

He held up the photo taken from about two hundred feet above the vessel, running at cruising speed across a calm blue sea. He held it so the bow was at the top of the picture, the wake at the bottom.

For a moment I didn't see it, and then it jumped out at me. The bow made a pointed hat. The life rings on the aft corners of the superstructure made the eyes. The half circle of padded bench around the aft of the cockpit made the clownish grin. "A face!" I said. "A damned face!"

"Which can be looked for from the air."

Which was worth a humpf from Meyer. His little blue eyes were bright with satisfaction. Meager as it was, it was still more of a starting point than I'd had before. The profile of a boat can be easily altered by someone intending to deceive. But that someone would not be thinking about how it looks from directly overhead.

So I locked away the photography, and we went out to eat. Meyer waited while I locked my old houseboat and activated my inconspicuous little security devices which would let me know when I returned if there was a stranger aboard, or if a stranger had been aboard while I was gone. In the old days Meyer seemed mildly amused by all this caution. But in recent years he has seen things in a different light, and now uses similar precautions, even though the chance of harm coming to that hairy economist is considerably less than of it coming to me.

Once you have made enough people sufficiently unhappy with your activities and the effect on their lives and fortunes, it is wise to live as though there is a small deadly snake in every shower stall, cyanide in the tastiest cookie. You can solve the problem by becoming a drifter, changing your base at random intervals. But my home is aboard the *Busted Flush* at Slip F-18, Bahia Mar Marina in Fort Lauderdale, and there I intend to stay until finally no one is able to either drink the water or breathe the air.

It was a pleasant night, so we walked the long mile to Benjamin's and had the good Irish stew at a table in the back. As we were finishing, two of Meyer's newest friends moved in on us. Denise and Frieda, visitors from England. He had met them on the beach that morning when one of them had asked him to identify something horrid which had washed up on the sand. Meyer is always being asked questions by strangers. He looks reliable. It was a sea slug. Both women were celebrating simultaneous divorces, and it was easy to see they would look splendid in beachwear. I managed to detach myself, and walked back to the marina alone.

When I opened the little panel in the port bulkhead outside the lounge, the fail-safe bulbs were all glowing, telling me everything was secure. I turned the system off and reactivated it once I was inside. I got out the photographs and sat and studied them.

It struck me that the young man and woman in the pictures—Cannon and McBride—looked dead. When you look at pictures of people you know are dead, there is something different about the eyes. As if they anticipated their particular fate. It is a visceral recognition. These two young lovers had that look. I told myself I was getting too fanciful, and went to bed.

It had been an oddly aimless year for me. Old friends had died in faraway places. In the spring of the year there had been some weeks shared with a lonely woman. We liked each other. We laughed at the same things. The sex was good. Nothing electric. More like cozy. Lois came down to manage a new health spa, one of a chain. What we tried to do, out of mutual loneliness, was make more out of the relationship than it could support. Then it becomes pretend, and you are both saying things cribbed from half-forgotten books and plays. So the structure slowly topples over, like vanilla ice cream piled too high. At the end of it there was an obscure impulse to shake hands.

So I had a few thousand stashed in my bulkhead bank forward, and the only recent expense of any moment was when I pulled out all the old music equipment, the tuner, amplifier, tape deck, turntable and speakers, and replaced it all with mostly Pioneer and Sony. The state of the art had left me far behind, and last summer I kept myself busy putting the best parts of the record collection onto cassettes, and the best parts of the reel-to-reel tapes onto cassettes as well. I set up a filing system. I was like a combination accountant, librarian and music director. I kept the editing function going for sixteen hours a day, and when everything was all neatened up and labeled, I found myself so sick of the sound of music I didn't want to hear any at all, even from a boat moored three slips away. I knew I would get back into it later, carefully. After I'd given the records and the reel-to-reel tapes away to the local jazz appreciation society, along with the equipment I'd discarded, I had twice the fidelity in half the space, very clean sound, crisp as bread sticks. And tired ears.

The only other expense was another Syd Solomon painting. I drove up to a gallery in Boca Raton where he was having a show and picked out a strong little one, twelve inches by sixteen inches, all storm fury and tidal race. He'd put a lot of energy into a small painting. If you want to screw paintings to the bulkheads of boats, you have to pick little ones.

I couldn't think of anything else I wanted to buy. The

Flush was running well. My old blue Rolls pickup, Miss Agnes, was docile and obedient. And there was still a few thousand down below in the waterproof box.

The search for the *Sundowner* didn't promise to elevate anyone's blood pressure. Except maybe Millis'. I knew that if the vessel was in the hands of the drug smugglers, I wanted no part of trying to yank it away from them. Maybe it could have been done six or seven years ago when there was still an innocence about it and the big money item was cannabis. That's when preppies and dropouts and commercial fishermen were going into business in competition with unaffiliated batches of Jamaicans, Colombianos, Cubans and poachers from the Everglades. It was a wild time, often turning ugly, but then the professionals came in and organized it. Those who wanted to stay in business for themselves were dropped into the Atlantic and the Caribbean wearing anchor chain, or they were given to the customs agents and Coast Guard as free gifts, along with their boats and gear. Once the import business was organized, the shoreside distribution was revised, along with the cash flow. The big money product became cocaine. Pot was too bulky. They pushed cocaine nationwide, and controlled the supply to keep the price up. A lot of it could be brought in by mules who could pass customs looking innocent. The Navy, Coast Guard and special agents made the small boat runs too risky for amateurs. The fun lads went under, and the business fell into the hands of fellows from the several Mafia families who, having always tried to keep Miami as a neutral zone, teamed up to run the money machine smartly and efficiently, corrupting and paying off enough customs agents of the DEA to reduce losses to an acceptable percentage.

Bringing Hubie's sloop back from Marigot Bay had been a good interlude for me. When we were pounding along on a good reach in hot sunshine, I spent a lot of hours working with the set of exercises Lois had taught me. She said that when you drive along the streets of Beijing in the morning, you see a lot of Chinese standing all alone, doing the same stretching exercises. It is called Tai Chi Chuan, and looks like a kind of imitation combat in slow motion, with no opponent. At first I felt like an idiot. "At your age," Lois said, "it is very important to stay flexible and limber. Each time you make the same move, you force yourself to bend a little further, reach further."

"At my age?" I had said.

"When there is a tendency to accept constricted movement of the joints."

"And how many push-ups can you do?"

"The question is irrelevant."

And so the post-Lois, post-sailing McGee was down very close to two hundred pounds, with a new layer of deep-water tan, and a match in slow-motion combat for any hundred-and-twelve-pound Chinese person.

On Thursday morning I found the Mick in his office in the back corner of a leased hangar, at the public-use airport at Southdale. He waved me into a ratty old wicker chair while he continued to poke two fingers at the keyboard of an Apple 11e computer, copying data from a yellow pad, grunting with annoyance whenever he made a mistake and had to correct it on the screen. He put the data on disk and then printed it and checked the printout against his yellow sheet. He then activated his modem and sent the data out over the phone. He leaned back in his squeaky chair, waiting. He punched a couple of the keys. Suddenly the printer chattered into life, ran off what looked like a full page of information and stopped.

He sighed, tore it off and studied it and flipped it aside. "Dad bang business is getting more frigging complicated all the time."

"What was that all about?"

"It's a couple of programs called DataPlan and OpsPlan. I got three birds I can get into the air and I have to file plans and routes for the next three days, charter work and package delivery. Key West to Marco to Fernandina Beach to Venice to Georgetown to Abaco to Great Exuma to Clearwater to Staniel Cay . . . to hell and gone, Trav. And you miss filing or change a flight plan without enough notice or run an hour early or late and they are all over you like bug worms, laying on the damn fines and penalties, and taking every removable panel off the aircraft, poking around for Lady Caine. Anyway, this gadget makes it easier than it was last year to run my little operation, but I had to pay a little old gal to set in here with me for a couple of weeks teaching me how to run it. I'd like to sell out. There's two different sets of people after me to do just that. But what the hell would I do with my time? Set on a porch? I hate golf and I hate TV and sunshine gives me the brown spots. What do you want from me this time?"

"You still do the aerial photography?"

"Indeed I do. And I still use that little old Aeronca Champ to do it."

"That old rag-wing still able to get it up?"

"And it'll keep on long after both of us are gone, if somebody loves her enough to get the parts made when they fail."

"Here's what I'm looking for. Confidentially." I slid the photograph across the desk, positioned so he would make out the face Meyer had found.

He stared at me, jaw sagging. "McGee, am I hearing you? You are looking for a damn boat? In Florida?"

"And wherever else you can fly that thing."

"You want to pay for a special mission?"

"Not if I can help it. There's no client picking up the tab. It's all me. I'd like you to work it in with your other business.

Just take pictures whenever you come to a big bunch of boats at a club or marina on city docks or wherever. And when you see the lone cruiser running a waterway or outside, see if it has a face."

"Face? Oh hell yes! I see it. But do you have any idea at all how many boats I fly over, me and my pilots, every day?"

"Just mail me the film. Here's mailers all stamped and addressed. I'll get prints made. Black and white. Fine grain."

"I'll work with wide angle, covers a bigger area. So get enlargements like maybe eight by ten. I got a Nikon C3 with a motor drive rigged to shoot straight down through a hole in the floor, with a long cord on the trigger. But I don't take the Champ to the islands. You said confidential, and I don't make that one by myself often. If I can get away, I like to use the Champ, low and slow. Now I'm ready to ask the big question."

"Thought you might be. What if you find it?" I asked.

"Like finding the head off a pin in seven haystacks. But what if I do?"

"Your piece of the action could be twenty to thirty thousand."

"What if I don't find it?"

"You're out a little film and a little air time, and we'll sit around and cry a little."

"Remind me never to ask you what you do for a living, McGee."

"It strikes me that all marinas look a lot alike from the air, so if . . ."

"I am a professional, friend. I list every shot in order and the list will be in with the exposed film every time."

A thin woman in a red and white jogging suit came into the office, clipboard in hand. "Everything is ready, Mick, except no passengers yet."

He cursed and then looked at the wall clock. "Give them

another ten minutes, Carleen, then go ahead and take off. The other stuff had to be in Key West by eleven-thirty. Carleen, this is a friend of mine named Travis McGee. Trav, this is Carleen Hooper, my best pilot, aside from me of course."

"Of course," she said, smiling as we shook hands. She went on out to wait for the passengers. Mick said she was a fool for work, and had three little kids to support. "She used to do aerobatics in a Mooney 231 with her husband in a twin version. He bought the farm and she doesn't want to do high-risk flying while her kids are little."

I hung around a little while to give him the usual chance to grouse about how too many regulations are ruining flying for the little guys, and too little regulation is ruining the cash flow for the big guys.

3

On Tuesday, the ninth of October, I got three rolls of film from the Mick. I took them to a big commercial lab and had over ninety eight-by-ten glossy prints in hand by five o'clock when they closed.

As soon as I was back aboard the *Flush*, by referring to the exposure notes Mick had enclosed, I was able to write the location where each picture had been taken on the back of the picture. The dimensions of the task became evident. The big marinas looked like so much uncooked rice scattered across a black maze. Under the magnifying glass the rice became the shiny toys of the yachtsmen, chrome and brass, varnish and plastic, cleats and davits, and aerials, canvas and teak.

It was going to take too much of the rest of my life to peer at each craft looking for the smiling face. Florida was too full of boats. I locked up and took the glass and the sheaf of prints down to Meyer's boat, the *Thorstein Veblen*. It is bigger and roomier, brighter and more open than the stuffy little cruiser he had before, the *John Maynard Keynes*. But already the hairy economist was beginning to wall himself in with books, pamphlets, charts, research papers and water glasses filled with sharp pencils.

He organized the search. It involved a screen, a plane projector and a drink while we waited for darkness. Each print required four projections, as the device could handle only a four-by-five area of the print comfortably. For each print he devised a template. Once we had identified a production boat we knew was fifty-four feet long, Meyer would then cut a U-shaped piece of cardboard to size. It was quick and easy work matching the template to the few fifty-four-footers in each segment of each print. Because the pictures had been taken at varying altitudes, from three hundred to five hundred feet, the template had to be recut for each print. As Meyer remarked, had we been searching for anything in the twenty-two-to-forty-two-foot range, we would have been wedged far up the creek. There were just too many of them. As we got used to looking, the templates became less necessary. Our eyes had adjusted to the relative sizes of the usual mix of pleasure boats, and we could immediately spot the marina areas where the larger ones were docked.

We came across several which could have been the *Sundowner*, but each close comparison with the color shot showed some basic structural differences unlikely to have been altered. We became instant experts at looking down on boats from aloft. We looked at them in marinas, in flotillas, in single-file parade on the waterways, tied up to backyard docks and out trolling the deeps.

It was a little after midnight when we finished the last print. Meyer turned off the projector. My eyes felt sandy and tired. Earlier on, Meyer had set out a package of his notorious chili to thaw. We divided it and I went sleepily back to the *Flush* to take a precautionary pair of antacid tablets before climbing into my lonely acre of bed in the master stateroom.

On Saturday I got four more rolls, too late to get them developed and printed before Monday, the fifteenth. The Monday-night session went a lot faster. Recognition of the right size and shape was more instantaneous. But it was dull work. I began to have the impression we were looking at the same half dozen prints over and over. We yawned a lot. The thought of jackpot can keep the adrenaline flowing, but when it seems indefinitely delayed, the brain sags.

And so, one week later, on the twenty-second, when the jackpot showed up in the second print of some seventy we were prepared to examine, it jolted us. "Hey!" we said. "How about that!" we said. "What do you know!" we said. It had all begun to seem so highly improbable, our elation was inappropriately large and lasting. I had scribbled the information from Mick's record on the back of the print. It said "west end Big Pine Key Sunday Oct 14." Meyer adjusted the focus to the sharpest image we could get. There were twenty-two boats in what seemed to be a shaggy little commercial marina on the Florida Bay side, not far from the south bridge. Several with outriggers looked like charter fishermen. The *Sundowner* was the biggest moored there. It smiled up at us.

I couldn't take my information to Billy because all we knew was that it had been there eight days ago.

On Tuesday morning at first light I was heading down toward the Keys, driving a battered old white Chevy pickup with big noisy beach-buggy tires and a Florida tag so old you could just about make out the green number on white from three feet away. But the sticker was up to date. I wore old khakis bleached by sun and salt, a faded red baseball cap which says, above the visor, Bay City Bandits. I wore an old pair of ratty gray New Balance running shoes, without socks. I wore aviator-style sunglasses. I wore a fishing knife in a sheath on my right hip. I wore a yellow windbreaker against the morning chill, and peeled it off as the sun came up.

I had borrowed the pickup from Sam Dandie. He lives aboard the *Merla S.* at Bahia Mar with one or another of his nieces. They like to come visit, he says solemnly, nodding. He invented the Dandie Flotation Gauge when he was thirty-eight, and hasn't worked since. He gives generously to his nieces. Borrowing his pickup is a trade-off. He enjoys driving Miss Agnes. He keeps trying to buy her. No way. I loan it to him and he takes a niece off to Disney World for a couple of days of fun and frolic. He takes one of those bungalows where you have everything sent in, if you wish. He has yet to see Epcot.

I reviewed my preparations as I drove. I had a grungy old cooler with ice and two six-packs of Bud. I had my old plug-casting bass rod, and my good spinner, heavy-duty graphite loaded with ten-pound test. I had the big black tackle box full of plugs, spinning lures, leader material, swivels, hooks and miscellany. And down in the bottom of it, under the last tray, lay the flat and deadly 9mm automatic pistol with the staggered box magazine holding fourteen rounds, wrapped in a piece of oily flannel. No extra rounds. If fourteen won't do it, then it can't be done.

Except for the weapon, I could see no reason in the world why if I said I worked in construction I wouldn't get instant belief.

It took a little while at Big Pine to orient myself. Things look different from on high. It turned out to be called the Starfish Marina. Beer, bait, boats, slips for rent, charter service, guides. The parking area was beside the marina building, a cement-block structure. I could see the slip where the *Sundowner* had been. It was gone, as I had expected. Luck comes floating by a morsel at a time.

The interior was cleaner and brighter than I expected. There were floor racks of fish-oriented merchandise, a display case of reels, a wall rack of rods, a couple of coolers and along one wall a line of bait bins with a constant flow of running water through them. A heavy man in a stained canvas apron was skimming off some dead bait fish which floated on top of the water in one of the middle bins, using a small dip net, and dropping them in a bucket.

"Make good chum," I said.

He turned and eyed me. "That's what they generally get used for."

"I meant that there kind, with the big eyes. They seem to cut up greasier than the others."

He finished and dropped the dip net into the bucket and stood up. "What can I do for you?"

"Has a fella name of Al been here looking for me?"

"Who are you?"

"My name is McGee."

"Far as I know nobody has been looking for you."

"He'll probably turn up. We would want to rent a boat. If he shows up. A green skiff like one of those out there would be fine. And twenty horse with a spare tank. Nothing fancy."

"Do you want to rent one or don't you?"

"Only if he shows up. Last time we were here we did good."

"I don't remember you being here."

"We didn't start right from this marina last time. It was one down the line. But we worked our way up this direction. Got some nice trouts off the grass out there."

"If he shows up, how long do you want the boat for?"

"We'd come in right at dusk. What would that be worth?"

"If you start in the next half hour, call it thirty dollars plus the gas."

"Little heavy, isn't it?"

"Going rate. Leave your car here, you don't have to make a deposit."

"It's the white pickup next to the power pole out there."

He glanced out the window and nodded. He went over to the cash register to get his cigarettes. As he lit one I said, "You own this place?"

"Me and the bank."

"You got the kind of work I'd like to do."

"What do you do, McGee?"

"Construction. But it isn't like it used to be. Nobody gives a shit anymore. Slap it together and sell it off and hope the sucker don't fall down before you get paid off."

"True, friend. True. I got a shipment of six reels in a couple weeks ago. Priced to sell at thirty-nine ninety-five each. Four of them defective. So I pay UPS to ship them back and I'll wait maybe two, three months for replacements or money back. I call up, I get to talk to a machine."

"Well, there's still some damn good merchandise being made in this world."

"Like what?"

"When me and Al went fishing last time, let me see, that would be on Sunday, a week ago last Sunday, when we went by here a couple times I noticed you had a big custom cruiser in here. Looked rich and sassy and really put together. I'd guess at least fifty feet, maybe more. Right out there it was, at that last slip."

"Good boat, but she wasn't kept up."

"Shame to let something like that go downhill. What was the name of it?"

"*Lazidays*. Registered out of Biloxi. Come across from Yucatan. A smart-ass redhead kid running it. Couple of girls aboard." He opened a blue notebook. "Kid's name was John Rogers. Came in Saturday night, took off Monday early. It was fifty-four feet. And it was a hog pen. When I saw how they were keeping her, I made them pay cash in advance."

"They came across from where?"

"Mexico, Yucatan. The redhead didn't tell me that. One of the girls, the blonde one, told me. She came in to buy beer and wanted to know if I'd take pesos. I said maybe, because my youngest, she likes coins. So I bought four different coins for a dollar. She kept scratching her legs and she said the bugs were terrible in Chetumal and I said where's that, and she waved west and said over in Yucatan there."

"I guess these days they check those boats out pretty good, the ones coming in from the west or the southwest."

He shrugged. "Sometimes yes, sometimes no. They're spread thin. Those from around here got into it, some are in the U.S. prison and some can't stop smiling. I wouldn't have the nerve for it. They even use satellites. So these days it's by airplane or real fast boats running at night. And it's none of my business if a boat I rent dock space to got checked or not."

"Mine either," I said. "What you get for this here Mirralure?"

"Four and quarter plus tax."

"Guess I'll take it. Big snook up in Chokoloskee Bay chewed mine raggedy."

"Hard to make them hit a plug."

"I put a little strip of white fish belly on the back-end gang hook and then work it like a wounded minnow. The ones that take it seem to usually be the big ones. Permit take this?"

"Permit'll hit anything at all or nothing at all, depending."

"Never have fastened on to one of those."

"You do, it's something to remember. Best to get a guide for them."

"Too rich for my blood, friend." I walked over and looked out the door. "Wish Al would show up."

"Want to use the phone, see what time he left?"

It seemed reasonable, so I telephoned Meyer collect

aboard the *Veblen* and when he answered, I said, "Al! Al, what the hell are you doing home? I've been waiting here at the Starfish Marina for you. You forget?"

"No, I didn't forget, McGee. I tried to get hold of you before you left but you'd already gone. I've got the flu."

"Couldn't you have phoned here?"

"I forgot the name of it. I remember where it is, but I couldn't remember the name."

"Thanks a lot, old buddy!" I said, and hung up on him.

I explained. The proprietor commiserated with me. I thanked him for his help, started out and turned back and said, "Did that *Lazidays* boat head back to Mexico?"

"I don't know and don't care. Why should you, McGee?"

He had the frosty look of sudden suspicion. I'd mentioned it once too often. I shrugged and came back to the register. "I don't know why I care. When I saw that thang tied up here, Al got pissed at me because I kept on coming by here to take just one more look at it. It was like seeing the boat you dreamed about your whole life. If I ever made it big—too late for any chance of that now—that's just what I'd buy myself. Matter of fact I told Al to meet me here because I thought I might get another look at her. So I guess I must have asked where she went so maybe I could get another look, if you knew where she went."

"You wouldn't like it so good you get a close look, believe me." His tone was casual, the flash of suspicion gone. "I don't know where they went. The redhead come in and bought a large-scale chart of this here end of Florida Bay. He topped off his tanks and took on provisions. See that gas station diagonal across the road to the left? He made some phone calls from that booth there out by the walk just beyond the station. He could have made the calls right on the phone here that you used. Anybody buys that much diesel, they get to use the phone if they pay the long-distance. I wanted a pay phone in here, but they have some damn reason they won't put it in. Going east, maybe he didn't want to run outside. But he has enough boat and the weather is holding. I don't know where he went."

I stopped at the next Key on the way back toward Miami, and bought the same Coast and Geodetic Survey chart. I sat in the pickup in the shade of a fairly big tree. There are no forest giants in the middle Keys. The hurricanes whip them to death. This one was thriving, awaiting the next big whirly. It had probably survived a couple when it was a sapling, able and willing to bend to the ground. I remembered Lois' message about staying limber. I sat and studied the bewilderment of islands and shoals north of the middle Keys. I phoned the Mick from a booth so hot I had to handle the phone in gingerly fashion. His machine told me to leave a message. My message involved where he could put his machine. I crossed the highway and got some fast food and a little further along the road I heard the three o'clock news. Nothing was happening except that a lot of little people were getting killed in a lot of little wars, and there was an out-of-season tropical disturbance forming beyond the Windwards.

I drove right to Mick's hangar at Southdale. Carleen Hooper was sitting beside the Mick's desk. She had on a pale green jogging outfit. Her blonde hair was short and tousled, her face sallow and lined, with big dark smudges under her eyes. She smiled at me and said, "McGee, I approve of your suggestion about the answering machine."

"Didn't think you'd be listening to it, Mrs. Hooper."

"Carlie, please. Mick should be here any minute. And I've got this big damned form to fill out for the FAA. This afternoon I am right in the groove, coming down from Orlando, assigned to twelve thousand, which is just above some clouds forming. I am skimming the top and all of a sudden this little ultralight pops right in front of me. What's he doing at twelve thousand anyway? I would call it two hundred feet. So I am at about two forty knots, which is about three hundred and fifty feet per second. I was just about to go onto autopilot, and if I had, he would have been dead. I had time for just one little twitch which lifted the right wing over him and I had a glance at his face. I think I took seven years off his life, and he took at least a week off mine. I came back around to get a number but those little suckers don't have to have one. It had an MX on the rudder surface. I was tempted to buzz him a couple of times for luck, but with my luck it would have ripped his wings off. He was heading on down pretty good anyway. He waved at me. Isn't that nice? Excuse me, I've got to get this dumb thing filled out. The way I see it, they should have an operational ceiling of one thousand feet and they shouldn't be allowed to operate those things within twenty-five miles of any airport. They look like big dumb mosquitoes."

I told her the fellow was lucky somebody with wonderful reflexes was flying her airplane. I roamed around, looking at the souvenirs the Mick has fastened to the two wooden walls of his office. The other two are glass from one yard on up so he can watch what's going on on the hangar floor. One picture was of the Mick standing on the hardpan in flying gear, helmet in hand, in front of what looked to be a World War II Navy torpedo bomber. It was dated February 10, 1942. The Mick looked about fifteen years old.

When he came in, I took him out into a corner of the hangar far from the two mechanics just finishing up their day, and I told him what I wanted. I showed him the chart. I'd marked the area I wanted covered.

"Okay," he said. "Lower level. Color. Check the hidey-holes. This is Tuesday. I can't do it before Saturday. It will take the whole day. I'll use the Champ and figure on two gas stops. How does four hundred sound? That's a special rate."

"Plus gas?"

"You called it."

"Damn it, Mick, they left the marina Monday morning, the fifteenth. Saturday is twelve days later. Any way anybody could do that tomorrow? Carlie? Somebody?"

"Big rush?"

"I've got a feeling in the lower spine. Lumbar four and five. That's the hunch area. Like they brought something across, and that's a transfer point. Or they're picking something up."

"Let me take another look at that schedule."

He was able to rework his little air force schedule so that he could do a half day tomorrow, in the morning, early.

He went into the back corner of the hangar to check his little yellow chum, his Aeronca 7AC Champion, about twenty-one feet of high-wing monoplane with a single wooden propeller, weighing 740 pounds empty, with room for two passengers, thirteen gallons of gas and 40 pounds of baggage, maximum speed at sea level: eighty-two knots.

"Take me along?" I asked him.

He looked me over and shook his head sadly. "You and me add up to three people, McGee, and I never stress my little friend here, the Champ. One time I put her right above stall speed heading into a steady forty-mile breeze, and she backed up at about five or six miles an hour. I could look down and make out the countryside going by the wrong way. Strange feeling. Tell you what. I can put a Polaroid back on the Nikon, and if the air is calm, I can keep peeling and reloading. Some wind and I'll be too dad bam busy. You could come by like maybe one in the afternoon."

4

Because I might have to take a run down the Keys again, I was once again costumed and equipped to match Sam Dandie's old Chevy pickup. I got to the hangar at quarter to one, and as I parked, the Mick came trotting heavily out, grinning broadly. "McGee, I just didn't dare tell you how bad I need that twenty to thirty big ones you mentioned. Superstition, I guess. Take a look."

He had four shots of it on thick Polaroid film, taken from a lower altitude than I had become accustomed to. Overhead, and one from a lot lower but behind the stern, so crisp I could read the name, and the third of the port side. The fourth was from a few hundred feet up, showing the vessel snugged up against mangrove.

"I think she's empty," he said.

"How so?"

"After I took this shot, this one where I was high over it, I came down and took this one from directly overhead, expecting people to run out on deck like they always do when they hear that little Continental coughing and sputtering like it's about to quit—and never does. When nobody came out, and I couldn't see any other boats around, I buzzed it from off the port side. I came across this piece of water here and pulled up. I got the camera fixed in place. Missed the first two shots. Water in one, mangrove in the other. Hit it clean the third time. I got the stern shot just right the first time. Couldn't get a bow shot on account of the way the mangrove curves around up here, see? After all that, nobody came on deck, and it was by then nine in the morning, and I came right back to the barn from there. She's empty but I don't think she's been stripped. See here? There's a good dinghy, and this up here is a rod with a star-drag reel somebody left on the side deck. So it can't have been empty too long. They strip an abandoned boat fast down in those waters."

"What's this here?"

"Somebody cut mangrove branches to hide her. But she's big. They didn't cut enough, and they've been cut long enough the leaves all curled up."

"Exactly where is she?"

"She's ten to twelve miles north-northwest of where I picked her up in the other picture at Big Pine Key. She's in a jumble of little islands to the north of Big Torch Key, sitting in a bay in this horseshoe-shaped island." He marked an X on my chart. "Look, in this shot you can see the channel coming in. Very tight. She's out of sight from the water in any direction. You'd have to feel your way into the bay to find her. You going to advise the owner?"

"After I take a look at her."

"Taking the law with you?"

"I think I'll take that look first."

"I don't want to see those funds slip away, friend."

"You won't, Mick."

. . .

At first light on Thursday morning I headed out from a place named Faulkner's Fish Camp on Ramrod Key in a wooden skiff with a twenty-horse motor, beer cooler, fly dope, tackle, tackle box, ten-power binoculars and a bait pail full of apprehensive shrimp. I pushed it as fast as the rig would go, and when I got to the area I got lost three or four times among the wrong islands before, at high noon, I found the channel into the little bay protected on one side by the horse-shoe island and on the other by a long narrow mangrove island. There was a gentle breeze from the north, just enough to riffle the surface of the bay. She was there, and the closer I got to her, the more disreputable she looked—like an elegant lady who had stepped into the wrong bar on New Year's Eve.

A lot of her varnish had been sprayed lavatory green and it had begun to flake off. I headed slowly for the stern. I could guess that under the new board, stained driftwood gray, screwed to the stern with LAZIDAYS painted thereon, I could find the thick golden word SUNDOWNER. A sudden shift of the breeze changed the look of the vessel and the shape of the day. It brought that thick ripe sweet stink of death and decay. I killed the motor and curved the skiff away from the stink, and as I did so, I noticed three buzzards in a dead mangrove which stood taller than the rest. Black sentinels defeated by the geography of a cruiser. They were never going to flap down to the cockpit deck, waddle down the steps to the feast. You seldom see them out on the islands, except after a red tide has washed the big dead fish onto the mud beaches. I have a friend who disbelieved the experts who say birds have no sense of smell, and so one summer out in the ranchlands northeast of Sarasota, he tested them. Before dawn he would put dead meat under a white wooden box, and spread several identical boxes around the area with nothing under them. The buzzards would circle above them for a time, and then would always come down to clumsy landings around the baited box, ignoring the others.

And then he realized that maybe it wasn't a keen sense of smell but instead remarkable eyesight. The carrion flies always arrive first. They have a shiny metallic-looking blue-green abdomen, and maybe the buzzards can spot the glintings from a thousand feet on high. Nature has many little tricks which reinforce the interdependence of the species.

It is one thing to look at a mistreated boat and another to look at a tomb. The silence of the bay seemed more intense. And I could see the glint of the carrion flies.

When you have time to think, use it. I wanted to go below and take a look. If somebody had killed people aboard, then trained investigators might find some useful clue. And if trained people were looking for clues, it would not be wise to leave any of my own. I had the illogical and uncomfortable feeling that at any moment a small boat would come in through the channel. I tied the skiff to the starboard corner of the stern, after I had sniffed a little bit of gasoline to deaden my sense of smell. I used the small rag to squeeze some gasoline from the spare tank into a little bottle from my tackle box which had held a remaining trace of reel oil. I wrapped the bottle in the gassy rag and put it in my shirt pocket. I checked the bottoms of the old gray running shoes. The last traces of tread were long gone. I found stiff old cotton fish gloves in the tackle box, kneaded them soft and put them on. I took the pistol from the bottom of the tackle box and shoved it inside the waistband of my khaki pants.

Double-check. My skiff was out of sight to anyone coming into the bay through the only navigable opening. Nothing could fall out of my pockets. I took the sunglasses off and placed them carefully on the rear ledge near the outboard motor. Then I clambered up quickly and levered myself over the transom and stepped down onto the red waterproof padding of the semicircular transom bench and from there to the deck, avoiding some broken glass and a dried puddle of something or other. I stopped there to use the little bottle and rag to kill my sense of smell again. Flies buzzed by me, coming and going. They had a traffic pattern. Down into the shadows of the main lounge through the open hatchway and back out again. One blundered into the side of my face as it went by.

Okay, McGee. If a fly can go down there, so can you. I turned and waved to the buzzards and went below, picking each step with care, pausing on the second one until my eyes adjusted to the shadows.

Someone had done horrid work. I looked at Howard Cannon first. He was the nearest. He was spread-eagled on his back on the floor, with a line from one wrist to the leg of a table that was screwed to the deck, and from the other wrist to the divider between two low lockers. I sat on my heels to get a closer look at what he had in his mouth. Somebody had pried his angular jaw open and inserted a thick roll of bills, of currency, between those buck teeth and then, from the look of the protruding inch of money, they had hammered it into place with the heel of a hand. There was a shiny blue plastic clothespin on his nose. His eyes were muddy slits of white with no iris showing. His face had a blue cyanotic look. I shut my eyes for a moment, breathing through my mouth, hoping no fly would get into one of the deep inhalations. There were some loose bills beside his head, a couple stuck in the blood that had run from the corner of his mouth. I carefully picked up two of the others. Both fifties. They looked perfectly good. Splendid money. Until I noticed that they had the same serial number. And I bent closer to one stuck in the dried blood and saw that it too had the same number. One could reasonably assume there had been some disagreement about the money. Howard Cannon a/k/a John Rogers had lost his argument. And his life. And Karen McBride's life as well. She lay face-down and forlorn on a couch, wearing only a polka-dot sun top. Her dead head lolled over the side of the couch, a tangle of blonde hair hanging. Her left arm hung down, the back of her hand resting against the deck. The flies seemed more interested in her than in her friend. I couldn't make out how she had been killed. I didn't want to touch her. Under the unkempt hair the skull looked misshapen to me, but I could not be sure. There was a dark matted area which could have been blood.

Only the more venturesome flies had gone beyond the main lounge into the forward cabin area. The slender naked girl who lay on her back on the bed had probably been beautiful in life. Dark hair. Clean features. But now the shape of the skull showed, the shape of the bones. She was dwindled the way a total loss of blood can cause. Her slender throat had been sliced from ear to ear, and the knife lay beside her head in the dark mat of blood, a kitchen knife from the galley. The insides of her thighs showed large blue bruised areas and I could guess she had been badly used before someone did her the favor of sending her on her way across the river.

I went back and gave Howard a gentle nudge in the hip area with the rubber toe of my shoe. The body was slack. I know that after death rigor sets in and later the body returns to a slackness of gas and rot, but I had no idea how long that would take. The interior of the *Sundowner* was stifling, a heat that made my shirt and pants cling to me, dark with sweat. The heat would hasten the process. I had a moment of dizziness and once again sniffed the gas. I looked around and realized that person or persons unknown had conducted a search. Drawers dumped, panels hacked open, engine hatches open, food spilled, the contents of lockers yanked out and spread around.

Maybe I could have found the *Sundowner* sooner. And if I had, maybe I too could be wearing a bright plastic clothespin and a mouthful of money.

I was not going to learn any more standing there. And almost without conscious transition, I was back in the skiff, sunglasses in place, chugging away from the *Sundowner*. I put the weapon back in the bottom of the tackle box. Out of some idiot impulse I poured what was left of the gas in the little bottle back into the spare tank. Mr. Neat. In spite of the sun's heat and the warmth of the breeze I felt cold. I stopped the motor in the middle of the bay and vomited over the side. I sucked a piece of ice from the cooler. I wanted to think some deep solemn thoughts about living and dying. But not here, where I felt exposed. I gave the thoughtful, patient buzzards a final wave of farewell and exited the bay, slowly and carefully. But there was no vessel and no aircraft in sight which could have spotted me leaving.

I made very good time returning to Faulkner's and turning the skiff in. There was some mild curiosity about a customer coming back early with no fish. But I said I hadn't felt too good out there, and when I began to feel worse, I thought I better come on in. It wasn't enough of an incident to make me memorable, I hoped.

I cruised ten miles toward home in the pickup before I found a phone booth in the shade, with a door that I could close instead of one of those stupid open shell-shaped things.

The voice on the other end said that it was indeed the Coast Guard I was speaking to, in the person of one rating named Bliss.

"I want to report a . . ."

"I must have your name first, sir."

"Look, what I want to do is report . . ."

"I must have your name and the location from which you are calling before you report the matter to which you refer, sir."

"Now goddamn it, Bliss . . ."

"Those are the regulations, sir."

"My name is Adam Smith and . . ."

"Will you spell that, sir."

I spelled it. "I am calling from Delancy's Grill in Homestead." And I spelled all that too.

"What is the nature of the matter you wish to report, sir?"

"Take this down, Bliss. Take it down carefully because I am not going to spell it. Get your people to take one of the big choppers that have pontoons, and take along three body bags and somebody who knows how to act at the scene of a crime, and tell them to search the small island area ten to twelve miles north-northwest of Big Pine Key, and they'll spot a fifty-four-foot cruiser parked against the mangrove shore of a crescent-shaped island."

"Is it . . ."

"Shut up, Bliss. Just write or tape or whatever you do. The cruiser was stolen last July fourth up on the east coast near Citrina. Its legal owner is William Ingraham. You people have this on record because you've looked for it."

"But, sir, we . . ."

"Aboard that cruiser, renamed the *Lazidays*, they will find the murdered bodies of Howard Cannon of Citrina and Karen McBride, also of Citrina, and also the body of an unidentified young female."

"Jesus Chr . . ."

"They've been dead a while and it is hot out there, so get

on it, Bliss. The island is a crescent pointed north and south, with the open side toward the west. You can tell it by the buzzards sitting in the tree nearby."

"But . . ."

"If they want to go out and tow that vessel in, they'll have to bring it out on a good high tide, right at the crest."

I hung up on him before his voice changed all the way to soprano.

After I gathered my wits I went back into the 7-Eleven and got another handful of change. Billy Ingraham was home. I told him I had located the *Sundowner*. I told him I had put the Coast Guard on it and he was to sit tight until he heard from them.

"Where is it? I can leave in ten minutes and . . ."

"Billy, don't make me sorry I told you. There are three dead bodies aboard her. The two kids from Citrina that were the suspects, and another girl."

"Good God!"

"They've been dead a while. It's one hell of a mess. They were killed in ugly ways, Billy. It's something to do with dope peddling or smuggling or counterfeiting. Listen carefully. I want to be out of this as of right now."

"How bad is my boat?"

"It would break your heart."

"Tell me."

"Okay, structurally she is probably okay. But it will need complete outfitting, above and below. New rugs, upholstery, paint, cabinetwork. I don't know if they can ever get the stink out. New paint and varnish. The heads were clogged. People have been crapping in the bilge. Billy, believe me, you don't want to see her. Lay back, and when they contact you, have her taken to the yard that built her for a complete overhaul, and then I think you ought to sell her after she's clean for whatever you can get."

"Let me be the judge of . . ."

"You be the judge. Okay. But one thing has to be clear, Billy. You never asked me to find her. I never looked for her. I never found her. Clear?"

"But why?"

"There has to be some very rough people involved in whatever was going on. And one team knocked off three people on the other team. I don't want anybody to get any idea that it could have been me."

"Oh."

"As far as you know, you may have asked me to look for her but I wasn't interested. I said the odds were too long."

"I didn't know you could get so nervous, Trav."

"Billy, I can get very nervous, and this is one of the times."

I knew when I reached the Mick I wouldn't have as much trouble making him see the point, and I didn't.

"Three deads," he said, and I heard him whistle softly.

"I am making a little bonfire of the photographs, and if you've got anything around there, you better roast a marshmallow too."

"Very good thinking. Let me see. Why were you trying to get in touch with me?"

"I changed my mind. Forgot what it was."

"What's your name again?"

"McGee. Travis McGee."

"Never heard of you, pal."

I made my final call from the outskirts of Fort Lauderdale to the newsroom at the Miami *Herald*. I told the woman who answered that the Coast Guard had recovered a stolen yacht down in the Keys with the bodies of three young people aboard, and hung up in the middle of the first question she asked. Calling her was easier than calling the Coast Guard. The Guard seems intent on making communication impossible.

I did not feel the inner knots unwind until I had returned the pickup to Sam Dandie, stowed my gear, bundled my sweaty khakis into the laundry sack, taken a long shower in my stall aboard the *Busted Flush*, big enough for a bridge game, dressed in cool whites and fixed myself a hearty flagon of Boodles over ice. I took the drink topside and sat on the sun deck and watched the lazy life of the marina and the homebound bustle of traffic over on the avenue.

Then I let myself think about being young and dying. One of the basic ingredients of good and bad poetry, good and bad drama the world over. The end of all as life is ere begun. A waste of the firm, springy, young flesh, of all the spices and juices. Tens of thousands of the young kill themselves every year. A pity. I wondered if it could be some kind of Darwinian design, getting rid of the ones unsuited for the rest of the ride. But that would leave out the earthquakes, the floods, the little and big wars, the famines and the deadly diseases that knock off the millions without regard to age or merit. No matter how many dead ones you see, indifference is never achieved except by the butchers. The dead young women had rocked me. A cruel waste. The dentist's daughter and somebody else's daughter. Grownups had helped each of them learn to walk, and had cried out their pleasure when the toddler, face screwed up in anxiety, had come tottering into the waiting arms. Somebody had proudly repeated their first words, read their first school papers, bought their first party dresses. And some people somewhere would have a wrenching, stinging, insatiable sense of loss.

I saw Meyer coming along the dock area and so I got up and walked back to the stern rail of the sun deck and asked him to come aboard. He said he would, as soon as he delivered one fine slab of dolphin to Slip E-10, to the Petersens aboard the *Rubiyacht*. I told him to stop below and fix a drink and bring it up. The long twilight is a fine time of day in October.

When he was in the neighboring deck chair I said, "May I tell you about my day?"

"Please do."

And that was another way of unwinding.

5

The weather held fine for the tag end of October and on further into November than we have any right to expect down here on the Gold Coast. The story of the murders and recovery of the *Sundowner* was a mini-sensation which died quickly. Buried in the gaudy news reports was speculation about the identity of the anonymous tipster who had phoned the Coast Guard with such knowing details about the identity of the vessel and the bodies aboard it. It was assumed that he had something to do with the murders and that it was related to the drug trade. There have been so many drug murders and so many deaths of the young in southeast Florida that nothing much new can be said.

There was another little flurry when the third victim was identified as Gigliermina Reyes y Fonseca, of Lima, Peru, daughter of a Peruvian diplomat. She had been traveling in Mexico with a companion and had been reported missing a month before the body was found.

On November 7, a Wednesday, Billy Ingraham called and said he had something for me, and I could come and get it anytime before Saturday. I drove up there the next morning and went up to the penthouse duplex at the top of Tower Alpha at Dias del Sol. Billy's tan had faded a little. He looked heavier and he seemed abrupt, almost surly. He led me into a little study on the lower floor of the duplex. He didn't ask me to sit down. He handed two thick manila envelopes to me.

"What's this, Billy?"

"Your money, McGee."

"How much?"

"Why don't you count it and find out?"

"What the hell is going on?"

"I'm paying you in cash. Isn't that the way you people like to get it?"

I sat down without invitation and tossed the two envelopes onto his desk. I began to realize what had happened. "Billy, I told you not to go look at the boat. But you did, didn't you?"

He perched a hip on a corner of his desk and looked dolefully down at me. "After the authorities were through with her, the yard sent a couple of men down. They got her cleaned up some and operating and brought her around to Jacksonville. Millis and me, we don't want that cruiser anymore. It's finished for us."

"Going to get another one?"

"I don't know. Maybe not. It's a lot of work and responsibility. Millis, she wants to spend the winter in the South of France."

"Why treat me so hardnose, Billy?"

"I don't know. Shit. You're part of the whole picture somehow. And that goddamn dentist calling me up and crying over the phone, and why did I leave the keys in the boat, his daughter would still be alive, and that damn insurance outfit saying take seventeen thousand three hundred or nothing at all, and people asking me how it felt to own a boat people got killed on. McGee, I just don't feel like being sweet and nice to anybody at all."

"How much is in the envelopes?"

"One ninety-three five."

"Okay."

"Don't you want to ask any questions?"

"Why should I? You're not the kind that screws friends."

"You got a right to know. It took eighty-eight thousand to get her back in decent shape to peddle. Part of that eighty-eight was the little piddle the insurance gave me. The yard says they can get four hundred and seventy-five for her. She nets out in recovery condition at three eighty-seven and you get half of that. Here's how I make out, if you care."

"I care."

"I had seven twenty in her that I put in. I put in a net seventy thousand seven hundred to get her in shape to sell. That makes seven ninety and seven hundred. Out of that I get back a hundred and ninety-three five hundred. In other words, McGee, I take a bath for five ninety-seven two."

"A boat is said to be a hole in the water into which the owner pours money."

He smiled for the first time, but it was a tired smile. "Bet your buns," he said. "The deal with you wasn't the best one I've ever made. I can't tell you how many times Millis has told me that. It never occurred to me that three damn kids could do eighty-eight thousand dollars' damage to a boat just living in it."

"And dying in it."

"Yes. That too." He sighed. "And I didn't know a custom boat would drop so much on the market. We designed it to suit us. People who can afford it, sooner get one built for their own tastes and lifestyle. And word got around it's the murder boat. That hurts chances of selling it. Superstition of the sea or something."

"Billy, you're breaking my heart. Want to renegotiate?"

"And you would, wouldn't you?"

"Just say the word."

He stood up and laughed and belted me on the arm hard enough to numb my fingertips. "Shit, McGee, I've got more money than Carter had pills. I just like to moan and groan. A deal is a deal. Don't insult me."

I got up and said, "Has anybody been by to find out who located your boat for you?"

"Three dapper little guys in three-piece suits about a week ago. Only one of them could speak English, and not a lot of it either. I told them the Coast Guard found my boat. They were some kind of Latins. They said somebody told the Coast Guard where to look. I said that was interesting, but I didn't know anything about it. They said that the person who tipped the Coast Guard knew whose boat it was. I said that was interesting too, and maybe it was my insurance company."

"Nice going. Thanks."

Millis sauntered in. She was wearing some kind of black silky jogging suit, and she smelled expensive. "Travis McGee! How good to see you!" she cried, and she did it so well I could almost believe her. "How clever you were to find the *Sundowner* for us."

"Just dumb luck," I said.

"I guess more luck for you than for us," she said. "Can you stay for lunch? Please?"

"Thanks, but I've got to get back."

Billy took me to the door. He said they were flying up to New York on Saturday because there were two shows Millis wanted to see, and also a friend of hers was having a show of his paintings in one of the galleries and they'd been invited to the opening. I told him I hoped he'd have a fine time. He said he hoped so too, but he didn't look as if he believed it.

I decided to give Mick the twenty rather than be picky and cut him to ten percent after expenses. I phoned him on Thursday to be sure he'd be in and then drove over with it. I gave it to him the same way I got it, half hundreds and half fifties in a manila envelope. He undid the clasp and peered in and then he beamed at me, and for an instant I saw how he must have looked as a little kid when he heard he was going to go to the movies.

"Hoo weee!" he said. "Makes my teeth hurt."

"Some well-dressed little Latin types came to my client to find out who found the boat."

"Nobody has come to me."

"They might."

"What boat is that?"

"I can't remember either."

"Wonder who wasted those kids," he said, frowning.

"What kids?"

"Okay, okay, okay," he said. "You get real cautious, don't you?"

"And I'm walking around, talking and everything."

That was the end of it, I thought. Before you tiptoe down the hall, you close all the doors, very carefully. And you don't make any noise until you are out of the neighborhood. Violent people tend to have dim little minds and a tendency to discount all explanations. They would rather hit than listen. The dim little minds have a short attention span, fortunately, and so when jingle-bell time came close, I had made some progress in forgetting the whole thing. There was the occasional unexpected glimpse of the roll of bills in the redhead's jaws, or of the flies crawling across the buttock mounds of the dentist's daughter, or of the kitchen filet knife with the red handle with finger grooves to make it more comfortable in the hand.

And then one day there was a card in my box to pick up a package at the window. It was book-sized, book-shaped, book-heft, and had a department store label, a hand-lettered address. I guessed the card would be inside. I was in a hurry, so I tossed it on the front seat of my blue Rolls pickup and headed over the bridge into town. A still, murky day with an eye-shadow sky and the stink of inversion. I needed an odd lot of boat items, some line, some triple-O steel wool, some brass grommets that would work with my grommeting tool, some paint thinner and a couple of small bronze cleats I had decided I needed to make certain lines aboard the *Flush* easier to manage. There is an open mall on the right a couple of blocks past U.S. 1, with a marine supply and hardware store at the far left end of it.

Even though I had a batch of other errands, I succumbed to my tendency to browse the hardware. I average three implausible gadgets per trip. Meyer predicts the *Flush* will eventually sink from the sheer weight of gadgetry.

As I was paying for my toys at checkout, there was a hard distant thudding sound, followed by some faint sounds in a higher register. I had once heard a head-on collision, and it had sounded much the same.

As I was driving out of the mall parking area, heading for the next errand, I heard the sirens coming.

That evening, three days before Christmas, I heard on the local news and weather that a bomb had exploded behind that shopping mall at a few minutes past ten, killing instantly one Emiliano Lopez, age fourteen, and one Horatio Sanchez, age thirteen. The explosion had blown a hole in the cinderblock wall that formed the back wall of the stock room of a dress shop in the middle of the mall, and done minor damage to a truck parked at a nearby loading dock. The explosion had been so violent only minute traces of the bomb had been found. Chemical analysis indicated an advanced type of plastic explosive, and the authorities said it was reasonable to assume it had a sophisticated arming mechanism. The dead youths had long records of juvenile offenses. As yet there seemed to be no motive.

In the pantheon there must be one god especially assigned to those of us who are amiable, stupid and lucky. I went out to the parking area at a half run and found my present was missing. And I had forgotten that in contemporary Fort Lauderdale one must always lock one's car.

The street children had opened my package.

It should have worked perfectly. I should have been blown to bloody mush. One big white flash in the brain, and nothingness from then on—unless, of course, John Tinker Meadows is correct in his television promises of golden streets and eternal life to come.

When I went back into the lounge, I fixed fresh drinks for myself and for Annabelle Everett. I had known her as Annabelle Harris when she had worked for Billy Ingraham back when Billy had his fingers in lots of pies. She'd married Stu Everett, a local TV weatherman, and gone with him when he'd moved to a bigger job in a bigger city, and she had come back without him when she caught him with the girl who did the eleven o'clock sports.

Annabelle is a tall, broad-shouldered blonde with an off-center way of looking at the world.

"What was that all about?" she demanded. "You look kinda funny."

"I thought I'd left something in the car."

"I turned off your little box, friend. They got from the news into weather, and I seriously doubt I will ever be interested in the weather again. Or sports. You can turn it back on if you are seriously concerned."

"No. No, thanks."

About five minutes later she said, "Hey, it would be nice to have somebody to talk to."

"What? Oh, I'm sorry, Annabelle. I was thinking."

"I wondered about that. Your forehead was all knotted up and you were sighing. I had to believe you were probably thinking. Want me to go so you can think a lot?"

"No, don't go. I was glad I ran into you. I didn't know you were back."

"I didn't expect to be back, but like I told you, things happen. Things happen to people every day. I didn't ever think very much was going to happen to me, but there you go. Married and divorced—well, almost divorced—in fourteen months. We should never have left here. Did you know I was born here?"

"Never knew it."

"The bad thing about that situation in Philadelphia, that sports girl is a little thing with hips out to here and a tiny mustache. I mean it hurts your pride along with everything else. Stu was okay until he started getting fan mail. He never got any down here because he had the wrong haircut. In Philadelphia they fixed him up. The mail started coming in. He grinned into every mirror he saw, and he kept doing that thing with his eyebrows. And taking an interest in sports. He always hated sports. He throws like a girl."

She got up and went into the galley and peered into the convection oven. "We got time for one more drink," she said.

"Smells great."

"Chicken Annabelle is always great, friend. You know why I said I'd come here and fix it?"

"Why?"

"Because you are just about the only one—you and Meyer too—who tried to tell me Stu is a silly shit. Why didn't I listen? The other guys I know here, since I've been back just over a month, they seem to think I'm some kind of practice target. They think they can take their shot and they can't miss. I guess the idea is that a married girl gets it so steady she gets used to it, and she misses it so bad all you got to do is get a hand on her and she gives up, and rolls onto her back. And that is a lot of crap. Right now I feel about screwing the way I feel about the weather."

"And sports."

"Right there! Stu and the Little Mustache can read his fan mail out loud."

As I handed her her drink I said, "I *did* have an ulterior motive in asking you aboard tonight."

"Oh my God, Travis! Not you too! I am twenty-nine and a half years old, and already I need a lift. I wear soft contacts and I can't carry a tune. My feet hurt and I feel about as sexy as Phyllis Schlafly. What is it with you guys?"

"We just can't help ourselves, ma'am."

"I guess I just don't realize how terrific I am. Anyway, what's the ulterior motive?"

"I've gotten very curious about Millis Hoover, also known as Mrs. Billy Ingraham. And I remember you worked with her when you worked for Billy."

"And there, friend Travis, you have your true barracuda. How is Billy? He was damn good to me."

"Right now he and Millis are in the South of France, and I don't think he is having the best time in the world. Last fourth of July some kids stole his new cruiser."

"Somebody wrote me something about that. Nothing but the best for Millis. She took aim at it and she got it all."

"They found the cruiser with three dead young people aboard it, down in the Keys. It was in bad shape."

"Why are you curious about Millis?"

"I saw her a couple of times when she worked for Billy. But not to talk to. I saw her twice up in that penthouse condo they have north of here. The first time she was cold as the well digger's proverbial. The last time she was real huggy."

"Then she either wanted something from you, or planned on getting something from Billy for being nice to you. Everything comes with price tags."

"Tell me about her."

"Not that I know a hell of a lot. Let me serve that chicken first, okay?"

And it was good. She didn't get back to Millis until the bird had been reduced to bones and there were but two more glasses of Mondavi Fumé Blanc left in the bottle.

She looked across at me through candlelight and said, "Old Millis. If I could trade bodies, I'd pick hers. Absolutely flawless. All silk and ivory. And those strange tilty eyes of green. Perfect features. And tough clean through, Travis. There is not an ounce of mercy in there anywhere. I'll tell you something I probably shouldn't. I found out by accident, and I never let on I knew. But she wangled old Billy into the sack long before Sadie died. A very hot, very heavy affair. That's one of the reasons he took Sadie's death so hard. Pure guilt. I'd guess from what I remember of the books that Billy would net out about ten to twelve million. Millis likes nice things. Millis lives for nice things."

"Background?"

"I do not know one damn thing for certain. This is all guesswork. And it was well over five years ago. She hadn't been working in the office very long. Several times men stopped in the office to see her. One at a time. It made her very angry. I had the feeling they were making demands and she was turning them down."

"What kind of men?"

"My old granddad would call them city slickers. Very tan men with hard eyes and Dior shirts and Gucci shoes. Men with fifty-dollar haircuts, imported convertibles, strong after-shave, gold chains and diamond rings. Men who stay in suites and know the number to call to have girls sent up. Maybe they were mob people, labor leaders, or maybe they were important lawyers. She used to get outside phone calls too. They made her furious."

"You mentioned guesswork, Annabelle."

"Okay. From her clothes and her habits it was easy to guess that she had been making more at her previous job than she was making for working for Billy. I think she was in-volved in something that paid good money but didn't have much of a future. So she got out of it maybe because she was scared or tired or something. They wanted her back, and kept after her for a little while. But she refused. Her office skills were rusty, but she got them back fast. And then she started looking around and saw Billy. A new career."

"Had she been living in Lauderdale before she went to work for Ingraham?"

"Oh, no. Miami."

About an hour later I drove her home. She had started yawning. We had agreed it had been a good evening, and we ought to try it again. "Next time I'll cook Duck Annabelle," she said drowsily. "Love this weird old truck of yours."

She was way down the beach in one of the prehistoric condos, renting a one-bedroom job that came cheap because it was on the sixth floor and the elevators had been out of service for a year. The roof leaked badly, but that was up on the tenth floor. There were no corridor lights, so she had to carry a flashlight in her purse. The Condominium Association had run out of funds when the big stuff started breaking. The pool was full of bushes, and the landscaping was returning to its original condition of pepper bushes and palmetto. Only a third of the units were occupied. Nobody knew who owned the empty ones, the city, the county, the banks or the estates of deceased retireds who'd moved into the Plaza del Rio long ago. She was anxious to get a job and move out before she got mugged in the stairwell. It was such a sad and sorry place I was tempted to ask her to move aboard the *Flush* until she got her life rearranged, but I was not ready for complications. She was pleasant and she was fun and she was a handsome woman, and she needed help but she wouldn't accept any.

I walked her up to her door, kissed the tip of her nose and felt my way back out into the night. The book bomb kept going off in the back of my mind, ripping Horatio and Emiliano to bits. That night I dreamed I was looking through a huge hole in a cement-block wall, staring in at racks and racks of bright dresses. I heard a ticking and looked down and saw the package addressed to me, right in front of my bare toes.

6

If someone makes a careful and sophisticated and almost foolproof attempt to kill you and they miss, it is, as Meyer announced on Sunday, two days before Christmas, a reasonable assumption they will try again.

"Also," he said, "one can expect the next attempt to be as subtle and as deadly as the first. You *do* realize, Travis, that the theft of a gift book and an explosion behind a mall may not be linked."

"But I should live as though they were."

"Precisely. Now let's see if we can come up with a list of people that anxious to send you to that big marina in the sky."

We discussed it for an hour and a half, and to my surprise we could come up with but six names, and they went way back, most of them. The seventh was not a name. The seventh, in Meyer's professorial script, read: "Someone who thinks you killed the three young people aboard the *Sundowner*."

"Let's break that last one down," Meyer said. "I say we rule out the dentist. If he thought you murdered his little girl, he might come after you with a gun. But with a certain hesitation. And from what you say, the Cannon clan would not care that much who did in their son Howard. So we have the girl from Peru. I happen to have the clipping right here. Gigliermina Reyes y Fonseca. A diplomat's daughter. Both those G's are pronounced as hard G's, as in 'begin.' "

"Thank you."

"But the contemporary nickname is usually with soft G's. Gigi. You're welcome."

"There were the three little men in business suits who came to Billy to find out who found his boat. Latins. Two didn't have any English, apparently. Why would they want to know?"

Meyer went into meditation for several minutes. He finally said, "We can play with another variation, Travis. Boat owner hires man to get boat back any way he can, and punish those who took it. You will say that it would be out of character for Billy Ingraham to give that kind of an order, and out of character for you to follow through if he did. Yet, in certain circles, that would be standard operating procedure. It might be difficult for them to imagine any other response to theft."

"Then Billy would be a target too."

"If they assume you were following his orders. You would be a hireling, a secondary target."

"Aren't we getting pretty fancy?"

"In testing any hypothesis, one useful method is to carry it to the ultimate limits of absurdity and find out if it still hangs together. This scenario assumes that Gigliermina was well connected with powerful people in Peru, and they are not concerned with degrees of intention or degrees of guilt. The girl is dead and vengeance requires that anyone who had anything to do with her death be killed."

"By a diplomat!?"

"By someone anxious to do him big favors."

"Okay. But back up a little, Meyer, damn it. Somebody *did* kill the three of them. See how absurd this is, for example. They came back from Yucatan with cocaine. Free-lance. He had some kind of contact, and he phoned from the gas station across the road from the Starfish Marina. He set up a meet, and somebody came with the money to buy it. Cannon or the McBride girl noticed that it was funny money, and that turned it into a bad scene."

"But from your description, Travis, it looked more as if the three aboard were trying to buy something with that money. It was discovered and they rammed it into his mouth. If the people who came aboard wanted to buy something with counterfeit, and it was discovered, they would have kept the counterfeit and whatever they came to buy. The ugly gesture said, 'Don't try to cheat us with counterfeit!' "

"It looked like very good quality."

"And probably could be passed one at a time with no trouble, but not in a batch."

"So maybe Cannon didn't notice it was counterfeit. Maybe he got paid already for what he brought in, and somebody hijacked them for the money, searched for it, made them tell where they had hidden it aboard, found it and found out it was no good."

Meyer shook his head sadly, a black bear who couldn't get at the honeycomb. "We're getting too far down too many roads, friend McGee. We need more bits and pieces."

"While they adjust their sights?"

Meyer looked grim, aimed a finger at me and said, "Bang, you're dead."

"That's very funny! That's truly hilarious. Maybe you'd write it down so I won't ever forget it."

"I'm sorry," he said, looking dismayed. "That was out of character. Just an impulse. Everybody steps out of character now and then."

"You seldom do."

"I am as surprised as you are."

On Christmas morning, in a hotel suite in Cannes, F. William Ingraham died of a massive cerebral hemorrhage. It was in the morning Lauderdale newspaper on Wednesday the twenty-sixth. The story covered his many accomplishments in altering the local landscape, and the awards and honors given him. They had contacted a few politicians on the state level, and the tenor of their response was that Ingraham had been a good citizen, civic-minded and responsible, and his death was a loss to all Floridians. The page one article said that the grieving widow, Millis Hoover Ingraham, was bringing the body home for burial.

I knew that Frank Payne, who is my lawyer whose services I seldom require, had been Ingraham's attorney for many years and would probably, along with the bank, be handling Billy's estate. So I went to see him that afternoon in his bank building offices. He was in a new firm. Those fellows group and regroup as often as square dancers. This one was Marhead, Carp, Payne and Guyler. I sat for fifteen minutes wondering how good the legs were on the receptionist. Her desk had what is called a privacy screen. Frank's secretary came and got me and took me back to a corner office that looked like a small library in a British club. Frank shook hands and patted his growing gut apologetically, saying he was about to join a health club. He always says that. I suggested Lois' outfit. He asked me if I had come to change my will, and I said that it was still okay as is, but I would like to talk about Billy Ingraham's estate.

We sat down across the desk from each other and he said it was a tragic thing that Billy had to lose out on a lot of good years remaining, and he said the estate was in very clean condition because Billy had done a lot of neatening up after he sold out his business interests, getting rid of little cats and dogs, small partnerships, shelters, tag ends of land. Everything that could be put into a discretionary trust had been put into it, so there would be very little to go through probate. Mostly the cars and his collection of western art.

"Millis the sole heir?"

"Looking to marry her, Trav?"

"Or get a job in a sideshow handling snakes? Sure. I don't really have to know how she's going to be fixed, Frank. I would guess she gets the bulk, less a few bequests to causes here and there. What I want to know about is insurance."

"Why?"

"Because if there are any policies on him that pay off double in the case of accidental death, there's a chance of collecting."

"Accidental! Look, the man was overweight and out of condition. He had high blood pressure. He had a lot of stress all his life. And he died in bed."

"Is murder an accidental death?"

"Are you nuts, McGee? Have you been watching TV?"

"You know about the *Sundowner* of course."

"I know all about it. I know how much of a bath he took. I know you found it for him. Don't look surprised. That's confidential information, lawyer and client. And I know what you were paid. A nice windfall. I hope you're going to declare it. That's my legal advice."

"I always declare everything that will show up in somebody else's tax records. You taught me that a long time ago."

"What's this murder nonsense?"

"Again, legal confidentiality, Frank, please."

"You've got it."

"Those two little kids who got killed by a bomb last Saturday. The bomb came to me in the mail. I forgot to lock the truck. I was parked in that mall lot. The package looked like a book. When I got home, it was missing. Those kids had petty-theft records."

He stared at me, biting his lip, then said, "And you haven't gone to the police?"

"You know all the good reasons I have to keep a low profile with the local law. Maybe the theft of the gift and the explosion are unrelated."

"Who wants you dead?"

"Maybe somebody who thinks I punished those kids for stealing the boat. And they might think Billy hired me to do just that. I don't know who. If I don't know who wanted to bomb me, then I don't know who killed the little boys, do I? What would I go to the police with?"

"Okay. But it sounds like a very outside chance."

"Can you get an autopsy?"

"Millis told me on the phone the body is being embalmed there. If they did an autopsy there, she would have mentioned it. Jesus, Trav, what basis have I got for ordering an autopsy? You know what would happen. Everybody would think it was Millis I was suspicious of. Somehow I don't want her mad at me."

"What's the timing?"

"Let me see here. She flies in late with the body on Friday, gets in at eleven-twenty at Miami. Decker and Sons will have a hearse there to bring it up to the funeral home. Services Sunday morning, the thirtieth, at United Baptist, and burial at noon out at Elysian Fields, next to Sadie."

"How about unofficial? It would just be the skull."

He thought it over. He shook his head. "I just can't do that and I'll tell you why. Suppose we do come up with evidence of a different cause of death? Even though it's way out of our jurisdiction I would have to advise the local law and I guess they would advise the French authorities. I never had one like this before. I think it can be done officially, but very quietly. I am going to have to use up some tickets I've got out all over town. Judge, assistant state's attorney, doctor, Floyd Decker. Jesus, I hate to waste all that clout, McGee."

"So they bury old Billy and we can sit around and wonder."

"Well, I'm going to have to make out an affidavit saying he came to me before they left for France and told me that if he died over there I was to make absolutely certain it was a natural death. So I'm doing my duty to a client. And maybe Billy told you to check up on me and make sure I do as he asked."

"Easy enough."

He sighed. "I've done dumber things, but I can't remember when."

The call came from Frank Payne at quarter to three on Sunday morning, the next-to-the-last day of the year, waking me from some kind of turbulent dream which faded before I could retain any part of it.

His voice was guarded. "I'm at Decker's. We're in real trouble, pal."

"What do you mean?"

"Leaving out all the medical gibberish, somebody

knocked him out somehow. Probably too late to find out if it was a drug. Maybe it was just a good whack on the skull with a sock full of sand. They then stuck something thin and sharp and curved right into the inside corner of his left eye. Something like a length of piano wire sharpened at one end, stiff wire. So they got it in there and turned it a little bit each time they jabbed. It was curved, so it created massive hemorrhaging, just as if a major artery in the brain had ruptured. No bleeding to speak of at the point of the puncture wound."

"So why are we in trouble?"

"We didn't think it through. There has to be an official report. The finding has to be verified by other medical authorities. We have to move into a full-scale autopsy with laboratory samples of the organs and so on and so on. There has to be a grand jury verdict of death at the hands of person or persons unknown, and everything will have to be turned over—copies at least—to the Sûreté or whatever they call it in France. And because Billy was prominent, everybody around here is going to want a piece of the action so they can get their name in the paper. Trav, the wire services and the networks are going to pick this up, and it is all going to point right at Millis, especially if they can find any trace of a strong sedative when they do the full-scale autopsy. The funeral is, let's say, indefinitely delayed. What they are going to do tomorrow at the church is have a memorial service. This is a real mess. Thanks a lot, McGee."

"Does it make the estate any bigger?"

"Maybe by a hundred and fifty thou, which is like saying the swimming pool is bigger if you pee in it."

"Millis know yet?"

"Not yet. I might go over to St. Kitts for a week. Get some rest."

"You need it, Frank."

"I'll take the wife and kiddies, and my spinning rod."

"I want you to think about something."

"Such as?"

"Millis is a bright, bright woman."

"Granted."

"She is careful with money."

"I'll buy that too."

"It costs a lot less to bring home an urn full of ashes, and if you killed somebody, it's a lot safer."

The silence was so long I thought he had hung up. "Frank?"

"I'm right here. I don't do the courtroom scene but Roger Carp does. I think he could get a lot of mileage out of what you just said. If she still wants us in her corner."

I was at the ten-thirty service at United Baptist. The big church was about half full. Had he still been in business, it would have been full. Commerce creates social obligations. Besides, it was the next-to-the-last day of the year.

I was early and I stood outside until Millis arrived. She'd taken the dark blue Continental out of storage and the man driving it seemed to be wearing the uniform of the security troops at Dias del Sol. One of Decker's pale young men went out and escorted her in, holding her in gingerly fashion by the elbow. She wore a tailored black suit, a small hat with a short black veil, no lipstick.

The Rev. Dr. Barnell Innerlake conducted the service. He seemed hesitant, as though working from a revised script. He recounted Billy's humble beginnings and his good works after God blessed his energies with some cash money.

So I was standing near the door of the big Continental when the guard held it open for the widow. She started to duck into the car and then stopped and faced me. I saw the green tilted glint through the veil.

"You heard?" she asked in a rusty voice.

She was too tough to play games with. "Yes, I heard."

"Come out to the penthouse, please."

"Right away?"

She looked at a diamond watch. "Noon?"

"Fine."

Away she went, small against the back-seat upholstery.

7

The young security types in the small foyer of Tower Alpha at Dias del Sol wore black armbands, and I guessed it was one of the services that went with a duplex penthouse. Or, I suppose, it could have been an expression of a genuine grief. Billy was a likable man, easy to work for and generous.

Millis opened the door as soon as I pressed the bell. She had changed to baggy white cotton slacks and an orange cotton shirt with long full sleeves. She had tied her hair back with a piece of orange yarn. She was barefoot.

She murmured a greeting, bolted the door and led the way back through the long living room with the wide glass expanse overlooking the sea, a room done in quiet blues and grays. I followed her down a short broad corridor into a small room which was evidently her dressing room. There was a dressing table with a tapestried bench and a mirror encircled by frosted bulbs. There was a French desk in dark wood with a maroon leather desk set. There was a love seat and two chairs, two walls of sliding doors which evidently concealed her wardrobe and an arched entrance into a much larger room with a queen-size pedestal bed.

She gestured vaguely toward the love seat. I lowered myself into it carefully. It looked fragile. There were no windows. The room was shadowed. The only light was that which shone through the arched entrance from the bedroom.

She turned the desk chair around and sat, hunching her shoulders and squeezing her eyes shut in a strange grimace.

"This isn't easy for me," she said.

"I'm sorry about Billy."

"He was fond of you. And I resented that, because I didn't want anybody to have any part of him, any part of his attention."

"I didn't know you cared. That much."

Her wistful smile was upside down. "Neither did I. I didn't at first. I thought I was going to marry Billy because I was looking for a safe haven. I thought I was going to marry him because it would mean an end to scuffling. But in the end I married him because I loved him. He made me feel loved. Nobody else ever did that. Wanted and loved."

"He was very proud of you."

She frowned. "So I had to keep living up to what he thought I was. Can that make you a better person, McGee?"

"Could happen. If you get into the habit."

"I guess. Maybe. Anyway, I've been awake since Frank Payne phoned me at five and told me somebody had killed Billy. I've been awake and thinking. There's a pattern to this. It's a very ugly pattern. Plus too many guesses."

"I'm not following you."

"I don't expect you to. Not without knowing more. So I have to tell you more. I don't like telling this to anybody. Did you ever hear of Enelio Fortez?"

It took a deep dip into memory. "Is he the one . . . about eight years ago . . . they found pieces of him all over Greater Miami?"

"Pieces of Nelly as reminders to the others to be careful. They planted the pieces near drug distribution centers. I'd been his live-in chum for three years when they killed him. Nelly got too greedy. It happens to people. He thought he could get away with it, but he couldn't. He just wasn't bright enough. I moved in with him just before I turned twenty. A big fun life. Lots of money, clothes, champagne, flights to Vegas and the islands. A very nice apartment. I heard later that some of them wanted to waste me too, just in case I'd been part of it. But a man named Arturo Jornalero said he would vouch for me. And I moved in with Art. Not full-time, like Nelly. Art has a wife and kids. But he's more important than Nelly could ever have become. He's right near the top, and it is a seventy-billion-dollar-a-year business. So at twenty-two I'd moved a couple of steps up the ladder. And when I was twenty-five I woke up. I saw some lines here by my eyes and some lines across my throat, and I knew that when I stopped being some kind of rarity that Art could show off to his buddies, I would be out on my keister with maybe a little gift of money to ease the transition. After I walked out and after Arturo located me, he sent some of his guys to talk me back home, but I wasn't having any. After a couple of phone calls he gave up. I had answered an ad in the local paper, and I wanted somebody who couldn't toss me out whenever he felt like it, so I took dead aim at my new boss, Billy Ingraham. I wanted a longer future than I was going to get in Miami. I have to tell you all this so you'll understand the rest of it."

"I wondered about you, Millis. You seemed a little out of focus."

"You've got a good eye. You made me nervous. Anyway, right after the identity of the girl from Peru broke in the news, Arturo got in touch with me. He said it was very important, and it had nothing to do with our previous friendship. That's what he called it. Friendship. So I sneaked off to a motel room and met him there.

"He told me that he was facing a very heavy situation. He said that the girl, Gigi, who got her throat cut, was the niece of the top man in the drug business in Peru, in Lima. This man, Isidro Reyes, is the brother of Gigi's father, the diplomat. It is a big powerful family, and apparently this Gigliermina was the darling, the apple of everybody's eye, and engaged to a young lawyer from another strong family down there. Everybody down there was enraged, and word had come through that they wanted everybody involved in that killing to be punished. Arturo said he had been keeping track of me, for old times' sake, and he said it was strange that our lives should cross again in this manner, but he had to find out if somehow Billy had gotten those kids killed in the process of getting his stolen boat back.

"We talked a long time. I told him about you and how you had found the *Sundowner* using aerial photography, and how you had phoned the Coast Guard and Billy the day you located the boat with the bodies aboard. He wanted to know if I was sure you hadn't found it several days earlier and then maybe got impatient when nobody else came across it and reported it. I said I was positive it had not happened that way. And I said Billy would never have told you to get the boat back no matter who you had to kill. And I said that the counterfeit money didn't make any sense in any scenario where you killed them. He thanked me for my time and said I'd been a big help. We shook hands and then we realized how funny that was and we laughed and I kissed him, and that was that. Now Billy is dead. Murdered. And I can't think of anyone who'd want him dead except some crazies in Peru who got the whole thing wrong."

So I told her all about my gift book, and the blood of children sprinkled to a height of fifteen feet on the back wall of the storage room of a dress shop named the Little Boutique. She looked at me in total consternation. "I *know* Arturo believed me. We had good communication. He'd gotten over being hurt and angry. I *know* he believed me. He said it was going to make it more difficult. Usually nobody would be interested in some bloody little mess down in the Keys. Somebody delivered too little or asked too much, or somebody else stepped into the picture at the wrong time. Nobody would care. But this time the wrong person died and so they would have to unravel it. It begins to sound like what I was thinking early this morning, McGee. They can't find out what happened, so they're killing people who *could* have done it, just to have something to show."

"There's another way to guess it."

"How?"

"They found out who really did it and they would rather not touch them."

She agreed, saying that could be possible. I then asked her if it would be a good idea to see if I could find Arturo Jornalero, and she turned and reached into a desk drawer and handed me his business card. Jornalero Management Associates. She said it was in a fairly new office building, the top two floors, two blocks south of the Miami *Herald* building on Biscayne, and half a block west, on the right-hand side of the street. No name on the building, just the huge gold numerals 202 over the entrance.

She wrote a note I could send in to him which might make it possible for me to see him. She sealed the envelope, handed it to me and I put it away.

She hunched her shoulders and said, "I feel as if I were falling and falling into some dark cold place, over and over, down through the dark."

She put her hand out to me, and when I took it, she led me into her bedroom. A very feminine room. Through a half-open door I could see into another bedroom, and on the far wall I saw the vital leaping curve of a stuffed game fish on a plaque. She turned by the bed and hugged me, her forehead against my chest. "Could you just hold me?" she asked. "Just hold me and if you don't mind maybe I'll cry a little."

So we stretched out on her queen-size bed, and I held her close and she cried. There wasn't much to her—just a slenderness, a vulnerability. The vulnerability was what had been missing before.

When the crying had ended, she said, "This is the first I've been able to cry for him. I wondered if I would, when I would. I guess I've never been able to feel very strongly about anyone, except Billy."

Her voice broke on his name, and the tears were not ended. When they finished for the second time, I thought she had gone to sleep. A narrow segment of jalousied window was open. I could hear the Atlantic swells curling and thudding on the beach far below. I could hear faint music from somewhere. Her head rested on my left arm. Her hair was fragrant. My right hand lay against the small of her back. A round hard knee pressed against my left thigh.

I wondered how I had gotten into this. I had not been with a woman since a few weeks before I had flown out to bring Hubie's sloop home. I could feel her warm and steady breathing. I thought about the time I had broken three ribs, and how it felt to breathe. I thought about icicles, hailstorms, broken glass. But nothing I thought of stopped my right hand from stretching the fingers wide and exerting a small pressure against her back. The knee pressure fell away and she came closer. I hoped she was still asleep and had not noticed a thing. But her breathing changed, and she pushed her hips so close she could not fail to notice what all thought of ice and pain had failed to quell.

She sat up abruptly and unbuttoned her blouse and took it off. She kept her eyes shut as though unwilling to watch what she was doing. She made a mouth, as the French say, a mouth of resignation and self-contempt. She knelt, put her thumbs inside the waist elastic of the baggy white slacks and peeled them down, rolled back and kicked them off. She had worn nothing under either the blouse or the slacks. Her body was elegant, sleek as fire-warm silk and ivory, with a deceptive flavor of immaturity about it, the nipples small and pink, the pubic hair a soft sooty smudge.

I would say that there was not a hell of a lot of tenderness going on. We were daytime thieves, rifling a strange bedroom, looking for the treasure as quickly and quietly as possible, hearts racing, hands trembling, small cries muffled. Found it all too quickly.

She came out of the bathroom in a long ivory-colored robe. I was dressed, and standing by the windows looking down at the sea. I turned and we looked at each other, partners in a small crime.

"That's not me," she said.

"Or me either. Wrong time, wrong place." I put my hands on her shoulders and bent and kissed her lightly on the lips. They were cool and slack. "Who can tell what anybody is like? Living and dying, loving and dying. We share the planet with some tiny critters which make love one time and then die. Nine months after earthquakes and floods and the dropping of bombs, lots of babies are born."

"It was my fault," she said.

"It wasn't intentional."

"Who knows from intentional? I gave it a chance to happen to prove that it couldn't. But it did. And I'm ashamed."

"Don't be. Don't be."

As I drove away from the glossy abode of the Widow Ingraham, I appealed to Billy Ingraham to please understand. And I told him we were both ashamed.

She had good reason to want to be held. And maybe one of the obscure reasons for what had happened was that she had confessed a somewhat grubby past to a stranger. The aftershock of confession is lessened if the stranger becomes a lover. Such confessions are more easily rationalized.

I knew I would not seek Meyer's judgment on the whole scene, and I realized that I want him to have a better opinion of McGee than I seem to have lately. The world was a bewilderment and I was having image problems. And so was Millis.

8

I had phoned ahead to be certain Mr. Jornalero was in. I did not make an appointment. I waited fifteen minutes after I sent the note in by way of the receptionist. The other five chairs were empty. There was a small table with a pile of architecture magazines. No windows. Indirect fluorescence. Handsome color prints of various structures on the walls. Small banks. Drive-ins. Office buildings. Each had a trim logo of the JMA initials in the bottom right corner. Elevator music was piped in. From time to time one of the phones on the receptionist's desk would ring or buzz and she would murmur into it, push buttons and hang up.

A phone buzzed. She answered it and told me how to find Mr. Jornalero's office. Through that door, second door on your left.

There was no desk in his office. Some leather furniture, bookshelves, a small conference table, windows with a view of a nearby windowless building and a small slice of the bay and the candy towers of the Beach.

He met me at the door and shook hands and ushered me over to a couple of leather chairs facing each other across a low coffee table. He was a big man, probably in his early fifties. Thick dark hair tinged with gray. Pale face, heavy features, a broad big-boned body with a look of sedentary softness in spite of some expensive custom tailoring. The patterned yellow silk tie had the Countess Mara logo. Yellow gold ring on his little finger with an emerald almost too big to be true. The flavor was of money and power and importance. And an unexpected friendliness.

"Millie and I were good friends for a long time," he said. "We've been out of touch lately. If there's any way I can help you . . ."

"She told me about your coming to see her back in October. She told you I located Billy Ingraham's boat. She said you were upset because the girl from Peru was important."

"Forgive me, Mr. McGee, if I seem a little disorganized. This is the third day of the new year. I've been out of the office for several days. I've been listening to problems since seven this morning and it is difficult to shift gears. I didn't realize why your name sounded familiar."

"You know about Millis' husband."

"Yes, of course. Stories like that get a lot of coverage. How is she handling it?"

"Well enough."

"The news stories imply she is under suspicion. That's nonsense, of course. From talking to her I know how fond she was of Mr. Ingraham."

"Billy's murder seems to have something to do with the girl from Peru."

He stared at me. "I don't see the connection."

"Did she convince you that Billy and I had nothing to do with what happened aboard the *Sundowner*?"

"Yes. Of course. As I told her, it seemed a strange and

horrible way for our lives to overlap again. Yes, she convinced me."

"When I went aboard the flies were working. I had to sniff at a gasoline rag to be able to stay below long enough to see what happened."

"I told you, Mr. McGee, she convinced me."

"On Saturday, three days before Christmas, a bomb went off behind a Lauderdale shopping center and killed two kids. Did you read about it?"

"Yes, I remember reading about it."

"The bomb that went off was, I think, a gift package I had gotten through the mail and hadn't opened. I went shopping there and didn't lock the car, and it is a good guess those kids swiped it and took it around behind the center to open it. The experts say it was a sophisticated bomb."

Arturo Jornalero frowned down at his right thumbnail. Then he took a delicate nibble at the edge of the nail, got up quickly and wandered over to the window, stood looking out, his hands locked behind him.

Without turning, he said, "Let us imagine that the young son of a dear friend or a valued business associate went down to Peru on vacation, and let us say he went up to Cuzco and was slain by thieves on a dark street at night. The bereaved father might come to me and I might make contact with business associates in Peru, and they might arrange to have the guilty punished without waiting for any slow process of law. It would be a matter of friendship and honor."

"Wouldn't they feel some kind of obligation to get the guilty parties?"

He came slowly back to the chair, settled into it and sighed audibly. "That *does* bother me, Mr. McGee. When the girl was identified, there was . . . considerable communication between Miami and Lima. The immediate suspicion was that whoever had tipped off the Coast Guard as to where to find the vessel could have been the one who killed the three of them. People have killed for a lot less money than you got for finding that boat. I told my associates that I knew Mr. Ingraham's wife and that I would look into it. I had a private meeting with her. After that I had someone look into your lifestyle and reputation, and also the character and reputation of your pilot friend out at Southdale Airport. I then reported to my associates that it was highly unlikely that you had anything to do with the trouble, or that Mr. Ingraham was involved in any way, except that it had happened aboard his boat, which had been stolen up at Citrina last July. I told them I thought the murders had been the result of a deal going bad."

"I was very nearly blown to bits and Billy was killed in Cannes with a wire shoved into his head. There was somebody you didn't convince."

"I haven't been keeping track. I am going to look into it."

There was enough of an edge behind his quiet and pleasant voice to make me guess he was going to make some people unhappy.

"What kind of business are you in, Mr. Jornalero?"

"We're an international management and consulting corporation. When, during consultation, we find an enterprise that pleases us, we try to buy into it. So, over the years, we've come up with a strange mix. We own pieces of motion picture distribution and production companies in South America and the Orient. We own portions of factoring companies and financial houses in the Bahamas, Cartagena, Bolivia, South Africa. We have a contracting branch and an architectural service here, and an employment agency and a large interest in a pipeline, and some small coastal freighters. When management is good, we believe in retaining it rather than get into the details of operation ourselves."

"And you're involved in a company in Lima?"

"Several, as a matter of fact. And some of those companies own pieces of companies in other countries, in partnership with us. It gets complex."

"I suppose you'd be in a pretty good position to invest at all times, because you have to handle such a big cash flow coming in from the drug business."

He stared at me, jaw sagging, and then he laughed and thumped himself on the thigh with a big white fist. "Millis has a very active and dramatic imagination. I must confess that while we were . . . together, I did tell her some melodramatic stories about my life. I am an ordinary businessman, and when a woman demands glamor and mystery, one tries to satisfy her. I can assure you, Mr. McGee, I have never *seen* a kilo of cocaine much less arranged for its purchase and sale. I have seen some foolish people at social gatherings snuffing it up their nostrils, an ugly and demeaning performance. You are the victim of a cliché, that any successful Latin businessman has to be involved somehow in drugs. We have a good cash flow because we arrange it that way. We get a good return from our investments and it is corporate policy to be ready at any time for the unexpected chance. Many good deals have fallen through because neither money nor credit was quickly available. Right now, this week, through our banking connection in Hong Kong we are buying some bonded warehouse facilities in Panama."

"Okay, then. If you are so completely aboveboard, what's all this about bypassing the police to do somebody a favor?"

"Do you know the word *pundonor*? It means a point of honor. The girl was sexually abused before they cut her throat. This is very distressing to her family. They are rich and powerful and very, very angry. And they know that convicted murderers can spend years and years in air-conditioned cells eating good food and watching television waiting for the execution that never happens. Personal vengeance is primitive. But in such a case it is satisfying."

"What about the counterfeit money?"

"As I told you and told them, I think it was a deal that fell through."

"Can you tell them again? Can you get to anybody who might know somebody who mailed me a bomb and tell them to get the word down the line to lay off? It makes me very nervous to be stalked by professionals."

"I think something can be done about it."

"I appreciate that, and I appreciate your giving me so much time."

"Tell Millis that if there is anything at all I can do, she need only ask."

After I parked my blue pickup and walked back to the *Flush*, I opened the little panel to see if I'd had visitors while I was away. I was so used to finding nothing wrong that I stood staring stupidly at the unlikely object which had been placed inside the recessed area where the lighted bulbs were. It was a stick figure of a cat made of red pipe cleaners, with whiskers made of nylon fishline. The bulbs were all lighted. I'd had no visitors who broke in, at least. If it was a message, the meaning eluded me.

And when I showed it to Meyer ten minutes later, it did not mean anything to him either, nor had I expected it to.

It was a clear day, chilly in the shade, hot in the bright sunlight, even at quarter to four. Meyer lay supine on a sun cot on my sun deck, his heavy chest pelt glistening with sweat from the exercises I'd talked him into. Meyer equates exercise with obligatory games and all the other enforced boredoms of childhood. But he is never in as bad shape as I expect him to be. I have accused him of secret calisthenics and he looks at me as if I had accused him of watching *General Hospital* or *Dallas*. He says his semi-fitness, a rubbery condition at best, is an inherited characteristic.

I sat in the lotus position on a beach towel on the deck, my back to the late sun as I replaced a broken eyelet on a boat rod, winding the waxed linen around and around and around.

"Jornalero could have been half right," he said from under the straw hat that shaded his face.

"Half right about what?"

"He wouldn't have to have any direct connection with the trade. He's perfectly set up to be a laundryman. If he could absorb two hundred million a year, spread it around the world and bring it back in as wages and bonuses and dividends and fees, he might earn three percent on the transactions, which would be six million."

"Somebody would have to trust him with the money."

"So he would know where it came from. Which, in a sense, would make him a part of the whole mess, wouldn't it?"

"He's very impressive. I'd trust him with money."

"From what he said, do you have any clue as to what could have happened?"

"I think he thought somebody got impatient. They got too eager to show some results and make the people in Peru happy. And it made him angry."

"That would fit," Meyer said. "From October into late December, with nothing happening. So they make some moves just to be doing something, whether it makes any sense or not."

"Maybe he can fix it. But I'm not going to unwrap any gifts."

"Why should they send gifts when they can put a man

with a rifle and a scope sight on any of those roofs over there?"

I looked over my shoulder at the roofs on the high buildings beyond the boat basin. When you aim down at a forty-five-degree angle, you cut the estimate of distance in half. That keeps it from throwing too high. The effect of gravity on the slug is diminished by the angle. I felt a circle of ice as big as a silver dollar three inches below the nape of my neck.

My little chore was done anyway. I had tied off the heavy thread. All that remained was the shellac, and I could do that below. I gathered up the towel and the spool of thread, the knife and the broken eyelet. When I turned to face the distant buildings, the circle of ice slid around my body as I turned, and ended up on the left side of my chest. I forced a yawn, and for an instant the ice was in the back of my throat, then reappeared on my chest.

"Sun's about gone," I said.

"If you say so," said Meyer.

I went below. He went back to his beamy cruiser to await the arrival from the airport of one of his female executive friends, a California lady who owns vineyards and sends him the occasional case of rare vintage wine. According to Meyer, whenever he takes her over to the islands, they sit around and discuss economic trends and international trade. And drink wine. Whatever happens, I do know that each one of his lady executive friends believes in her heart that she is the great love of Meyer's whole life. It shows when they say goodbye. And in Meyer's special way, perhaps it is true. They all are. Not that there have ever been that many of them. Six perhaps. Or seven.

And that evening when I wasn't thinking about dying, I nearly did. Again.

9

I had planned to stay aboard that Thursday night. Christmas and New Year's Eve had been duds. I had long ago given up expecting too much of them. But this time it was even less than usual. The little toss with Millis had made me feel listless and grubby. I had been reading Lewis Thomas and for the first time he depressed me, even when he said that the glue that seems to hold mankind in some kind of lasting stasis is everyone's desire to be useful. Maybe I had a desire to be useful which had no outlet.

For once there was such a fat sum in the hidey-hole that the next segment of my retirement stretched into the misty future. But I couldn't think of any way I wanted to spend it. Maybe get on an airplane and fly to Peru.

Airplanes made me think of the Mick, and reminded me that I hadn't warned him of the remote chance of something unpleasant happening to him too. For once he answered instead of his machine.

After I finished telling him why it might be well for him to keep his back against the wall, he told me I wasn't making very much sense. I told him that a lot of things weren't making good sense lately, but that's the way the world was at the moment. All over the planet, I told him, people were trying to make sense out of chaos.

"What are you drinking?" he asked me.

"At the moment, coffee."

"Keep right on with it, pal," he said, and hung up.

Ten seconds later came the muted bong as somebody trod on the mat at the head of my stubby gangplank to the aft deck, and moments later a fast rapping on the door to the lounge, and a voice calling, "Hey, Trav! Hey, McGee!"

It was Annabelle Everett, with a wide happy smile and a bottle of chilled domestic champagne, to tell me she had, that morning, gone to work in a travel agency, loved the people she was working with, had found the computer easy to operate and was going to move in with one of the girls who worked there because the one who had quit, whose job she had taken, was getting married and moving out to Texas. Annabelle was on a high. I got out the ice bucket and opened the champagne and put on some music. She had gotten all her morale back in one fell swoop. So she wanted to celebrate with one person who had tried to tell her that marrying Stu the weatherman was not a really outstanding idea.

The champagne was slightly acidic, and later on at the steak house the steaks were stringy, the drinks watery, but nothing could quell her spirits. I drove her back to her sixth-floor walk-up apartment in that dying condominium, the Plaza del Rio, walked up with her and went in on invitation. She was beginning to unravel at the edges. Her eyes began wobbling. I insisted we have one more little drink. She had some cheap scotch and I made hers stiff. Then I took my time drinking my weak one. When I had finished I took our glasses out into the small kitchen and rinsed them and put them upside down on the drainboard.

I checked the bedroom and found a king-size bed. I turned it down, went out and gathered her up and carried her in and put her on the bed. I felt very prim and sanctimonious. And then I realized that, after all, she had been celebrating, and she had made it clear what she wanted the end of the evening to be. I shook her to make certain she couldn't wake up, and then I stripped her and left her clothes in what would look like hasty disarray, some on the floor, some on a chair. I covered her up, then rumpled up the bed, both on her side and on what was intended to be mine.

I found a lipstick and wrote on her bathroom mirror: "Thanks for everything, Trav." I left a night light on and let myself out, making certain the door locked when I closed it. After all, a girl needs her pride.

I was so pleased with myself I almost missed the slight movement of a shadow in the condo parking area. The parking area had not been lighted at night for a long time. What light there was came from the high white glare of a fast-food enterprise a half block away. Half the area was in blackness, and in the other half, where I had parked, the distant light made long black shadows on the broken asphalt, shadows of the cars and the overgrown bushes. There were maybe twenty cars in the lot, and they were parked fairly close together in that part of the lot closest to the entrance.

I backed up and waited for a car to start up, or for the sound of someone breaking into a car. Caution is a habit, dearly acquired. Caution must be accompanied, whenever required, by the necessary flow of adrenaline, to make the machinery work all the better. I was in the best shape of the past two years. I am gifted from birth with a lot of quick. The hand-eye coordination is better than most. The four inches over six feet provides leverage. Looking slow and lazy helps also.

When nothing happened, I eased along the side of the building, staying in blackness, feeling ahead with each foot before putting my weight on it. The shadow could have been a neighborhood dog, angling across the area. When I reached the rear corner of the building, I waited again. There was a faint light from the other direction, and if I went further I would step out into it. My night vision was improving the longer I waited. I could see the outline of my Rolls pickup. And as I watched it, the outline changed. A man was on the far side of it, moving from the cab toward the tailgate, moving from my left to my right. I saw a faint red arc as he lifted a cigarette into view above the truck bed, moved it to his mouth and lowered it again, then turned and walked back. When his silhouette disappeared behind the cab, I ran silently toward the dark shadow of the nearest car, bending low, running at half speed. It was three cars from my own. The only way I could avoid the light was to work my way under the cars. I stretched out on my back and eased under two cars, pulling myself along by finding handholds on the undersides of the cars.

I crouched quietly in the shadow of the car parked next to mine.

"Son of a bitch'll probably stay up there with her and screw her all night."

The voice was startlingly close. A bad-tempered voice, muttering. And too close. I did not understand it until I felt the car I was touching move slightly. The voice was sitting in the car. I made myself smaller against the side of the car.

"Shut your face, Sully," a thinner, higher voice said. It was inside the car also. It had the flavor of command.

There was a scrape of leather on hardpan, and then a

third voice, and I guessed it was Cigarette moving over from my truck to the far side of the sedan. "What's with the conversation, guys?" His voice was soft and guarded.

"Sully's getting tired of waiting."

"So am I," Cigarette said. "Want we should go up there and take him?"

"Forget it," said the voice of command. "Too much can go wrong."

Sully said, "We were lucky nothing went wrong already, the way you followed so close."

"Knock it off, both of you. Cappy wants it done soon as we can. An accident. Shut up and wait."

I spent ten silent minutes wondering what the hell I was going to do next. Three of them, planning to give me a fatal accident. Let me count the ways. I had not spotted anyone following me. I am always on the watch for a tail. So the man was good. Maybe he had the car rigged for two sets of headlights. That would do it, at night.

Sully made my mind up for me. "I'm going to get out and move around some."

"Go ahead."

He got out my side. It was a four-door sedan, and he opened the back door as I squirmed back away from him. If he headed toward the rear of the car, I was fine for the moment. But he came toward me and his knee hit my shoulder.

As he grunted with surprise, I lunged up and grabbed him by the clothing and yanked him down, turning him as I brought him down, turning him away from the car, using leverage to drop him on his back. His head made a melony sound against the hardpan and he went loose. Somebody yelled, and as I got up, I drove my shoulder into the reopening door of the car, hammering it shut. But it didn't slam. It bounced off something, and a man screamed so loudly I guessed that he had his hand on the doorframe to pull himself up out of the seat. I scooted around the back end of the sedan, looking hard and fast for Cigarette. Nowhere in sight. I froze and then, as I heard a grunt of effort behind me, I dropped with the top of my left shoulder ablaze, swung my legs around and kicked his legs out from under him. As he went down I saw the glint of the blade in his hand. I bounded up before he did, and kicked him in the face with the side of my shoe as he started up. He rolled all the way over and ended up on his hands and knees, and so I kicked him again. Hands can be fragile. Broken hands hurt like sin. He ended up on his back, knife tinkling away under one of the cars. I didn't want to stay for names and serial numbers. I didn't know how badly I was bleeding. I piled into the pickup, started it in a hurry and backed out in a big swing, turning my lights on as I started forward. The one I had thumped first came wobbling out from beyond the other car. He came right out in front of the pickup, then tried to turn and run, but he entangled his feet and fell. I swerved away from the major portion of him, but my right front wheel went over both his knees, making a sickening celery sound, accompanied by a high gargling scream.

I kept checking myself on the fast ride back, listening to see if I felt faint or dizzy. My shirt was sopping wet in the shoulder area. I got aboard without incident, peeled the shirt off as soon as I was aboard and buttoned up.

Then I checked myself with mirrors. It was such a tiny gouge I almost felt let down. I had ducked almost all the way beneath the thrust. It had sliced the very top ridge of the muscle, torn some nerves, opened some blood vessels, but could almost be covered by a Band-Aid. I held cold-water pads on it until the bleeding stopped, and then used a mild antiseptic and pulled the edges together with narrow strips of tape. It was awkward having to work using the mirror, and the final product looked clumsy, but it was a lot better than where he had wanted to plant the blade—right to the hilt, six inches lower. And how had they planned to make *that* look like an accident? Maybe they had planned an accident so totally messy nobody would notice a knife wound.

I stretched out and unwound with a flagon of Boodles and ice. I had ruined one hand, one set of knees and the lower half of a face. Three men, one of whom was named Sully, taking orders from someone named Cappy. Reasonably competent professionals waiting for me in the dark, to inflict an accidental death. Maybe Jornalero had not moved quickly enough. Or had not believed me. At least I could give Jornalero a name now. And I could watch him closely to see what happened when I gave him the name.

On Friday morning Jornalero saw me immediately. He said it was a beautiful morning. No dispute. Bright and cool. He said he had been up very early for a sunrise sail on his catamaran. He said that his resolution for the new year was to do more sailing and get in better shape. I said my resolution was to keep breathing.

"Is there any reason to think you might not, Mr. McGee?"

I told him my three reasons. I could not give good descriptions of the men, but I had noticed that it was a recent dark-colored, four-door Pontiac, license USL 901. And the three men discussed giving me an accidental death on the orders of one Cappy. The only other name I had was Sully, who would probably never walk really well again. The expression on his face showed dismay and concern.

"I don't understand this at all," he said. "I was told there could have been a misunderstanding and I said that it would be wise to correct it, and I was told that it would be corrected right away. Would you please go back out to reception while I make a few phone calls."

It was a long fifteen minutes before he sent for me. He seemed depressed. "Sit down, Mr. McGee. Certain people found your performance last night impressive. I must say that I do too."

"I made a call last night to a friend to see if it was police business, but there was no sheet on it, so I guess they didn't check into a Lauderdale hospital."

"They managed to drive to . . . a different city. They're receiving medical attention."

"Why the foul-up?"

"I'm very sorry, but I have been told not to discuss this with you any further."

"What the hell does that mean?"

"They want to settle for you. And close the books."

"Look, does anybody disagree that Billy didn't order the killings and I didn't do them?"

"I think it's understood."

"Then *why*, damn it?"

"Let's just say it cleans up a certain situation."

"There are men doing life in the slam because somebody wanted to clean up a certain situation."

"Precisely."

"And you are not kidding me?"

"I *am* telling you more than I should. I will even suggest to you that you take the money you received for recovering that yacht, and go away for a year or two."

"Can you introduce me to somebody I can talk to about this mess?"

"Out of the question. Sorry I can't be of any more help." He stood up. My signal to go.

"I have the funny feeling, Arturo, you would have helped if you could."

"Sometimes there are no choices," he said.

I kept hearing him say that as I drove through heavy

traffic out of the city and north on the Interstate. I could eliminate my choices one by one. Go to the authorities? And what seems to be the trouble, sir? Well, some people want to kill me. Why is that? Because I located a boat with dead people on it. Did you kill them? No, sir. Oh, I see. They think you did! No, they know I didn't. Then why do they want to kill you? I think because they have to kill somebody—just to show they're on the job. Okay, who are these people? I haven't any idea. How do you know they want to kill you? They keep trying. I see. Mr. McGee, I am going to arrange an appointment for you with a man whose job it is to listen to people's troubles and problems.

Or I could undo the umbilical cords that affix the *Busted Flush* to the slip, and head down around the peninsula and somewhere up the other side. Find a place where I could anchor out, and use the dinghy for shoreside supplies, live small and careful. And longer.

Or close up the *Flush* and fly to Cairns up there at the top end of Australia. Summer there, and the fishing is good. Walk over to the aquarium at feeding time and study the dwarf crocodiles and think about Jornalero's associates. Sample the brawny Australian beach lassies who can windsurf all day without tiring a single muscle.

Hang around and let them keep trying.

When I walked out to the *Flush* I found a man sitting on the finger pier, legs dangling, staring at the *Flush* and tapping cigar ashes into the water. He looked fat, but from the way he came to his feet, all in one motion, I knew he was in better shape than he looked. He wore a blue work shirt and khaki pants, a Greek seaman's cap and thick leather sandals. He was short and broad with a square jaw, no neck, a deep red sunburn, small brown eyes, deep-set, white eyebrows and lashes.

I was a good ten inches taller than he. He tilted his head

and looked up at me and said, barely moving his lips, "Three four nine one two three eight. In ten minutes. Now point to something over near the motel."

I did as asked. He thanked me, touched his cap and went trudging away. I called that number ten minutes later.

"Hello?"

"This is McGee."

"Trav, how the hell are you? Tommy T. told me to look you up when I got here."

"How is old Tom?"

"He's fine. You going to be aboard about eight? I want to just stop on by and say hello."

"I'll be right here."

"Great! See you."

Whoever he was, he was careful.

Even though my security system indicated nobody had been aboard, I checked the whole houseboat carefully. And when I was through I put on snorkel and fins and took the big underwater light and checked the hull and all the adjacent pilings. I came up shivering and took a hot shower. And then there was nothing to do but cook something and wait for the man in the Greek hat.

10

I left one dim fantail light on. He tapped at the door at three minutes past eight. Same careful fellow. Or maybe not careful enough. I opened the door and he said, "My name is Browder."

"McGee," I said, and stuck my hand out. He took it and I pulled him in and held tight as Meyer slid in behind him, closed the door with one hand and jabbed him once in the back with the barrel of my Colt Diamondback and then moved back away from him to what I had told Meyer is a safe and appropriate distance.

"Browder, the man behind you is not very familiar with firearms. The revolver is cocked. There is a shell in the chamber. His finger is on the trigger. If you do anything quick and funny, it might twitch."

"Nothing quick. Nothing funny. Believe me."

After I had tied him to a stanchion with a length of braided nylon line, Meyer was able to take a deep breath again. I emptied his pockets and put everything on the table.

He had a silver money clip in the shape of a dollar sign, worn
from long use, with four hundred and twenty dollars in it. He
had some crumpled ones and some change in the same pocket
as a Swiss Army knife with a cracked red handle. I patted him
down and found an ankle holster with a little two-shot derringer in it, two rounds of .22 Magnum hollowpoints. He
stood as patiently as a horse being groomed.

"Going to do it with the derringer?" I asked him.

"It wouldn't look like an accident, would it?"

"Why does it have to be an accident anyway?"

"I'll give you a number and you dial it and let me say
something into it. They will get a voiceprint, okay? Then
they'll clear me."

I had to retie him where the phone would reach. He said
the phone was manned twenty-four hours a day. I wasn't
familiar with the area code. It was answered on the second
ring by a male voice repeating the last four digits of the number I'd dialed. I held the phone to Browder's face and he said,
"Okay, Browder for clearance. Give them a description."

"Hold," the voice said.

We all waited for a long ninety seconds and then the voice
said, "Browder, Scott Ellis. Five foot seven, one hundred and
seventy-five pounds, age thirty-eight, brown eyes, ruddy
complexion, S-shaped scar inside of left forearm, first joint of
little finger of left hand missing, hairy mole right shoulder,
faded blue tattoo right forearm of anchor and five stars in a
circle around it. Browder is on detached duty with the Drug
Enforcement Administration."

I said thank you to a dead line and untied him.

"You don't want to check the hairy mole?" he asked.

"No, thanks."

"It isn't all that hairy anyway."

"Just for luck, I'll hang on to the derringer, though."

"Don't let me leave without it."

"Mr. Scott Browder, this is Meyer."

They nodded at each other. He massaged his wrists and said, "I could guess you'd be careful. What I hoped was no whop on the skull first. Hits on the head make me throw up. After the bomb thing they really wondered if they should go after somebody with all that amount of luck."

"Sit down. Drink?"

"Thanks. Scotch, no ice, little bit of water. You can guess why I wouldn't carry an official ID."

"Infiltration?" I asked.

"After Operation Southern Comfort a lot of our guys were made, so I'm one of the new batch."

"Operation what?"

He looked disappointed. "It was big, like five tons of coke by plane, with a relay strip in the Bahamas. Anyway, I'm involved with the people who never see it or touch it or have a direct contact with anybody who *does* see it and touch it. I'm after the arrangers. Not like Jornalero. He just does money for them. Long ago he used to hire the mules for the Colombianos. He worked his way up and, because he's smart, mostly out of it. They could get him for currency violations if they thought they could make it stick. But he covers his tracks good."

"Can you tell me who wants me killed?" I asked, giving him his drink.

He sipped it, nodded approval and said, "What would you do if I gave you names?"

"Pay visits."

He looked at me with disapproval. "McGee, I am not going to tell you how much I know about you. You are big and you are lucky and you have some good moves. If I wanted to get you killed quick, I'd give you some names. How can I impress you? We are talking about very big money and very smart people. Listen and believe. It would be like sending a twelve-year-old girl on a naked reverse against the Raiders. It is a class you will never be in."

"Who is Cappy?"

"Short for the Capataz. That isn't his name. It means the Foreman. He's way down the list. He's enforcement. You scrambled three of his people. Rick Sullivan is having his knees rebuilt. Louis LaLieu will spend a year with his dental surgeon. Dean Matan has four broken bones and some ripped tendons in his left hand. And Cappy is annoyed."

"Who did it to Billy?"

"I don't know and I don't think Cappy knows, and I would guess that the man in Marseille Cappy contacted for a favor wouldn't know either exactly who did it. Just like nobody really knows who put your bomb together or who mailed it. Incidentally, word went back to Marseille that the wire job was sloppy. They wanted it done so that it wouldn't be picked up in an autopsy. They should have used a big injection of insulin."

"A bomb isn't exactly accidental-looking."

"After that missed, they decided on accidents. Too many killings and you have a lot of official attention, and that is bad for business. The people in Peru would understand the accidents were arranged."

"What was my accident going to be?"

"I couldn't say exactly, but I think you were supposed to walk out into heavy traffic. Those three were standby talent, strictly second-class, McGee."

Meyer asked his first question. "Mr. Browder, if Mr. McGee stays here, what are his chances of staying alive?"

Browder looked at Meyer with more interest. "Slim to none."

"And why is that so important to somebody?"

"Friend Meyer, you ask the hard ones, don't you? Something is stirring. What you've got in the Miami-Atlanta area is a loose amalgamation of two groups. They work very cozy together. It's in their interest. Let's call one the Old-timers. Some syndicate families, gambling interests, vice, narcotics. But not down on the nitty-gritty level. Making policy, suggesting arrangements, selecting the right people. Let's call the other group the New Boys. Rednecks, Cubans, Jamaicans, Puerto Ricans, Mexicans, Guatemalans, Peruvians, Bolivians. Smuggling narcotics, peddling weapons, murder and arson for hire. And again you have a top layer of policy people, negotiators. For a while the Old-timers and the New Boys were killing each other off. Wiser heads prevailed. They have the same problems of product and cash flow. So they have been working together. Now there is trouble in paradise. It has something to do with you, McGee, and with Ingraham and his wife and Jornalero and that stolen boat and Gigi Reyes. I've discussed matters with my associates and my superiors, and the general feeling is that if we can find the right buttons and push them, there is going to be a full-scale war again. Crazy Marieleños running around in panel trucks full of automatic weapons and grenades. And some fruit may drop off the tree. We may get enough to build some tight cases.

"Lately, it's getting a little better. When we can't build a solid criminal prosecution, we can bring a civil action and tell the clown to either show up on the stand and explain his income taxes for the past fifteen years, and how come he could buy a two-million-dollar home on the beach, or we take the house off his hands. It stings them pretty good. But I like the tight cases better."

"Which side wants me dead?"

"The Old-timers, mostly."

"What can I do?"

"I don't know yet, McGee. First I want to know every detail about the boat. How you looked, where you located it. What you did aboard. The whole thing."

He made me go over the part about the boat coming over from Yucatan twice. And he wanted every detail about the interior of the *Sundowner*, known then as the *Lazidays*. The exact position and condition of each body. The placement of the roll of fifties, and the spare fifties around the head of Howard Cannon. The shape and placement of the bruises on the thighs of the Peruvian girl. The clothing on the others. I closed my eyes and rebuilt the scene. It came back so vividly I could hear the lazy buzzing of the carrion flies, feel the sodden weight of my sweat-soaked clothes.

"I got to think," Browder said.

He was a pacer. He frowned and paced and, with fresh drink in hand, made little grunts, mumbles and hand gestures.

He stopped in front of me and pointed down at me. "You! Have you got any cowboy clothes? Hat, shirts, boots?"

"Nothing."

"Buy them tomorrow morning. Get high heels on the boots and a big high crown on the hat. I want you seven and a half feet tall. I want you looked at. I'll bring the eye patch. He's dead, but they won't know that in the Yucatan, will they?"

"Is that a question?"

"Hell no. Shut up. Let me think." And he went back to pacing.

Finally he dropped into a chair and clapped his thick hands together. "It's a chance, but maybe the only chance you got, McGee. Bring money. A good chunk of it. Can you bring fifty big ones?"

"To where, for what?"

"You and me, we're going on a buying trip."

"I thought you were up there on the policy level, Browder."

"Hell no. I'm third or fourth string. If I want to go buying and have a source, why should they stop me? They let people turn a dime. They don't want them to get greedy and foolish. I had been working on the idea they came over from Veracruz or Tampico. If it was from Chetumal, and they made a buy, I know the name. It had to be through him or somebody close to him. I know the name but I don't know how to make the contact. We can't roam around asking. I think I know who can tell me how to make the contact. What you do, McGee, you stay low. Buy the cowhand clothes. Wait for a call from me day after tomorrow. I think we'll be taking the Monday or Tuesday afternoon flight on AeroMexico to Cancún."

"I can hardly wait," I said.

"Save the funny routines. This can get us both shot."

"If you take more than five thousand out of the country, they . . ."

"Fifty big ones makes a pack of hundreds this thick." He held up a hand, thumb and finger about two and a half inches apart. "Got a passport? . . . Good. I'll take the money in. Pack a carryon with what you'll need for three or four days. I don't know this minute if it's on or off. Maybe they think so much of me they don't want me to go out on a buy because I could get picked up coming back. On the other hand, if I'm coming up with the money and they're getting their percentage when they buy back from me for the wholesale market, what is there to lose? I'll let you know."

"If it happens," I asked, "who am I supposed to be?"

"I never heard his real name. They called him Bucky. Didn't look much like you. He had a round pink face. But tall. Real tall. He lost an eye in a bar. He walked into a dart game. Drunk. He didn't say much. He smiled a lot. He could do a pretty good John Wayne imitation. He did a lot of field work, so all the sources knew what he looked like. Word gets around. They called him the Estanciero. It means the Rancher. Bucky was never on a ranch in his life, except the night he got killed. It was a routine landing on a ranch strip in Pasco County and Bucky was there with a van to off-load the product and take it up north somewhere. Birmingham, I think. Some locals tried to hijack the load but they got cut down. Two of them got it. One of the others fired from long range, in the dark, probably just aiming in the general direction of the airplane, and took Bucky right in the throat. So one of the two people off the plane took the truck north, after the two of them had loaded Bucky and the two dead hotshots into the cabin. The pilot took it fifty miles out over the Gulf, put it on automatic pilot and heaved them out. What happened hasn't exactly been advertised. I know because it is part of my job to find out things like that, and the pilot likes brandy."

He looked at his watch and stood up. "Got to go. Look, I don't want to make you nervous. There's very little rough stuff going on these days. I'll be in touch."

After he had been gone ten minutes I said to Meyer, "If he is after my fifty thousand, that's the most elaborate con I ever ran into."

"I think he's real," Meyer said.

"Is that the right word?"

"Probably not. The man is basically unreal. But he's what he says he is."

"You're saying I should do it? I should go with him?"

"Do you think that's the kind of decision I should make for you?"

"Why do you keep answering a question with a question?"

"Doesn't everyone?"

"Okay, Meyer. Seriously. Life is full of signs and portents. Something hides in the shadows and keeps trying to tell you things you should know. But the language is never clear. You aimed a finger at me a while back and said, 'Bang, you're dead.' It is so unlike you to do a kid thing like that, I get the feeling something was trying to talk to me through you."

"It was just a dumb impulse."

"I guess the whole situation is making me too jumpy."

"And if you stay right here and make no moves at all, you're going to get jumpier."

"Probably."

"But be very, very careful, Travis."

11

Browder and I bought tickets, open return, at the Aero-Mexico counter at Miami International on Monday afternoon. It was still the busy season for Cancún, but there were a lot more coming back than going by this seventh day of the new year. We were put on standby, but after we were bused over to a newer building, Browder quietly bought us the top slots on the standby list.

The old fat jet was jam-packed. There was a holiday flavor, an anticipation of vacation aboard. There were a couple of tour groups, shouting back and forth to each other. It reminded me of the time Meyer and I had flown down to the Yucatan, the time when we found the man we had looked for over a long time. At that time we were hunting, and this time I was the hunted. That time I was with Meyer, and this time with a man I did not know. Reason said he could be trusted. But the phone identification could have been rigged. This time I would not return with a prize as rare as the one I had brought back to Lauderdale the last time. I told myself to relax and roll with it. But I could not shuck the moody, twitchy feeling. Besides, I felt like a clown, even after I had stowed the tall pale nineteen-gallon hat in the overhead compartment. Browder had brought the eye patch, one of those small black shiny ones with a black elastic band that was a little too tight, so that the edge of the patch pressed against the bones around the socket of my right eye. My shirt had pale shiny buttons, my pants were too tight in the crotch and the high boots of imitation lizard hurt my feet.

When I had asked Browder in the airport what was going on, he told me we'd talk later. He approved of the way I looked. He was not impressed with how much the boots hurt. I towered over him in the terminal. He leaned back and looked up at me like a pedestrian checking the stop light. In past years I had exaggerated my height as a method of disguise. But this time it bothered me more. I was a figure of fun. My clothes were too new. And I wondered if anybody wanted to do harm to the Estanciero.

One of the overworked flight attendants, charged with serving a hot meal on the short flight, smiled at me and said, "Hello there! We haven't seen you in a long time, Bucky."

"Nice to be aboard, ma'am," I said. The recognition made me more uncomfortable. She paused and looked back at me, with a small frown. And that didn't help either.

Also I felt uneasy when I thought of the fifty thousand. I had handed it in a rubber-banded block in a brown paper bag to Browder. He had taken it into a stall in the men's room. When he came out he led me into a quiet corner of the terminal and showed me his hard-cover Spanish/English dictionary. He had divided the cash into three packets and placed them inside the hollowed-out book. He kept the book closed with a red rubber band.

"Won't they look in that?"

"They don't hassle the tourist business. And if they do

check us and if they look, and if they find it, the going *mordida* is five hundred bucks. You and I are going through the clearance separate. Don't sweat it. It'll be fine."

Several other big passenger aircraft had landed at Cancún ahead of us, and a couple more came in right after we did. The modern airport is, for practical purposes, divided in half. The departure area with ticket counters, departure tax counters and security inspection is three times as large as the arrival lounge. Not a lounge. Long, long slow lines piled up at high counters where bored and indifferent little bureaucrats, male and female, glanced at passports and stamped tourist permits which had been filled out on the flights. I was able to stroll right on out of the customs area into the outer area of the arrival section without interception. The customs counters were unmanned. But several attentive men stood back by a wall, and every now and then one of them would step out and flag down a passenger and check his luggage.

Beyond the glass wall was total chaos. Passengers were finding their tour group, and the place to stand for their hotel buses. Avis, Hertz and Budget were doing big business. I looked back through the glass wall and saw Browder in there, working his way through the crowd toward the doorway. People charged into me, then backed off and stared up at me in obvious astonishment. I saw a whole pack of chubby people of indeterminate age, all wearing name tags with tridents on them, and I realized they were all destined for Club Med. They had that look, a batch of lonesome loners who had decided to try to take a big chance in the sunshine.

"Let's go," Browder said, pushing at me. I do not like being pushed at. He went ahead in a half trot and I followed along, walking carefully on sore feet. He stood in the Budget line and, after he spent five minutes at the counter, we went out to the far curb, walking between a couple of the tour buses parked in a long line at the first curb. It was bright and hot in Cancún. The buses stood there snoring and stinking, big beasts drowsing in the heat. The drivers sat high behind the wheels, wiry little brown men with that same look of apathy and cynicism you see on the faces of big-city cab-drivers.

It was ten minutes before our rental car arrived, a dark blue Renault 12 with eighteen thousand kilometers on the meter, a mini-station wagon with four doors. Browder got behind the wheel. If I could have fitted there, I couldn't have worked the pedals with those boots on. I tossed the big hat in back and took off the eye patch.

"You gotta wear that at all times!" Browder said.

"And off come the boots too, friend. You just drive the car."

"You getting smart-ass on me?"

I knelt on the seat and reached back and slipped the dictionary out of his carryon and put it in mine as he turned and watched me.

"If two of us are going to run this," he said, "we are going to run it into a tree."

"Get out of the crush here and park a minute."

He drove out of the airport proper and turned onto the long wide road that led out to the main highway that runs from Puerto Juárez all the way down to Chetumal, the capital city of Quintana Roo (pronounced "row" as in "row your boat"). He pulled way over to the side and turned the engine off. No air conditioning, and the dark car was like a convection oven when the windows were open and it was moving, and like a barbecue pit when it was standing still.

"Now what?" he asked.

"We are a long way from anything," I told him. "Up ahead turn left and we're fifteen or twenty minutes from Cancún. Turn right and you've got a batch of sixty miles of nothing. So who are we seeing, where is he and how do you get in touch?"

"It will unfold as we go along. Okay?"

"Not okay."

He studied me for a few moments. Sweat ran down his thick red cheek. "So I'll hold your hand, McGee. We've got two singles at the Sheraton. We locate a pool attendant, a towel boy named Ricky, and we tell him that we've come to do some business with the banker. We give him a room number and sit tight. Somebody will get in touch."

"Soon?"

"Maybe. Maybe not. We just wait and see."

At the hotel restaurant near the pool, I excited so much awe and interest I doubt anyone noticed Browder. The employees wore little name plates above the shirt pocket. No trace of any Ricky, and Browder didn't want to ask about him.

He was there in the morning, on Tuesday. He was a tall sallow Mexican lad who had dyed his hair yellow a couple of months back. It was half grown out, a startling sight indeed. He wore a gold snake bracelet around his wrist and a bangle in his ear.

Browder roamed until he could intercept Ricky out of earshot of the other employees and the tourists. He came back angry. "Christ, I don't know. I told him, and I told him the room number. Son of a bitch is asleep on his feet. He yawned at me. He needs dental work. From now on one of us is in my room at all times."

It was a relief to spend a little time away from him. In spite of his objections, I discarded the hat and boots for the time being. At his urgent request I kept the eye patch on until I bought some swim trunks and used the pool. Water kept getting behind the patch. So I left it off while swimming, put it back on when I knew I'd be seeing him. When I was out, he had to stay in the room. Whoever was in the room could watch the junk television from the States on the satellite disk, if they so chose. It's a funny thing about television and cigarettes. Hardly anybody I know anymore smokes cigarettes or watches the tube. One stunts the body and one stunts the mind.

I went and looked at the little Mayan ruin north of the hotel. The hotel itself is like a segment sliced out of a giant flat-topped Mayan pyramid. They are building condominiums nearby, the same size and shape. I wandered over and took a look at construction. Mexico is full of magic buildings. You never find anybody hard at work but the buildings go up.

Wednesday afternoon when I took my fast laps in the pool, there was more of an edge in the northeast breeze. I had tucked the hard eye patch on its black elastic cord into the locker-key pocket of my swim trunks. When I climbed out of the pool and tried to put it back on, it slipped out of my wet fingers and, propelled by the elastic, went skittering off behind me, across cement and tile, way over to a line of sun cots positioned five or six feet apart. It was under the second cot. I said, "Parm me," knelt and retrieved it and stood up to put it on.

"At least wipe it off," said the woman on the sun cot, reaching out to me with a Kleenex.

I thanked her and wiped the plastic patch off and put it back on. She looked up at me with a skeptical frown. She wore a swimsuit but looked as if she could manage a bikini nicely. Brown hair, blue eyes, a three-day tourist burn.

"Why are you wearing that thing?" she asked.

"How do you mean?"

"You take it off to go in the pool and put it on when you come out."

"What I've got is some kind of hypersensitivity to light."

"I *bet* you have."

"You sound as if you don't believe me."

"Maybe because it's the wrong kind of patch. I had a friend who had to wear one of those. That's what you wear when the eyeball is gone."

"Mine is still right here."

"I know. So, well, it made me wonder. We put out a lot of spy novels."

"We?"

"I write copy for a publishing house in New York. And right now I'm just about as far away from it as I can afford to get. For ten whole days. But my mind is still in the shop, I guess. That patch is like a clue or a signal. I had to ask or worry about it forever."

"Try to think of it as an election bet. Will that help?"

She frowned, sighed, checked the degree of burn on her shoulder. "I'll have to make do with that, won't I? Because you're not going to tell me anything else." She stuck her hand up and said, "Nancy Sheppard, New York."

I took it and said, "Travis McGee, Florida. Happy to meet you. I might be having a drink later over at the . . ."

"Don't get ahead of yourself," she said. "I just wanted to know about the patch." And she rolled facedown on her sun cot in total dismissal.

So the patch was on and I decided to keep it on at all times. If people from publishing houses could nail me that easily, I was probably being stupid about the patch. And probably the boots and the hat. But everything hurt except the hat.

Nancy Sheppard's observation had jolted me out of a curious listlessness I had felt ever since the awareness of being hunted for reasons no one would or could explain. As quarry, I was acting much like the persons I had hunted. Aware of pursuit, they do not become more sly. They become careless, random, disheartened. Easier to bring down. They seem to welcome the end of the play, just to find out what is going on. So I was being precisely that kind of a horse's ass. Out of control.

I had been in control when I had gone hunting the *Sundowner*. I found it and then the world turned upside down. I had not reacted this way when I had been hunted other times in other places. But then I knew who was after me and why. For perhaps the first time in my life I appreciated the corrosive effects of total uncertainty. And it was something I could use, if I survived to use it. In Kafka's story *The Trial*, the prisoner disintegrated because he could never find out what he was guilty of. So I vowed to tighten up. By being a fool, I was handicapping Browder.

Word came on Thursday afternoon. I was on room duty. I wrote it down. There was no point in going to find Browder. He came back a half hour later. He read my note.

"What kind of a voice?"

"Male. Heavy and deep and slow."

"Accent?"

"Some, but not Mexican. More like German or Scandinavian. But slight."

"Okay. That's not our guy. So we've got to go to Tulum. Hand me the map."

"Right down the road past the airport, say eighty-five miles from here, two hours to be safe."

"You've been there before?"

"A while back."

He looked at me and when I didn't continue he shrugged and said, "Suit yourself. You have any Spanish?"

"Kitchen Spanish, without verbs. And not much of that. I've noticed you do a little better than that."

"A little. So to make it by eleven we leave at nine."

"Unless you want to get there earlier and look around."
"I don't want to do anything to make the birds fly."

We parked at Tulum a little before eleven. The parking lot was across the road from the Mayan ruins. There were a dozen big tour buses and about fifty cars. Two sides of the parking lot were lined with ramshackle shops strung with bright flags and plastic gadgetry. The shops were selling clothing, jewelry, junk, fake Mayan carvings, T-shirts, souvenirs, tacos, enchiladas, beer, soft drinks, seashells and paper flowers. The shops and small restaurants extended down both sides of the approach to the ruins from the main highway.

We locked the little blue station wagon and walked diagonally across the lot and back along the way we had come, to the sign Browder had spotted on the way in. Restaurante Tía Juanita. It was dim inside, out of the white glare of sunlight. There were six crude wooden tables on a dirt floor, mismatched chairs, a counter along the back with a heavy woman behind it. The place smelled of fried grease, beer and urine. One table was occupied by two Mexican kids drinking Coca-Cola out of oversized bottles.

We took the table on the left just inside the door. An electric fan on the counter top turned back and forth, giving us a brief blast of warm moving air every twenty seconds. Browder went to the counter and brought back two bottles of León Negra dark beer. We were halfway through the beer when a man came in, paused to let his eyes adjust to the diminished light and then sat down with us. He was big and he looked fit. He had a full beard, ponytail, cotton pullover shirt with narrow red and white horizontal stripes, cutoff jeans and, as I noticed later, old army boots worn without laces or socks. He was a relic from the past, a time traveler from San Francisco in the sixties. Mexico is full of them. Aging hippies, last survivors, drifting down toward the Mayan ruins, burned-out cases, languid and ragged in the heat, traveling with dirty duffel bags, listlessly thumbing the sparse traffic.

He looked at me and said, "Heard of you. I thought it was going to be somebody after the good Oaxaca bush. Very heavy and clean. But you'd be looking for the white lady out of Belize."

"And for that we'd see the Brujo?" Browder asked.

"He's hard to see lately. He's just set up a new market to handle all he brings in."

"Out of Bogotá to Belize, then by boat to Chetumal, sure. But where from here? I don't get it, this new market. If it's coming into the States, our people get it anyway."

"Maybe the Brujo is a little pissed at your people. Maybe he's got a Canadian outlet."

"We've never given him a bad deal."

"That isn't what he says. And that isn't what I know."

"Who are you?" Browder asked.

"How much were you thinking to buy?"

"Enough."

"You know what happens sometimes," the man said. "Sometimes people who deal in it, they use a little. Then they begin to think they are smarter than anybody. So they try a little angle here, a little angle there, and then they crap in their own nest."

"No chance of seeing the Brujo?"

"I don't know. He might want to tell you some kind of a message. He's still hot about it."

"Tell me about it," Browder said.

"That's up to him. A man gets taken, he doesn't want other people telling people about it."

"How would we get to see him?"

"I can take a shot at it. But you could be wasting your time."

"Now?"

"Let's go. We'll have to use my truck."

We followed him to where he had parked an old red Ford pickup. The fenders were gone to provide space for the huge tires which lifted the chassis so high we had to climb up into it. Going through the crowd I attracted the same awed attention as before. Take my six four and add another twelve inches of heels plus hat and it made the children's eyes bug. I realized what it would feel like to be in a carnival.

We went down an old road that followed the shore, down past a fish camp at Boca de Paila, and at last the road petered out to a mere rocky trace which he crawled over in low gear, avoiding rocks big enough to hit the underside of the battered truck. He pulled into the dirt yard of a typical Mayan hut, though bigger than most, scattering turkeys, dogs and ducks. He told us to wait beside the truck. The hut was round, made of wattle and sticks plastered with a lime mix and heavily thatched with old brown palm fronds. The man brushed against copper bells strung by the entrance as he entered the dark interior. Dogs stretched out again in the shade. Turkeys and ducks were pecking around.

The man came out and said, "They sent somebody after him. They'll come back with him or with a message from him."

"Take long?"

"Ten, fifteen minutes."

"Then he lives near?"

"I've never seen where he lives, friend." He gestured. "Somewhere beyond all that jungle stuff."

Finally a man appeared in the doorway of the hut and beckoned to us. He stood there as we approached and then stepped aside to let us enter. He was Mayan, maybe fifty years old, with the broad impassive face of a Siberian peasant, and the great hooked nose of Egyptian wall paintings. His skin color was a deep golden brown. A young man in black shorts and a white shirt stood in the narrow rear doorway of the hut, holding an automatic weapon at ready, aimed at our ankles. He gave us his total attention all the time we were there.

The Brujo wore white trousers and a long white shirt with four pockets and with broad stripes of blue embroidery down the front of it. There were hammocks strung inside the hut, and several heavy wooden boxes.

He sat on a carved chest, and motioned us toward the boxes.

As I was wondering if he spoke English, he said, "When I get the seventy-five thousand American dollars you tricky bastards owe me, maybe we can start doing business again."

12

"We haven't tricked anyone," Browder said. "Believe me."

"So why are you coming here with a man trying to look like the Estanciero? The real Estanciero, Bucky, had a girl's face. Not this one here."

"Now I can take this damn thing off," I said, and removed the hat with the tall crown and huge brim so I could slip the eye patch off. I noticed out of the corner of my eye that the gun barrel in the doorway moved up to give me some individual attention, then sagged as I replaced the hat and put the patch in my pocket.

"Jesus Christ, McGee!" Browder said angrily.

I looked at the impassive man sitting on the chest and said, "Sir, your honor, señor or El Brujo, or whatever . . ."

"Señor is fine."

"Señor, I would be very grateful if you would tell me who cheated you and how. I do not deal drugs. I do not use drugs. I prevailed upon this fine fellow here, Mr. Scott Ellis Browder, to bring me along with him. He *does* deal drugs. I dressed up like Bucky at his request, so I would maybe be recognized as him, and that would make us more believable. We know something went wrong down here but we don't know what. Back home in Florida, people are trying to kill me, and I don't know why, but it has something to do with what happened down here, I think."

"But my main mission is to make a buy," Browder said hurriedly.

"For how much?"

"Fifty thousand dollars' worth."

"Where is the money?"

"In a lock box at the hotel," I said.

El Brujo stared into my eyes. I tried to look earnest, troubled and sincere. "A man named Ruffino Marino has been buying from me for a year and a half. Italian-American," he said.

Browder grunted with surprise and El Brujo stared at him and said, "You have a problem with that?"

"Big heavy man about sixty, with a limp?"

"No, indeed. A handsome young man about twenty-eight. Slender. Mustache."

"Thank you. You have very good English, señor."

"I have a degree in business administration from Stanford," he said, so flatly I knew he was trying to hide his pride in it.

El Brujo turned back to me. "Marino flew the product out of the Tulum airstrip to an airstrip on a Florida ranch near Fort Myers. He made four trips. He complained about increasing surveillance. He flew over the last time in early August. He did not fly the product back. He brought here a young man with red hair. John Rogers. He said Rogers would take the product back by boat. I said it was more risky by water than by air. He said they had worked out something. John Rogers' boat was docked at Cozumel. I sent a man up there to help him find safe anchorage down here. You have to know the waters, and know the reefs. The boat anchored in good protected water in the Bahia de la Ascensión. Rogers had a young woman with him. I had to wait for more product to fill the order. We loaned them a jeep. Marino had flown back. Rogers and the woman explored the area. When I supplied the product, they left. They came back in September. Again I had to wait for product. They paid me and left. They left with a young woman who had been traveling here with relatives. Apparently she wanted to go with them and see the United States. I would have stopped them taking her had I known she was an important person. This was big police business, big rewards. She was a reckless young woman. The family in Lima had sent her traveling with relatives to get her mind off an unsuitable young man. She was to have been married to a lawyer. We heard here that she had been killed in the United States, in Florida. I receive the International Edition of the Miami *Herald* every afternoon. And I watch your television. I have a twelve-foot dish antenna. I was careless about the money. After all, it came from Marino, who had been doing business with me for over a year. I didn't notice it was counterfeit until I was just about to send it by courier to my bank on Grand Cayman." He took two fifties out of his pocket and held them out toward Browder, who jumped up and walked over and got them, the gun muzzle following him. He examined them and handed them to me. They looked crisp but felt damp. Same familiar serial number. F38865729D.

"If you get the paper," I said, "then you know the redhead and his girl were killed too."

"Of course. And Rogers wasn't his name. All I know is that Marino owes me seventy-five thousand dollars. If you and your people want to do any business here for any kind of product, they have to clear that matter up first." He frowned.

"I can't understand why it hasn't been cleared up. I know the mathematics as well as they do. What costs you people seventy-five thousand, you wholesale for two hundred thousand. The wholesaler sells it to the distributor for four hundred thousand. The distributor sells it to the area dealers and they sell it to the street dealers and they sell it to the consumers after adulteration for a million dollars."

"Maybe," Browder said, "we've been pinching down on supply to hold the price."

"Why would you come to me to make a buy knowing I was cheated?"

"I didn't know you'd been cheated."

"I'm not a fool! You don't have any independent importers anymore."

"Maybe Marino was the very last."

"And so I am out of luck? Is that it?"

"That could be it, Mr. Brujo."

"There will be no sales until I am reimbursed."

"I'm in no position to decide that. I'm not high enough up the ladder. But I will go back and report. I have the feeling enough product is coming in from other directions. But it's good policy to keep all the channels open."

"Martin, you can drive these men back, please."

As we stood up, Browder said, "What was it they worked out to cut down the risk of taking it in by boat, sir?"

"Didn't you look into that, Martin?" Brujo asked.

"Yes, sir. The product would go into one of those aluminum Haliburton cases with a good watertight seal, with enough lead to make negative buoyancy. The case had two eyes welded onto the two corners on one end, and there was a wire cable, thin, fastened to the eyes, making a Y like a ski towline. They had about fifty feet of cable and the other end was fastened to a large eye bolt screwed into the keel amidships. They kept the case on the transom. Oh, the case had two little fins welded or brazed onto the sides so that if they had to tow the case at cruising speed it would come up near the surface but wouldn't broach. The fins were adjustable so they could take some practice runs with the case full to see how it behaved. If there was any chance of being boarded and searched, they would just shove the case overboard. If they traveled, it stayed below the surface. If they stopped, it hung straight down toward the bottom. After the danger was over, they could get up to speed, pick up the cable with a boat hook and bring the case back aboard. Unless someone sent a diver over to look at the hull, they were safe, and even then he might not see the cable."

"Thanks for your time," I said to El Brujo.

After we had climbed into the red truck I asked Browder what *brujo* meant. Martin answered for him. "Wizard or magician. More like magician."

"I wonder if he contributes to the alumni fund," I said.

"Probably," said Martin. "He uses his education. He has commercial ventures in Cancún, Mérida, Valladolid, Chetumal and Villahermosa. He's got a radiotelephone back in there somewhere. He's a very serious man. It wasn't smart to cheat him."

As we rode, I looked sidelong at Martin. There were flecks of gray in that beard. Deep wrinkles at the corners of his eyes. The hippie look was a perfect disguise for the environment in which he worked. He lacked the dazed vapid manner of the strung-out homeless ones, but I guessed that he could assume the role whenever it seemed useful.

I wondered how Martin felt about the business he was in. But I knew Browder wouldn't like it if I asked him. And I probably wouldn't understand the answer.

Browder held it all in until we were back inside the little blue Renault and heading north. Then he hit the top of the steering wheel with the heel of his hand. "Wowee!" yelled

Browder. "Hey ho!" yelled Browder. "Gottum!" yelled Browder.

"Got who?"

"Whoever falls out of the tree when we shake it. Like this, McGee. Mr. Ruffino Marino, who lives in a million-dollar condo at Sailfish Lagoon, is a respected investment adviser. He fought his way up through one of the families. He invests mob money in restaurants and hotels and dry cleaning and car washes and liquor stores. And he probably has a little sit-down dinner once in a while with old friends and they make policy about who to be friends with and what to buy next. Ruffi Junior has always been a wild-ass kid. Not exactly a kid any longer, but his habits haven't changed. Stock cars, speedboats, airplanes, actresses. So it was the kid had the deal with Brujo, and that is crazy because the last thing the old man would want for his sons and daughters would be anything illegal. He bought respectability and he wants to keep it. Nothing should mar the Marino name, so it is dead-ass certain he didn't know about this until it had been going on for a while."

"How would Ruffi Junior dispose of the product?"

"Use the Marino name to get to a wholesaler, and then sell it to him for a little bit under the going price to keep the man's mouth shut. A personal deal. There could be other ways. I'm just brainstorming it. The thing to know is that the old man would blow a gasket if he knew any of his kids, especially the oldest son, was dealing."

"Why would he deal?"

"I heard a rumor he wanted to be a movie star like Stallone. He financed a movie using a tax shelter plan and it was a bomb, a dead loss. He could make a million a year buying from Brujo. Maybe he wants to make another movie."

"What about the dead people?"

"I can make up a scenario for you. Ruffi Junior is contacted by Howard Cannon by phone once he is back safe in the Keys with the product. So they arrange a pickup by Ruffi, by fast runabout or float plane, back there where you found the boat. I think Ruffi Junior would come along. He doesn't want to be very public about what he's doing. So he goes down and boards the boat to pick up the product and give the redhead his cut. The redhead is proud of how cute he was. He'd probably bought that funny money for fifteen cents on the dollar. Eleven thousand two hundred fifty for seventy-five. But he probably bought a round hundred. He wants to buy into the action. He still has the seventy-five in good money Ruffi gave him. So he tells Ruffi what he did and shows him the rest of the funny money.

"Okay. So Ruffi is known for having a temper. He beat up on a girl once a couple of years ago. It was in the papers. But he got off. There he is looking in horror at that dumb turd redhead telling him how smart he is. Ruffi knows it is a stolen boat. He knows that he can never make the redhead understand what an idiot he's been. Then maybe the redhead tells him he has the seventy-five thousand hidden, just in case Ruffi doesn't want to deal him in. I think that's in character. Do you?"

"Please watch the road, Browder. This is a very narrow road. Those oil trucks are doing eighty-five."

"Would you say that would be in character?"

"Yes. I noticed some broken mangrove. He probably hid the money ashore. Sealed it in a plastic bag and tied it to a mangrove knee. The way the boat was moored, you could jump into the shallows and wade into the mangroves."

"Okay, so he faked the redhead out of position, cold-cocked him, then turned and busted the skull on the blonde girl, knocking her back onto the bunk. Then he tied up the redhead the way you found him, and then he went in and had his fun and games with the little lady from Peru until he heard the redhead start bellowing. He knew the blonde girl was dead. He cut the throat of the little brunette. Why shouldn't he? He thought they were just three pieces of garbage, a half step ahead of the law. The redhead had closed off Ruffi's source, and Ruffi didn't think he should be walking around talking about how cute he had been.

"So he came out and sat down beside the redhead and put a clothespin on his nose and then clamped a hand over his mouth. When the redhead began to pass out, Ruffi would let him breathe again, and each time he would ask where the redhead had hidden the product and hidden the money. He let the redhead know both the women were dead. When he had answers he liked, he went looking, and when he found the goods and knew the answers had been on target, he went back and took those fifties and made a roll that would just fit into the redhead's mouth, pried his jaws open, jammed the bills in and hammered them home. Then he probably sat and watched the redhead asphyxiate. It would have taken a while because he could probably suck in a little bit of air around the wad of money. And while he was on the way to dying, Ruffi was probably telling him what a horse's ass he had been. Then he picked up his goods and his money and got into his boat or airplane and left the area in a hurry. From Ruffi's point of view, a reasonable solution. Brujo had no good way to contact him and probably wouldn't try. Ruffi took his goods to market before the murder story broke, and there was no way to connect him to it anyway."

"Write me into your scenario, friend. Where do I fit? Where did Billy Ingraham fit?"

"Young Ruffi is not dumb. When he found out he had killed the niece of a very heavy dealer in Lima, he knew it would be as if somebody had killed one of his sisters. The pressure would never quit. Sooner or later, unless they had a story they could buy, they would backtrack all the way to

Ruffino Marino Junior. You know what I think? I think he went to his old man and confessed. The old man has more brains than Ruffi. And he couldn't throw his kid to the dogs, or even admit his kid had been dealing. So the alternate theory was that Billy Ingraham had told you to get his boat back and punish whoever had taken it. And you got to it four days before you notified the Coast Guard. They sold that story to the people in Lima, named names. They promised to take you out. At first it was going to be quick and dirty. But then somebody, maybe the senior Marino, decided that might cause too much investigation. When you escaped the bomb, they decided on accidental. After all, if the right newspaper clippings were mailed to Peru, it would end right there no matter how you and Ingraham died. Honor would be served, and all that shit. But the Ingraham accident was messed up, and by a freak of chance, Jornalero knew the new Mrs. Ingraham. The world can be a small place. You and Millis Ingraham convinced Jornalero you were not guilty and Ingraham wasn't guilty. But when Jornalero tried to get the thing stopped right there, they wouldn't listen. They told him they were going to do it their way. Reason? Pressure from Ruffino Marino Senior. To hide the participation of his dear boy. To stifle any further investigation. Mail your ears to Peru, and everybody can breathe deep and slow."

"Look out!"

"Jesus Christ, McGee! I saw him. I wasn't going to run into him."

A pair of toucans flew over the road twenty feet high and a hundred feet ahead of us. They fly with their bills hanging down. They make little irregular swoops as they fly. They do not look as if they really enjoyed getting around that way. Their breast is of the interior colors of their favorite diet, papaya.

"So what makes you so happy, Browder?"

"The Old-timers against the New Boys. It is going to be tough to split them up because they are both antsy about the Canadians moving into the Miami area. Canadian mobs. But this whole thing about the girl from Peru offended the New Boys. Latin heritage and all. So when they find out she was raped and killed by the son of one of the Old-timers, and the Old-timers have been trying to throw you to the Peruvians to get the pressure off and save their kinfolk, it isn't going to sit too well. Shake the tree and things fall down."

And so we went skimming up the rough and narrow highway to Cancún, passing the trucks and buses at a hundred and twenty kilometers an hour, the hot wind whipping at us. Browder hummed happily over the sounds of wind and engine and from time to time he would laugh.

"If they found out you're in drug enforcement, what would happen?"

"It would depend on how much they think I know. Maybe only a good thumping by persons unknown. Or maybe I would drive into a canal."

"Rough way to live, isn't it?"

"I came looking for it. We've got a fifteen-year-old daughter—no, she's sixteen now—she OD'd on some kind of a crazy mix of speed and horse two years ago. The high school was full of it. She passed out and in the hospital she stopped breathing, but they got her going again, except she's a vegetable. She used to be a pretty girl. Our marriage wasn't solid enough to handle that. So I'm undercover and my ex-wife teaches in night school so she can spend more time with Nan. What I want to do, one way or another, is nail some of the sanctimonious bastards who control the drug trade without ever getting their hands dirty. When you make any kind of a case against one of them and by some miracle get a conviction, the appeal procedures take five to seven years, and if guilty is still the verdict, they spend ten months in a federal country club. The ones we haul in are the people who bring the product in and handle it and peddle it. They get the long sentences and they can be replaced overnight. What I want to see is a nice drug war. Like six or eight years ago. Car bombs, fire bombs, bodies in the trunks of Cadillacs. Important bodies."

"What's going to happen with me, Browder?"

"As soon as I can spread the word, they will be off your case."

"How soon will that be?"

"I'm working on how I should do it."

"Don't let me spoil your concentration."

The jungle grew deep on both sides of the road, grew tall right up to the edges of the two traffic lanes, a green blur as we sped past. From time to time we came to a tall stick with something on top of it, a marker for the path that would lead back to one of the jungle huts of the descendants of the Maya. On top of the stick would be a piece of plastic, a tire, a celluloid doll or a beer can. Buzzards circled aloft, dipping down to chomp the slain creatures on the concrete.

Browder was a fast driver and not a good driver. He would get too close to a slow-moving vehicle before edging out to take a look down the highway. When he passed he cut in quickly even with nothing approaching and nothing bullying him from behind. The expert driver moves out into the passing lane when he is at least fifteen car lengths from the vehicle he is passing. Then he can move back without haste if it is not a good time to pass. Once by, he makes his angle of return to his lane as long and gradual as is consistent with what is ahead of and behind him. The good driver takes his foot off the gas when there is anything ahead he does not understand. We came to a place where big green branches had been cut and put in the oncoming lane. It was a warning. There was a disabled VW camper with branches in the road behind it as well, a hundred yards and more from the camper. Browder didn't slow. As we approached at high speed he saw a tanker truck beginning to turn out to pass the camper. It was coming toward us. Browder accelerated and got as far to the right as he could. We brushed the jungle as we sped by the big high bumper of the tanker truck. Browder yelled curses. "Goddamn maniac truck driver!" he hollered

I said, "You are a rotten driver." This is like telling someone he has no sense of humor, or that he's a poor judge of character.

"I am an excellent driver!" he said. "Excellent! What's wrong with you?"

"I know. You've never had a serious accident."

"Never!"

"Then you are a very lucky man. You are a rotten driver. You are a hazard on the road. You go too fast for conditions. You don't know how to pass. You don't slow down when you should. You want everybody to get out of your way."

After he stopped being very, very angry he said, "You're serious, aren't you?"

"Absolutely. And I don't want to be found dead in this comedy outfit."

"Want to drive?"

"Soon as you can find a place to get off the road and I can get these boots off."

"And then I'll tell you what's wrong with your driving, McGee."

"Always eager to learn."

through a security X ray, and once cleared you carried them on into some sort of big lounge with plastic chairs to await the announcement of your flight.

No matter how many times you vow you will never stand in line again for anything, you get trapped. The lighting inside the big terminal was dim. The brighter light was at the check-in counters and outside the glass doors over on the other side of the big room we were in.

I was a half step ahead of Browder. He was close and to my left. Beyond him were a man and a woman, short and smiling, wearing identical yellow shirts which said "I Love Cancún." They were kicking a duffel bag and an imitation Gucci suitcase ahead of them.

Browder lurched against me and clutched at my left arm. I thought he had tripped over his carryon. As I turned to steady him, his grasp loosened and he slipped away from me, and fell loosely, facedown, limbs sprawling. He had bought a pale gray guayabera shirt that morning in the hotel shop where I bought the sandals. It was nailed to the left side of his back, fairly low but angled upward, by something that had a narrow three-inch handle wrapped in black electrician's tape. There was a spreading red stain around the point of entry. His carryon was gone. I could not see anyone leaving in a hurry. The people behind him looked absolutely normal and quite horrified.

A woman screamed. I put my fingertips on the absolute silence of his throat. He seemed to settle more closely to the floor. "Who did it?" I asked the people who'd been behind us.

"Who did it? Who knows? Somebody hurrying. I didn't look."

There were sharp whistles and the security guards came on the run. The people closest to it had moved back away

13

Saturday was a big departure day at the Cancún airport.
Eastern, American, AeroMexico, Mexicana, charter services,
everybody was leaving in the middle of the day. Once again
Browder bought a couple of top slots on the wait list. The line
heading toward the departure tax counter was three or four
people wide and sixty yards long. People sighed, kicked their
luggage along the tile floor and told each other to have the six
hundred pesos ready for the departure tax.

I had discarded the hat, which had cost me thirty-three
dollars. I had put it on the head of a twelve-year-old Mexican,
to his infinite delight. The imitation-lizard boots I left under
the bed, after I had bought sandals at a hotel shop. I kept the
eye patch in my pocket, but I don't know why. I thought if I
saw Nancy Sheppard again by the pool, I would present her
with the damn ugly thing. Anyway, I was a lot less conspicuous. Which was, as it turned out, a good thing.

The line seemed endless. When I stood tall I could see
that after the payment of departure tax, the carryons went

from the body. Then the line continued. It merely curved around the fallen man, everybody on their way to pay their six hundred pesos, catch their flight. They kicked their luggage along. I wore my carryon with my elbow clamped down on it. I edged into the moving line a little ahead of where I had been.

"Wasn't that man with you?" a woman asked me.

"No. We were just chatting."

"What happened back there?" a man asked.

"Somebody fainted. Some man," the woman said.

I had made my choice just quickly enough. I looked back. The police were stopping people, hauling them back to the scene of the crime and trying to interrogate them. It was obvious that El Brujo, a very serious man, had decided to cut the loss he had suffered. Or one of his people, Martin or the man with the weapon, had decided that the money would be worth some risk. Browder had come to make the buy, so he would be the one with the money, too bulky to wear in a money belt. I could feel the book through the canvas of my carryon. They would expect Browder to have the money. Even though I did not think they would risk a second chance as soon as they discovered they were wrong, I was anxious to get past Security and into the departure lounge.

Browder had made his own life decisions. He had taken his own risks. He had bought his own ticket. Nothing would be gained by my hanging around. And if I did, I might be invited to join Browder. I had not liked the man, even though I respected his dedication and his courage. In spite of all my rationalizations, in spite of all my very good reasons for melting into the crowd and fading away, I still felt chickenshit about it. It didn't help at all to realize that I was doing exactly what Browder would have done had the narrow blade punched into my heart with equal professionalism of thrust and angle. Staying would have done absolutely no good at all. But it would have felt better than leaving. Once through Security I found an empty chair that backed up to a wall. There I pretended to read the book I had picked up at the hotel newsstand. I had gotten to the part where a buried cat came back to life, but couldn't walk well.

Two official-looking men came in and stood looking carefully around at the people waiting. I tried to make myself a size smaller. They gave it a good long look and went out. My flight was called. I had no boarding pass and so I was stopped at the glass doorway. There were about a dozen of us.

A flight attendant came out to the head of the ladderway from inside the aircraft and held up four fingers. The man at the doorway waved and she went back. "Broo-dare? Broo-dare?" he called out, looking inquisitively at us. No luck. Broodare was not answering any more calls. Not on this earth.

"McGay?" he said. "McGay?"

I showed him my ticket and he gave me a boarding pass. I got on and the attendant said, "Thirty-one C, sir."

Three abreast. I was on the aisle, next to a bald priest who was next to a fat brassy blonde in the window seat. I kept willing the airplane off the ground. I kept trying to make myself a few pounds lighter. After an interminable time we trundled out to the runway, lumbered down to the end, turned, came back and suddenly broke free, rising and turning, looking down to see the white lines of beaches, jumbles of concrete, blue sea, green jungle, cars and buses crawling.

It was full dark by the time I boarded my houseboat. I checked my security system and then felt for the lock with the key. I unlocked it and then when I put my hand on the latch, I yanked it back quickly. I thought I had put my hand over some sort of large bristly bug on the latch. I moved to the side so my shadow wouldn't be on the latch. And I saw that it was a stick figure of a cat made of pipe cleaners. This one was blue and it was taped to the latch. I pulled it free when I went in, and I put it with the other one I had found. There was an innocence about the cats, but at the same time a sinister flavor. They did not represent somebody having fun. Communication is a process of interpreting symbols. Words are symbols. Gestures and gifts and touchings are symbols. In any life we misinterpret more than we should, perhaps because our deepest intentions are at odds with the messages we project. The cats bothered me because they touched a memory I could not completely unearth. I could see an edge of it, but I could not make out the whole. It was a fossil, deep in my geology, in a stratum long covered.

I had no wish to turn on lights. I was thirsty. I found the water jug in the refrigerator and drank directly from the jug, deep and long. Then I stripped off what was left of my clown suit with the pearl buttons and the oversized zippers. The shirt smelled of airplane, of people jammed into an airless intimacy for too long—tobacco smoke, perfume, beer, engine oil and sweat.

I stretched out on my double-king bed, hands laced behind my head, looking up at the dark overhead. Somebody came burbling into their slip, and the *Busted Flush* heaved a little, sighed a little, as the slow bow wave came by. A line creaked, and something in the galley tinkled. I felt grainy and spent. Tongue tip found the edge of a questionable tooth. A cramp began to knot my right calf and so with thumb and forefinger I pinched my nose shut with considerable force and held the pressure until the cramp faded away. A Chinese solution. Acupressure, just as steady pressure at the right point on the inside of the wrist, three finger widths from the heel of the hand, will inhibit nausea.

Another surge moved the *Flush*. In the sense of movement a boat is a living thing. It is a companion in the night. Each boat has its own manner and character. The *Flush* is an amiable, stubborn old brute. Like a fat dog, she can be made to run, but not for very long, and then will pretend more exhaustion than she feels.

My mind wheeled in concentric circles until, with nowhere else to go, it lit on Browder. I got up and turned a light on to find the phone number I had scribbled. I dialed it. A voice answered as before, repeating the last four digits of the number. A male voice with a robotic tinniness to it, like a talking toy.

I said, "Scott Ellis Browder was knifed to death in the Cancún airport at one-fifteen today."

There was no answer. I wondered if anybody had heard me. And then a voice said, in a low heavy tone full of exhaustion and despair, "Oh shit!" And the connection was broken.

I wondered what Browder's real name had been. I wondered what agency he was on loan from. I would have given odds of seven to three that when he died, it would have been on the highway, passing something at the wrong time and place.

I was trying to make myself get up, take a shower, brush teeth, when I fell asleep. When I woke up a little before four in the morning, a stiff wind was whining through the boat basin and the *Flush* was making small erratic motions as it snubbed against the lines. And I was frozen. One of those wintertime slabs of Siberia had come sliding down into South Florida, freezing the citrus and strawberries, puckering the tourist skin, whitecapping the bays and emptying the beaches.

I got an extra blanket, got shivering into the bed and pulled the covers over me. The cold had awakened me from a dream. I had been in a poker game at an oval table, with the center green-shaded light hung so low I could not make out the faces of the men at the table. They all wore dark clothing. The game was three-card draw, jacks to open. They were red Bicycle cards. Every time I picked up my five cards, I found the faces absolutely blank. Just white paper. I wanted to complain about this, but for some reason I was reluctant. I threw each hand in, blank faces up, hoping they would notice. All the rest of the cards were normal. I could see that each time a winner exposed his hand. There was a lot of betting, all in silence. A lot of money. And then I picked up one hand and found they were real cards. I did not sort them. I never sort poker hands or bridge hands. The act gives too much away to an observant opponent. I had three kings of clubs and two jacks of diamonds. In the dream I did not think this odd. They were waiting for me to bet when the cold woke me up. In the dream I had been shivering with the tension of having a good hand. The shivering was real.

It was the coldest morning I could remember in Fort Lauderdale. I dug out my old black leather jacket, rock-climbing trousers and watch cap. The tops of my ears felt good tucked into the watch cap. People were standing around in wonder looking at the frost on the bushes, and huffing so they could see their breath before the wind whipped it away. And the wind had also whipped all the urban smutch out to sea, all the stink of diesel, gasoline, chemicals and garbage fires, leaving a sky so blue it was like the sky of childhood.

Ever since I had awakened I had a picture that flashed into my mind and winked out, over and over, a slide projector inside my head with but one slide. It showed Browder with his right cheek against the tile, his mouth and eyes half open. It showed the pattern of his hair in the left sideburn and at the nape of his neck. It showed the shape of his ear, and it showed my hand reaching into the frame to rest my fingertips against the left side of his throat. It is a very quick way. It snaps a man from life into death. When the heart is stopped with such brutal precision, blood flow ceases and the brain stops making its electrical images and all the muscles go slack. So he was Browder walking and three seconds later he was dead meat on the floor and somebody, in a hurry, was leaving the terminal with his carryon.

If I were king of the country I would decree that on a certain date, three months hence, all green money in denominations of twenty dollars and up would become valueless. Everyone possessing that money could, during the three months, bring it in and exchange it for orange-colored money. One exchange per person. Bring in all your cash, and if you have more than one thousand dollars, fill out a form explaining where you got it and how long you'd had it. There's untold billions of sleazy money out there. Untold billions that would never be turned in because possession of it cannot be explained. Bureaucracy gone quite mad, of course. But then we would be starting over, and because the gangster types would be afraid it could happen again, they would be wary about too much accumulation. By simple bookkeeping you could compute the unreturned green money and figure it as a deduction from the federal deficit, as though it had been a contribution to the government. Which, of course, it would be—as any piece of currency is a claim against the government, against society.

I tried this on Meyer at Sunday breakfast. He peered across the table at me as if he thought I had lost my wits. As an economist, he was appalled. "Please stick with what you know. Please," he said.

"If Archimedes had stuck with what . . ."

"McGee, listen. It is the anticipation of the declining value of money that triggers inflation. If the public anticipated that money would be worth nothing in three months, they would spend it. And they would make it come true. Too much money after too few goods."

"But . . ."

"Please. Your motives are pure. Your monetary knowledge

is infantile. Don't spoil my hash browns. If you want to be serious about it, I will loan you some texts."

"I just stopped being serious."

"Good. Now let's get back to what you were talking about before. You have a target. The young Marino. Or his father. Or both. They are public people. I read about them from time to time, mostly about the young ones. Four children?"

"Two boys and two girls. Ruffi is the eldest."

"So you can reach them, approach them, whatever. Luckily, before anybody reaches you again. But is that what Browder would have done? If we are going to make moral judgments, take what we conceive to be moral actions, then we should set in motion what Browder hoped to set in motion."

"I don't know how he was going to do it."

"You mean you don't know what particular pipeline he was going to use. But is it important to know that? I would think that your Mr. Jornalero would get the information to the right people. If Browder's guess was right, you can then lay back until the fireworks are over, and if young Marino survives it, you have your target. But after the fireworks, if indeed they happen, no one will be coming after you anymore. So you could quit right there."

"If I should happen to want to."

"But you won't?"

"No. If I read about that boat in the paper, maybe I could quit. But I was there. I saw them. I didn't know them, but I think I owe them. If they were garbage, they were young garbage. Whoever did it, it ought to be hung around his neck like a sign. Unclean. He ought to have to carry a little bell to warn people he's coming."

"The white knight rides again."

"With rusty armor, bent lance and swaybacked steed.

Why not? Billy was a friend. I had good luck and the two little thieves had bad luck. So I'll follow your suggestion. I thank you for it. Browder thanks you. I'll buy the breakfast."

"I think you should. Anyone who can carry that much money into Mexico and bring it all back out can always buy my breakfast."

"When I counted it, I was down two thousand. Browder took out expenses, I think."

"Strange man. He didn't sound persuasive. He didn't look persuasive. But he was."

In the afternoon I tried to get in touch with Jornalero. There was no listing for a home phone. I phoned Millis. Her voice was subdued and listless.

"How are you making it?" I asked her.

"It isn't easy. And the cold in the night killed my whole garden. Everything is black and sagging and ugly. Like some kind of message. All of a sudden this place seems huge. I want to get out of it and yet I don't."

"How do you mean?"

"Frank keeps asking me to come in and sign things but I make excuses and he has to bring the papers here, and bring a notary and witnesses along. It's a terrible nuisance for him."

"He'll bill you for it."

"Of course. McGee, I kind of thought I'd hear from you sooner than this."

"I was out of town."

"Oh?"

"I was out of the country."

"Really? All I wanted, I wanted a chance to tell you that I tried to feel guilty and ashamed of us, but I couldn't manage that either. And then I've been worried about somebody trying to hurt you again."

"I had to do some scrambling about four days or so after I last saw you. But they didn't try hard enough."

"I hate to even *think* about it. Can you come see me today?"

"I called you to ask if you have any phone number for Jornalero. For his home?"

"Let me go look. I doubt it."

She took so long I got tired of waiting and switched the speaker phone on. I was pouring myself a cup of coffee I didn't need when she came back on the line. She told me I sounded as if I was in the bottom of a well. I told her that was because I have a cheap speaker phone. She said she found Jornalero's home address, but no phone number. He lived at 22 Sailfish Lagoon, Miami. As, I remembered, did the elder Marino.

"Are you going to stop by, Travis?"

"Let me have a rain check, Millis. I've got some people coming over."

"Sure you have. Okay. Forget I asked."

"Maybe after they leave. I'll phone first."

No one was coming over. Sometimes I lie well, with hearty conviction. I probably hadn't lied well to Millis because I didn't want to get involved with her, but I couldn't help wondering if just a little bit of involvement would hurt anything.

So of course, to punish bad lying, some people came over. Two people, two men in their thirties, conservative tweed jackets, neckties, a look of desks and offices. Wisner and Torbell. Employed by the DEA. Polite, impassive, with the cop air of habitual disbelief. Nothing the world had told them had been totally true, and would never be true, here or in the hereafter.

"Browder gave us a pre-operational report by phone. We'd like to check it out with you, Mr. McGee," Wisner said.

14

In the lounge I got Wisner into the big chair and Torbell onto the curved yellow couch. I brought the desk chair closer and sat in it, thus making myself a foot taller than they were. If you suspect someone wishes to give you a hard time, never arrange yourself so that he or she can look down at you.

They refused a drink. Torbell cleared his throat and took out a small notebook. He leafed back and forth through the pages, wearing a frown of self-importance which made a little knot between his brows.

I let them have their silence. So they gave up finally and Torbell said, "May we assume that you phoned in the report of his death?"

"You may so assume."

"You took fifty thousand dollars down there with you?"

"I did."

"And brought it back?"

"I brought forty-eight back. Browder took out expenses, I think."

"Where did you get the money?"

"That's irrelevant."

"We have the power to make arrests."

I held both fists out toward him. "Be my guest."

Wisner took his turn, saying, "Your attitude isn't getting us anywhere."

"Our attitudes, let's say."

"All right. Did you go down with Browder to buy cocaine?"

"No."

"Then for God's sake, man, why were you carrying all that money around?"

"Browder carried it into Mexico. I asked him at one point why his employers couldn't provide the money. He said the government was cutting back on expenses."

"Why did you provide it?"

"There was a Jack Benny skit years ago where a robber jumped out at him with a gun and said, 'Your money or your life!' And it was the long, long silence that got laughs."

"Are you saying Browder threatened you?"

"I'm saying there have been two unsuccessful attempts on my life lately and Browder heard about them from the other end. He also heard, from the other end, that the orders to kill Billy Ingraham came from Miami. Browder seemed to think that if I sat still, they'd finally get to me."

"Was this Ingraham a smuggler?"

"Why don't you people do some homework before you come out of the office to hassle somebody? Ingraham was a retired millionaire developer killed in Cannes in a hotel last month by somebody shoving a wire into his brain."

Wisner and Torbell looked at each other and Torbell said, "I think I read about that. He was the one owned the yacht three people were killed on."

"And I'm the one who found the yacht with the bodies

aboard and notified the Coast Guard. I had a deal with Billy to try to find it. And I did. And one of the bodies was of a young Peruvian girl from an important family. Her uncle is in the drug business. He demanded that the Miami group find out who killed his niece. They decided it was easier to nominate Billy and me than look for the right one. I'd found out the cruiser had come across from the Yucatan. So Browder found a way to make contact over there, and I could provide the money to make it look real, and he had me rigged out to impersonate a dead smuggler named Bucky, the Estanciero."

"Who?"

"Forget it. Forget the whole thing."

Torbell's face got red. "It took a long time to plant Browder on the inside, to plant him at a level where he could provide us now and then with some very useful information on delivery systems. It's a giant step backward to have him taken out."

"He wouldn't think so."

"What do you mean?" Wisner asked.

"He implied that all he was doing was help nail the replaceables. He was more interested in the men behind the scenes."

"I know he was," Torbell said. "The impossible dream. The men who run things never put anything on paper. They never say anything usable on a telephone. They deal strictly in cash, and by the time it is in hand, it has a history that is squeaky-clean. It has been through the big laundromat."

I almost said, "Run by Jornalero," but stopped in time. That would have led to the unlikely connection between Jornalero and Billy Ingraham, something that would have creased their bureaucratic brows with new suspicions.

Torbell perused his notebook again. He verified the date we had flown to Cancún. I took him through the travelogue, step by step. I was pleasantly surprised to find they knew about El Brujo. I told them I did not know exactly how Browder had made contact with him, and I could not remember the name of the man we met who drove us down the coast road to see the wizard.

I told them that a man had been flying into the airstrip at Tulum and buying from Brujo and flying back to a ranch strip in Florida. But each flight was more dangerous than the last, so he had brought in the kids who had stolen Ingraham's boat, and they took a shipment back in the boat in August. They came back in September and paid Brujo seventy-five thousand in counterfeit money. Brujo said he would not deal with the Florida people until somebody reimbursed him for his loss. He said he was dealing with Canadians, who were taking all he could offer.

"Browder told me it was his guess that the man who had been flying the product out of Yucatan to Florida arranged to pick up the shipment in the Keys from the kids. When he got there he learned they had paid off Brujo in counterfeit, thus cutting off the source. So he killed them and took back his seventy-five thousand along with the shipment."

"Who was this person?"

I had been turning the dilemma over and over in my mind, knowing they would come to that key question sooner or later. I became ever more convinced that this pair would blow it. Better they should be back in the office reading the computer screens.

"We never did get his name. I don't think Brujo knew it. We got a description. He was a thin man, prematurely bald, deeply tanned, wearing glasses with gold rims."

Torbell wrote this neatly in his little book.

Wisner asked, "Who killed Browder?"

"The light was strange in there. We were far from the windows and doors. The line was dense, jam-packed, and it was so long that people kept edging through it from both directions, because it was blocking the way to the airline check-in stations. It was very quick. Nobody noticed who did it."

"And they took his carryon bag?"

"He had the strap over his right shoulder. I think they hit him and slipped it off in the same motion. They thought they had a clean fifty thousand. He was the one trying to make the buy, so he was the one logically to rob. The bulk is too big for a money belt."

"One of Brujo's people?"

"Sure. Who else knew? But my guess would be it was an independent action, not directed by El Brujo. Whoever did it had all the necessary skills."

So then, of course, being bureaucrats, they took me through it again, in greater detail. They were not in operations. They were in reports. When they left, they did not thank me. After all, they were making me do my duty as a law-abiding citizen. They said they might be back if they thought of something else to ask.

Funny how your body keeps tricking your brain. Mine seems to do it far oftener than I would care to admit. I began to think there probably was a lot more about Jornalero that Millis knew and had not had a chance to tell me. And the more I could learn about Jornalero, the more useful he would be.

And maybe the thing to do—without getting involved with her, of course—was to give her a ring and sort of drop on by and chat. It could be important, I thought, to tell her she might also be in danger. But she wouldn't buy that and neither could I. Arturo Jornalero would provide a certain amount of insulation, and even had she never known him, Latino *pundonor* would not countenance the vengeance slaying of women. I decided to stop giving myself vapid excuses for seeing her.

It was a chill and early dusk when I walked into the foyer of Tower Alpha, Dias del Sol, and said, "Hi, guys," to the security personnel on duty. Their response was bleak. I understood. They were entitled to their own fantasies. So I rode to the top. Were I to guess the amount of time we spent in discussing the life and times of Arturo Jornalero, I would say it was probably eleven or twelve minutes.

The first reprise was as hasty and hungry as the time before. But the next was slower, longer and far more inventive. She had pink night lights which showed her lovely face pulled tight with straining, teeth set in the plump lower lip. She was as quick, sleek and graceful in movement as a dolphin.

She fell gasping beside me, hanging on to keep from falling off the planet. She burrowed her head into my neck and when her heart and her breathing had slowed, she said, "I made some phone calls Friday."

"What about?"

"To my friendly travel agent."

"Going somewhere?"

"Maybe we are."

"We?"

"Us. The two of us. Millis and Travis. The choice I like best, we fly to Los Angeles about February fifth—I think that's the date—and we get on the *Royal Viking Sky* and take it all the way across the Pacific, to wonderful ports, and up through the Suez Canal and the Mediterranean to London, and we fly back to Miami on the Concorde."

"We do all that? I hardly know you."

"It can be our getting-acquainted cruise. It's like eighty days, I think."

"This is so sudden."

She shook me. "Are you in there? Are you awake? Listening? A penthouse suite, man, and I buy all the goodies."

"I'm not that kind," I said.

She laughed and then said, "Seriously, do you ever think you've worn it all out around here?"

It hit a little too close to home. Too many had gone away and too many had died. Without my realizing it, it had happened so slowly, I had moved a generation away from the beach people. To them I had become a sun-brown rough-looking fellow of an indeterminate age who did not quite understand their dialect, did not share their habits—either sexual or pharmacological—who thought their music unmusical, their lyrics banal and repetitive, a square fellow who read books and wore yesterday's clothes. But the worst realization was that they bored me. The laughing, clean-limbed lovely young girls were as bright, functional and vapid as cereal boxes. And their young men—all hair and lethargy—were so laid back as to have become immobile. Meyer was increasingly grumpy, and sometimes almost hostile. I couldn't remember the last time I had tried to stop laughing and couldn't. I could hang around while the rest of the old friends slid away. I couldn't remember the last time I'd had twenty people aboard the *Flush* at the same time. When the green ripper dropped around and took the Alabama Tiger off for permanent and much-needed rest, the heirs had sold the *'Bama Gal* to a fellow who moved her around to Mobile. For a time ladies of an overwhelmingly female persuasion had stopped by to ask me where the hell the Tiger had gone. I told them he had died smiling, and they had toted him off to the family plot, and the longest floating house party in the world had at last ended. Always, they wept. The party was over.

The management had changed. Irv Deibert had departed. The city was changing. It was getting ugly and dirty and brutal. Locks and chains sold well. People full of speed and angel dust beat each other to death on the night beaches. There is a high in the life cycle of any city. I had seen it in Fort Lauderdale, and we had passed it and it was going to be a long downslope. I could ride it down or leave it and hope that memory would gradually replace the "now" with the "once upon a time."

"Seriously, Millis, maybe I have."

"Are you saying yes?"

"I'm saying let's us take a little nap. Let's sleep on it."

"The agent said those suites have their own little sun decks. Completely private."

"Uh-huh."

"It anchors in Cook's Bay at Mooréa. Billy told me that is the most beautiful place he ever saw in his whole life."

"Uh-huh."

"Frank's tax man estimates that after estate taxes I'll have an income of about seven hundred thousand, mostly tax-free —more if I sell this place, but I want to give that a lot more thought."

"Uh-huh," I said, and heard nothing of what she might have said after that.

On Monday I tried to see Mr. Jornalero at his office in Miami. He was in but did not wish to see me. I threatened to stay until he decided he could, but the tiny receptionist phoned down and two security men were sent up. I went peacefully. I drove out of my way and took a look at Sailfish Lagoon. It looked as if the same architect had designed Dias del Sol. But it had more of a fortress look than did Millis' place. And there seemed to be some elegant private homes behind the high wall, near the yacht basin.

A man who wishes nothing further to do with you presents a problem. Though I had not seen the procedure, I could guess that Arturo, between his fortress and his office, traveled in a chauffeured limousine, and that when he walked to a nearby restaurant for a business lunch, there would be a muscled fellow a half step behind him, and maybe another a few steps ahead. Rich men walk carefully in Miami.

When I had worked out a plan, I hurried back to Bahia Mar and began working on overdue maintenance on my aging runabout, the *Muñequita*, a two-ton T-Craft with a pair of one-hundred-and-twenty-horsepower stern-drive units. It shares the same slip with the houseboat. Usually I am very good about taking care of my gear, but it had been too long since I had given the *Muñequita* the loving attention she needs. I had not noticed the five-inch rip in the custom tarp cover near the gunwale on the port side, amidships. It was damp and grungy under the tarp, with mildew thriving. The automatic bilge pump had tried to take care of the incoming rain until it killed the batteries. The tarp was faded, the paint was faded and the white letters of her name on the transom had turned to ivory.

We all do penance in our own strange ways. Mine was to risk getting killed while I paid my dues. By late Wednesday afternoon, the sixteenth, the batteries were up, bilge dry, mildew swabbed away, tanks topped, tarp mended. I had taken her outside into a pretty good sea and punished my spine and kidneys jumping her head on into the swells to knock a lot of the accumulated marine crud off the bottom. The Calmec autopilot was working again. The bilge pump was operational, the ice chest cleaned and stocked, the power lifts greased, the lights checked and replaced where necessary. She wasn't at her best, but she was a hell of a lot better than before. I wondered why I had spent all that time revamping a music system and indexing tapes when the *Muñequita* needed help so badly. Meyer wandered over a couple of times to watch me at work. He wanted to know what I was doing about my personal problem, and I said I was working on it. He said it looked to him as though I was working on a boat. I didn't explain, though I should have. It wasn't fair to Meyer. But, then again, we had gotten into a game of surly. Old friends do that from time to time. To loosen the bonds, I guess.

At times it seems as if arranging to have no commitment of any kind to anyone would be a special freedom. But in fact the whole idea works in reverse. The most deadly commitment of all is to be committed only to one's self. Some come to realize this after they are in the nursing home.

With an hour of daylight left, and the day growing chillier, I headed down toward Miami, traveling inside. Black leather jacket and watch cap, and the winds of passage strumming the canvas overhead, an NPR station on the FM, speaking mildly of the news of the day on *All Things Considered*, without hype or fury. The little doll growled along, at the lowest speed that would keep her on plane, white wake hissing behind her. There was comfort in being able to enjoy the boat. I had driven myself hard to get her back in shape. I had sore muscles, barked knuckles, a torn thumbnail and tired knees. Penance. Memory of the rumbling voice of the grandpa long ago: "Anything you can't take care of, kid, you don't deserve to own. A dog, a gun, a reel, a bike or a woman. You learn how to do it and you do it, because if you don't you hate yourself."

An out-of-date morality. Anything you don't take care of, you replace. Of course, the ERA wouldn't cotton to Grandpa's including a woman in his list of ownership items. Grandma seemed a happy woman, however.

It was long past full dark when I came to the marina I had stopped at in other years. I lugged down until I had minimum headway, folded the top down, stood up with the portable spotlight and picked up the private channel markers as I made my way in. The place had expanded. I went to the gas dock and when a man sauntered out to take a line, I asked him if Wendy was around. He said she had sold the place almost two years ago, and it was now owned by Sea and Marine Ventures. They had a slip, though. I tied up, locked up, walked two blocks for pizza and beer, came back and stretched out on one of the narrow bunks in the bow and set my wrist alarm for five-thirty.

15

On Thursday morning at six-thirty I was making long slow lazy eights way out in the bay outside the sunlit structures of Sailfish Lagoon. By ten o'clock I gave up and dawdled back to the marina. The same little slip was still available, and there was a marine supplies store close at hand, so I bought various medicines and unguents, salves and brighteners for the little doll, and spent the rest of daylight improving her outward appearance, quitting at nightfall with sore arms and an easier conscience. About all that would remain to do would be to order a new custom tarp cover, and have her hauled for a bottom job.

On Friday I was on station at six, making my eights in the sunrise, binoculars handy. At twenty past six a triangular sail and a small jib went up in among a small forest of sticks, and soon a catamaran came out into the lagoon, heading for the bay. The sail was green and white. The figure aboard had on a dark red jogging suit and a white knit cap. I decided that it was not Arturo, but then when he came closer and I had him in good focus, I saw that it was. I abandoned my station and went off down the bay, heading south at a goodly pace, but keeping watch on Jornalero.

The morning breeze had freshened, and he began to zip right along. When he was far enough from his base, I swung around and came back at high speed and got between him and the lagoon. Apparently he did not notice me, or at least he did not notice the point of the maneuver. When I turned and came back out toward him, more slowly, he was moving well. He got on a long reach, and pulled his sail to the angle where one pontoon lifted out of the water, with Jornalero leaning far back for balance, hissing along at perhaps twenty to twenty-five miles an hour. It began to look trickier than I had expected.

I pushed both throttles and came up on the windward side of him. He jerked his head around and stared at me in astonishment and waved me off. The cat turned into the wind and the pontoon dropped back into the water. The empty sail flapped. I yelled over to him. "It's me! McGee! Got to talk to you."

"No!" he yelled, and came about and started off on another reach, not as productive a one, but one that would take him back into the lagoon. I caught up and moved in front of him so that he had to shear away. I bumped into a pontoon and nearly knocked him overboard. A moment later I had snagged a halyard with my boat hook. He was one very angry sailor.

"I've got nothing to say to you!"

"I don't want you to talk, Mr. Jornalero. I want you to listen. Okay? Come aboard. I'll take that thing in tow."

He was a sensible man. It took him half a minute to realize he had very little choice. We were well out from shore. I gave him a hand. He stepped on the gunwale and hopped down to the deck lightly and handily.

He sat on the engine hatch and said, "So talk."

I moved out to a broader section of the bay, towing the cat, and then I killed the engines in the *Muñequita*. There was lots of silence to talk into. The sail flapped idly on the cat.

"What I am going to say to you doesn't mean anything and won't mean anything unless you arrange to have somebody check it out. Do you know a wholesaler down in the Yucatan south of Cancún, down below Tulum? A man they call Brujo?"

"I'm listening. You're talking."

"Okay. I'll assume you don't, but I'll assume that you can get in touch with some people who do know him or know about him and who can arrange to go see him about something. They are to ask him about a man who flew in from Florida in a light plane to the Tulum airstrip four times, and made buys from Brujo and flew the product back to a ranch strip. The surveillance was getting tighter, so that same man hired the kids who stole Billy Ingraham's boat to come over and take it out by boat. He was there for the first buy, but sent them over by boat with the money for the second buy."

His expression had changed, lips pursed and twisted into contemptuous disbelief. The sun was high enough to have lost all the orange look of sunrise light, and the bay had changed from gunmetal to blue. Boat traffic was increasing. I had swiveled the pilot seat around to face him.

"Something bothering you?"

"You're talking."

"They had worked out a way to bring it in by boat."

"The people who stop boats know every way there is."

"Now we're both talking. Okay, a discussion is better than a monologue."

"McGee, there's no point in talking to me about bringing in drugs. I don't have anything to do with it."

"Not since you used to recruit mules in Colombia?"

It jolted him. I could see his intent to deny, but he backed away from that. "Not many people know that, or remember that. I worked my way up . . . and out. I head up my own corporation. It's a legitimate business all the way."

I smiled at him. "Want a beer, Arturo?"

"Before breakfast? Why not?"

I uncapped two from the cooler and handed him one. He took a long thirsty drink and wiped his mouth on the dark red sleeve.

I said, "They'd figured out a new way of bringing it in by boat." I told him about the eye bolt in the keel, the length of cable and the adjustable fins on the aluminum case. He listened carefully.

"So? A thing like that, it gets around," he said. "Others try it. Someone gets caught, and then it will no longer work. Towing a dead shark with the kilos sewn inside doesn't work anymore. Filling the hollow radio aerial with it doesn't work anymore. Dropping it in shallow water with an electronic beeper fastened to it doesn't work anymore." He stopped abruptly, took another swallow of beer and said, "I hear these things, but they have nothing to do with me. What's the point in what you are telling me?"

"When the kids came back to make a buy on their own, they had to wait around for product. They hooked up with Gigi Reyes and took her along willingly when they left. When they left they stiffed El Brujo with seventy-five thousand of funny money."

"They were very lucky they didn't die right there."

"They were too dumb to know how lucky they were. They were being tricky. When they got back to the Keys they set up a meet with the fellow who had hired them, the fellow who had given up flying across the Gulf and the Caribbean. He met them in the Keys. They had hidden the product and the good money, which they hadn't used, and tried to pry a piece of the action out of their employer. They showed him how smart they were. They showed him the rest of the funny money."

"And so," Jornalero said, faking a yawn, "he killed them as soon as he'd made them reveal the hiding place. They had cut off his source of supply. And he had no idea how stupid it was to kill the Reyes woman."

"Right. And that angry man was—in here we insert a drum roll for suspense—that man was . . . Ruffino Marino, Junior."

You often see people open their eyes wide, but it is rare to see the eyes bulge. It must have something to do with some sort of pressure in the brain. Arturo Jornalero's eyes bulged. His mouth hung open. His big white hand collapsed the almost empty beer can. I watched him pull himself together, but it took time. Lots of thoughts were spinning through his mind.

And then another thought brought him up short. "Wait a minute! Nobody in their right mind would give their true name when making a buy. The money talks."

"Mr. Jornalero, you wouldn't get the people off my back. At first you thought you could and then you decided you couldn't. I had a chance to find out what this whole scam was about. I sat and listened to Brujo say that it had been Ruffino Marino. How do I know how he knew the name? Maybe it was painted on the side of his little airplane. Maybe he gave it because he thought Brujo had seen his movie. Maybe he introduced himself because he is simply stupid. But that's the man."

Slowly and reluctantly, he bought it. He shook his head. "That explains it."

"Explains what?"

"Never mind."

"Is this going to get me off the hook? Hey!"

He raised his head and frowned at me as if he had forgotten I was there. "What? Oh, I think you can probably forget about the whole situation. Yes." He got up and got the line and pulled his cat close and climbed down into it. He freed my line and tossed it back aboard, pulled his sail taut, worked the rudder and began to head without haste toward the lagoon. He didn't turn or wave. I was out of sight and out of mind. He had a lot of other things to think about.

The breeze was from the mainland. The sea was flat. I took the *Muñequita* outside and ran north up the coast at close to forty knots, promising myself as I have so many times before that the only sane way to get from Lauderdale to Miami and back is by water, and I would never drive again.

On that Friday afternoon I made my peace with Meyer and related all the action up to date, leaving out any mention of Millis. She was not a pertinent factor. He is a good listener. The questions were infrequent. We talked aboard the *Flush*. While we talked, we worked on a jug of wine, a Gallo red. Meyer wore a white turtleneck and his cold-weather overalls. He looked more dockhand than economist.

When the tale had been told, Meyer sighed, got up and went over and looked at my tapes, and selected one of his favorites, a CBS release, *Suite for Flute and Jazz Piano*, with Jean-Pierre Rampal on flute, Claude Bolling on piano, Marcel Sabiani on drums and Max Hédiguer on string bass. Meyer likes the next-to-the-last number on side two called "Versatile," where Rampal plays a bass flute. Meyer says you can hardly ever get to hear a bass flute solo anymore.

He slotted the tape, turned on the rig, adjusted the volume. Then he fiddled with the equalizer. He likes more treble emphasis than I do. I think he is beginning to lose the higher registers. They're the ones which go first.

He sipped wine and listened to the music with his eyes closed, legs outstretched, ankles crossed. A potato-nose Buddha in meditation, totally at ease and complete within his hairy carapace. He listened all the way through the tape, and got up slowly and turned it off just as "Versatile" ended. He doesn't care for the last number. Fidgety, he calls it. It is titled "Veloce."

"It could work," he said.

"What?"

"The families of the so-called Mafia are no longer rooted in the Sicilian tradition, where even though they were in dirty businesses, there was a sense of unity and honor and loyalty within the group. They aren't families anymore. They have taken in too many outsiders. They've mongrelized the group with everything from Swensen to Pokulsnik to Moran. Honest Italian-Americans no longer have to resent the press coverage of their Sicilian brethren. But even back in the olden times, it never resembled the sentimental idiocy of *The Godfather*. These groups of gangsters, their only loyalty is to money. They've joined forces with the Latins and the rednecks because without contention and with control of the marketplace, the money is better. On the other hand, the Latins still have the sense of family and duty and honor that the Mafia had fifty years ago. The money is almost everything, but not quite. So I think Browder is right. This will cause a split. The way they are interlinked, too many people know too much. So it will tend to get bloody. Each side can turn loose the enforcers they've been using in solving normal business problems. Send them after bigger game. We can sit in the stands and cheer."

"Maybe these people have gotten soft," I said, "but if it gets bloody, they'll bring in out-of-town talent."

Meyer nodded. "Roofing contractors from Toledo."

"What do you mean?"

"That's what they used to call button men. Roofing workers they call them now."

"How did you get to know that, Meyer?"

He smiled sleepily. "You think I'm some kind of recluse?"

The Miami *Herald* put it on page one on Monday morning: DRUG WAR BREAKS OUT. Most of the action had taken place on Sunday. One Walter Hanrahan, a prominent developer and land speculator in Boca Raton, had turned the key in his golf cart and blown himself and his son as high as the roof on the pro shop. Person or persons unknown had lobbed a grenade into Francisco Puchero's convertible as he was driving along Collins Avenue in Miami Beach. It had blown his legs off and he had died en route to the emergency ward. Puchero had been prominent in community affairs. Firemen responded to an alarm regarding a Lincoln Continental on fire near a landfill in Homestead. When the fire had been doused, they found Manuel Samuro and Guillero "Pappy" Labrador wedged into the large trunk. The two men controlled the privately held corporation called Federated Trucking Express of Coral Gables. They each left a wife and three children. Samuro had recently received an award of merit from the Chamber of Commerce for his work in attracting new light industry to the area. Two masked gunmen had forced their way into a private club in Hollywood, Florida, had gone to an upstairs room where a poker game was in session and had killed five of the six players, each with two or three shots to the head. They had left the money, several thousand dollars, on the table. It had happened at 1 a.m. on Saturday. The dead were Collins, Silvestre, Zabala, Shorter and Cawley. The survivor, Brett Slusarski, had two .22 caliber bullets in his brain and was not expected to live. All were prominent long-term residents of the Gold Coast, active in business and social life.

I had a sudden vision of Browder standing in one of the anterooms of hell, welcoming the newcomers aboard with merry smile and hearty handshake.

The thing that apparently sewed it all together for the Miami *Herald* newsroom was when three Cubans broke down the gate and the door to a warehouse in Miami Shores by driving a white Ford panel delivery truck through them at five o'clock Saturday afternoon, and then hopped out with automatic weapons, killed the three men working in the warehouse with about a hundred more rounds than necessary, and then firebombed the warehouse and drove away. An unexpectedly efficient sprinkler system had contained the fire, and the authorities had recovered an estimated seven hundred kilos, or three quarters of a long ton, of pure cocaine. Ownership of the warehouse was being traced.

That brought the murders into a sharper focus, and explained the money being left on the table when the poker game was invaded. And it darkened considerably the public reputations, posthumously, of men who had given a great deal of time and thought over the years to presenting a picture of good characters and good works.

The violent deaths continued that week. The owner of a fleet of shrimp boats was killed when a car pulled up beside his on Alligator Alley and somebody shot him in the face. A man came screaming down out of the top floor of a high-rise hotel on the Beach, the Contessa. He had owned twelve points in the hotel. A commodities broker was found hanging from a live oak tree in his backyard in Fort Lauderdale, with his hands tied behind him. His daughter found him. She was five years old.

And then on Thursday the name jumped out at me. Ruffino Marino. But it was the papa. He had employed additional bodyguards, stationing one in the sixteenth-floor foyer at Sailfish Lagoon, outside his apartment door, and the other down in the lobby by the elevator that served the sixteenth to twenty-second floors. Somebody had gained entrance to the apartment above Marino's, tied and gagged the occupants, waited until nightfall, climbed from the upper balcony down to Marino's, forced the door, sliced the throat of the elder Marino as he slept, without disturbing Mrs. Marino in the nearby bed, climbed the rope back to the upper balcony, walked down the fire stairs to the parking-garage level and disappeared. Once in the clear they phoned the police so that the people they had bound and gagged could be released. Marino had been a prominent citizen, an investment adviser, with personal holdings in hotels, restaurants, beer franchises, magazine and book distribution, parking garages, linen service and liquor stores. The lengthy story about him said that he had been under investigation several times for possible racketeering, but no indictment had ever been returned.

The lengthy newspaper account described in great detail the sophisticated security system with its computerized video and audio scanning, its perimeter sensors which could detect all prowlers. In fact, the account did so much marveling about how clever the murderers had been that it was quite clear the reporters believed that some of the fellows operating all that great equipment had been bribed to turn deaf and blind and dumb during the murder. And that, of course, is the vulnerable segment of all foolproof systems, the fools who take care of it.

The picture showed a broad-faced, bull-necked bald man with heavy black eyebrows and a toothy smile so broad it produced a squint. He wore a sport coat and a shirt with an open collar. A thick thatch of gray hair sprouted from the V of the open shirt, and a medal on a chain dangled against the hair below the wide throat the knife had sought and found in the darkness. The piece spoke of the widow, Rose Ellen Marino, and her work with handicapped children. The four children of the marriage were named, and only Ruffi Junior got any specific mention, as a producer and director of motion pictures and an investor in theatrical properties. It listed the powerboat races he had won.

The weekend papers had editorials about the bloodbath, as did the national news magazines. It had been correctly pegged as a war between the old-time underworld and the new drug barons, after several years of uneasy peace. One newspaper, *USA Today*, was perceptive enough to note that the Canadian mobs were probably standing on the sidelines smiling. The editorials bemoaned the existence of the cocaine trade. The dollar value of the business was pegged at one hundred billion dollars, with an estimated one hundred metric tons coming in each year, with no more than six percent of it confiscated by the authorities. There had been seventeen violent deaths over a very few days, which became eighteen when Slusarski died without regaining consciousness. Had they known the connection, they could have counted up to twenty-five—a federal employee, two street urchins, two boat thieves, a Peruvian debutante and an old man in Cannes. It was the prominence and the civic reputation of so many of the suddenly and violently dead which led to so much coverage. The two standard shots were of the smoking remains of a golf cart, and of a side view of the Contessa Hotel, with a dotted line curving down from a high floor to a Germanic X on the pavement. Local television hit a new low in taste with the remarkable question "And how did you feel, Karen, when you found your daddy hanging from that tree?"

A guest column in *The New York Times*, reprinted in local papers, was by an ex-employee of the DEA. He said, in part, "It is valuable, small, easy to smuggle. As easy as diamonds, but unlike diamonds it is a fashionable consumable. It is psychologically habituating without being physiologically addictive. It is the smart party snort for the young, middle-class, half-successful, upwardly mobile professional, as well as for the career thief. It can provide a rush of extreme confidence accompanied by erotic fervor and torrents of oratory. It can also rot the nose and encourage suicidal driving habits. It is so expensive it has the cachet of conspicuous consumption at parties peopled by musicians, artists and writers, the sign of a gracious contemporary hostess.

"A vast and deadly infrastructure provides it—from the plucking of the leaves of the highland bushes to the tiny gold straw that sucks a line into the delicate nostril of a mayor's mistress in Oregon and makes her eyes sparkle. Within the present context, nothing can stop it. The losses of officialdom are within the limits, say, of spoilage in the vegetable business. It has been brought in by drone aircraft, radio-controlled. It has been brought in by one-man submarine. It has been shot ashore by slingshot from freighters docking at Tampa. Even were importation to be punished by death it would still go on, because the lifetime wages of a laborer can be carried in a single pocket.

"The only possible solution to this deadly trade is to ignore it. Legalize it along with marijuana. Then the infrastructure will sag and collapse. It will no longer be fashionable. Street dealers will no longer hustle new customers on high school sidewalks. And men won't die in the squalid massacres we have seen recently in southeast Florida.

"But maybe it is too late for legalization. The bureaucracy of detection and control has a huge national payroll. Florida's economy is as dependent on Lady Caine as it is on cattle or fishing. Legalization will be fought bitterly by politicians who will say that to do so will imperil our children. Are they not now imperiled?"

Meyer brought that guest column to my attention. He is a newspaper freak. He has to have an oversized postal drawer instead of a box.

The killings had stopped. On Saturday evening I went over to Meyer's boat and told him I thought we ought to go to a special Mass at St. Matthew's on Sunday, to pay our respects to the dear departed Ruffino Marino, a Knight of Malta.

16

A friend of a friend of an independent motion picture distributor in Miami found me a glossy eight-by-ten publicity shot of young Ruffino Marino in full living color. The typed data stuck to the back told me I was looking at Mark Hardin, the star of the newest release by Feature Masterworks, Inc., entitled *Fate's Holiday*.

Ruffi looked directly into my eyes. He was handsomely tanned. He had a very large amount of shiny black hair that curled around his ears, hiding all but the lower lobes. He had long eyelashes, a smallish puffy mouth with the lips parted just enough to reveal the gleam of wet teeth, very white. Black hair was combed across the broad tanned forehead. He wore one eyebrow higher than the other. Sort of quizzical. He had a cute cleft in his chin. He wore a gold choker chain of a size useful for restraining Great Danes. He had long hollows in his cheeks and a fuzzy hollow in his throat. His eyes looked wet, like his teeth.

But the film star did not attend his daddy's Mass. A lot of cops were there, and a lot of burly men in civilian clothes who kept whipping their heads from side to side, looking at everything. A lot of women in veils. A lot of important-looking couples arriving by private limo. Very, very few politicians. Very, very few public figures. Had he died of a coronary on the seventeenth hole at the club, all the politicians would have been there.

We had a third-floor front room in a hotel diagonally across the boulevard from St. Matthew's. The day was clear and bright. We both had binoculars. We looked for people the same size as Ruffi. We looked for anybody scooting in, hiding his face. We watched them go in and we watched them come out, the family last of all. Ruffi hadn't been able to make it.

On the way back in my blue pickup Meyer voiced the opinion that Ruffi might be way off to our right somewhere, wedged into a drum which had later been filled with wet cement, allowed to harden, and rolled off the deck of a coastal freighter. And perhaps a picture of him in the drum, prior to cementing him in, had been delivered in Lima.

"I'm sorry you had to say that, Meyer. I've been thinking it, but I hoped nobody would say it. I mean, it would be a nice thing to know, but damn little chance of my getting to know it for sure. And unless I know it for sure, I am going to have to go around flinching at every little noise behind me."

"No sources? Nobody to ask?"

"I thought of Willy Nucci, but last I heard he was retired. He sold the hotel and he was going to travel, but he got sick, they say. I think he's still in Miami. Things change a lot faster than they used to. I don't know who to ask anymore."

"Maybe I can find out where Willy is."

"You, Meyer? How?"

"Details of the sale. It had to be a big dollar value. Trace it through public records. Dade County Courthouse records. How long back?"

I had to think about that, and relate it to other things that had happened in my life. "Right about two years, maybe a little less."

It took Meyer all of Monday and half of Tuesday to nail it down. He went there, back and forth, on a Trailways bus. Meyer likes riding buses. He says it is the ultimate privacy. Nobody ever talks to you. You sit high enough to look over the tops of the cars and the bridge railings and see the world. You can read and think. He says tourists on cruises get off their luxury vessels and clamber onto buses, paying large fees to stare at the foreign scenery while somebody yaps at them about what they are looking at over a PA system so dreadful they catch one word in three. He says he has seen things out of bus windows so absurd, so grotesque, so fantastic, that riding the bus is sometimes like gliding through someone else's dream.

But he came back with the information that I could find Willy Nucci in #4 at 33 Northeast 7th Street. The company that had made the sale had been WiNu Enterprises, from whom Willy, as a private citizen, had purchased the first mortgage. The mortgage money was paid into Willy's account at a branch of the Sun Banks. When cash withdrawals were made, a young woman with a limited power of attorney would bring Willy's check to the branch bank and be given the cash.

On Wednesday, the thirtieth, I picked up a rental Buick from my local Budget outlet and drove down. I felt better in the rental than in the blue truck. Miss Agnes was too conspicuous and too well known. I wondered if I should get rid of her. And also unload the *Busted Flush* and the *Muñequita*. They were signs and symbols of my lingering adolescence. I could make do with rent-a-car, rent-a-boat, rent-a-girl, rent-a-life. Anything busts, mister, you get hold of us right away and we come over and replace whatever it is. You can buy full insurance coverage right here, so you'll never have another worry. Lose a friend and we can replace him or her with a working model, same size, age, education and repartee. Lose or break yourself and we will replace you too, insert you right back into the same hole in reality from which you were ejected.

It was a smaller street than I expected, and it wandered aimlessly under old trees. Number thirty-three was old Moorish, a faded orange-yellow with vines crawling on it, looking for cracks. There was an ornamental iron fence around the small yard, and a walk that bisected the yard and went up three steps to two doors under an overhang. One and two were on the left, three and four on the right. Beside the four was an arrow pointing up, and a button. I pushed the button.

A woman's voice came out of the little round speaker. "Whizzit?"

"McGee. Travis McGee to see Willy Nucci."

"Sec." In a little while the door buzzed and I went in and up narrow stairs. There was a window of fixed glass at the top of the stairs, looking east, looking across a broad reach of bay toward the concrete puzzle of Miami Beach. Down below was a walled garden, beautifully tended.

I tapped on the door and a big girl let me in. She was a standard-issue plastic, pneumatic blonde with wide happy blue eyes, sun-streaked hair, snub nose, smiling mouth and a suggestion of overbite. She wore a white knee-length T-shirt, and across her substantial breasts were the big red letters M A S C O T.

"Aren't *you* the big one!" she said. "Come on in."

"We make some kind of matched set," I said.

"Get off that already!" Willy said in a frail voice. He was grinning at me from a nest of bright pillows on an oversized couch. I hoped I hadn't revealed the shock I felt upon seeing him. Willy has always been a small man, pale and scrawny. Now he looked about as big as a starving child. His hair was gone, and the yellow skin was pulled tight to the skull shape. We had done a little business from time to time in years past. He had always been cool, remote, careful. I was one of the very few who knew that he actually owned the hotel he worked at.

Now here he was, grinning at me, delighted to see me—a character change. The handshake was like taking hold of a few little breadsticks.

"Pull up a chair, McGee. Tell me what you're doing for laughs."

"Come to think of it, I haven't been laughing very much lately, Willy."

"Having no fun?"

"Not very much."

"Then you're not thinking good. There's a Hungarian proverb: Before you get a chance to look around, the picnic is over. What'll you drink?"

"A beer would be fine."

"I got Carta Blanca."

"Better than fine."

"Briney, get my friend McGee a Carta Blanca, love."

She left the big room. I looked around at it. "Great place here, Willy."

He shook his head. "I was going to live great. Everything I wanted. The timing was terrible."

"I heard you were sick."

He grinned at me, a merry grin. "What I'm doing here is

dying. Right before your very eyes. I was getting chemo-
therapy, but I finally had them stop that shit. The only way I
could be half-ass comfortable was smoke pot all day, and that
fogged up my head so I couldn't keep track of anything.
Where I got it is in the pancreas, and I don't even know what
that is or what it does. Or used to do."

Briney brought the beer in a big frosty mug. I said,
"Thanks, Briney. What does that stand for?"

"Well, it was Brenda and then Brenny and then I got hung
up on surfing and I was out there all day riding waves and
so it was Briney. Like salt."

"California meat," Willy said in that whispery voice.
"Stuff Greenberg sent her to me as a free gift. You ever meet
him? No, I guess you wouldn't. She owed him one and he
owed me one, and so it goes. What I'll do, McGee, if you're
going sour, I'll will her to you."

"Human bondage is against the law," I said.

"McGee," he said in his tiny voice, "she's had nurse train-
ing. We had her twenty-fifth birthday party last week. She's
healthy as horses and she can cook anything you can think
up, and she keeps this place clean, and she loves to eat and
sleep and cook and dance and sunbathe."

I stared at him and then at her. "You're serious?"

"What am I going to do?" he said. "I send her back to
Stuff, I'm ungrateful. Almost everybody I know is a mean
bastard except you. You are mean too, but in another kind of
way than the other guys. And if you're not having any fun,
she'll be a nice change for you."

"Don't you have any say in this?" I asked her.

"Where do you live, McGee?" she asked.

"In a houseboat at Bahia Mar in Fort Lauderdale."

"Hey, I've never lived on a boat! Neat-o!"

"Don't you have something you'd rather do? Someplace
you'd rather go?"

She grinned at me. There was one gold filling, way back. "Shit, man. Everybody has to be *someplace*."

Willy said, "It's a load off my mind. I've got everything pretty well straightened out except Briney. And now that's done."

"Have you heard me say yes?" I said.

"Jesus, Nooch. Maybe you came on him too fast. Maybe he's got a girl there to take care of him. Maybe he's married. Maybe he's gay."

"None of the above," I heard myself say.

"You hear about me, you come get her, okay?" Willy asked. "Briney'll have cash money to pay her own way."

"I've never seen anybody so enthusiastic," she said, and walked out.

"What are you trying to do to me, Willy?"

"She sees a dumb bird in a tree singing, it's the greatest bird ever, singing the best song in the world. It sets her up for hours. She hops up for the sunrise, and it starts off the best day she ever had—every day. She hums to herself all the day long. I turn on the TV, she leaves the room. She says it is like living secondhand. Every morning, every night, she stands on her head in a corner fifteen minutes."

"Willy, you can't give people to people."

"You heard me say I'm dying? A dying guy can do what he wants. You hurt her feelings, right? In ten minutes she won't even remember. Okay, you had a reason to come here. You've never come to see me without a reason."

"Do you stay in touch?"

"Guys stop by. We do a little talking. I've been dropping business, spreading it around, mostly unloading it on the people doing the work. All I got left is a little bit of numbers and some sharking that is being paid off slow. So I know mostly what is going on."

"So you lost some friends lately?"

"What I lost was some guys I knew."

"What about Ruffino Marino?"

"One of the ones I knew. Not too bad of a guy. I read once about a cowboy escaping from the Indians. What he did, he walked backward across a sandy place and he had this big leafy tree limb and he brushed out his footprints. That was Big Ruffi. He got big in the Church, and all that. A thousand years ago he was a button man out of Cleveland, doing invitation jobs in Vegas and Pittsburgh and wherever. So he gets to be a big man in the community, million-dollar condo, wife and four kids, the youngest nineteen and all of them out of the house, and they come in and stick him like a pig."

"Why?"

"I don't know. I heard what people are guessing, though. I heard he tried to put the lid on something Ruffi Junior did. There's a legitimate crazy. He wants to be some kind of a hero but he doesn't know what kind. Some girl from a very important South American family that works close with the drug people here, she got herself raped and killed during some kind of drug hustle, and it wouldn't have happened if anybody knew who she really was. Anyway, Ruffi Junior went to his old man and confessed he'd been a part of the scene. He swore he hadn't killed anybody, and didn't know that his pal, Bobby Dermon, was going to kill three people until it was done.

"Big Ruffi was probably sore as boils that his oldest kid was getting into a drug thing after the old man had dry-cleaned the family name. Ruffi Junior had boats, airplanes, fast cars, anything he wanted. The old man tried to put the lid on it. After all, his son hadn't killed anybody. It was his son's friend, Bobby. But somehow the whole Latin crowd got word that Ruffi Junior had killed the girl. They came after Big Ruffi and he gave them Dermon.

"They took Dermon someplace and they didn't kill him. I

heard they probably took him to a warehouse where it wouldn't matter if he screamed, and they hot-wired him and kept plugging him in until they got the very same story over and over, and it turned out it had been Ruffi Junior all along. People think that by then Dermon wasn't going to live anyway, so they took a Polaroid shot of him, and they sent the photo and the tape to Big Ruffi, and they put Dermon into a condo foundation one of them was building down past Dinner Key. They asked for Ruffi Junior. Big Ruffi said he was gone, and he didn't know where. Frank Puchero had been involved in the Dermon thing, so they threw a grenade into his convertible. Then Hanrahan was blown up on general principles, and it spread from there. A war, like old times."

"Now it's quiet?"

"I hear it is quiet but it is tense. Big Ruffi got it for trying to put the lid on and not telling them where to find his kid."

"Why all the others?"

"Why not? All it ever was was a working arrangement. When it starts to come apart, then people get what maybe they asked for in other deals a while back. Maybe short weight or short money—just a suspicion, not enough to rock the boat for. Once it opens up you pay back old scores. And new ones."

"Anybody have any idea where Ruffi Junior is?"

"Nobody knows. Maybe he's in Toronto, or maybe he's in Tampa. Wherever he is, he's scared shitless. He's sending out for food, booze and broads."

"He wasn't at the Mass."

"So I heard. Nobody thought he'd be there, but they covered it anyway. You were there?"

"I kind of want him."

"Do yourself a favor. You get a line on him, don't dirty your hands. Call me and I'll get the word to the right place."

"It's a little more personal than that."

"Why should it be personal?"

"I got to the three people he killed before the law did."

He smiled and shook his head. "You are a nutcake like Ruffi Junior. Not the same kind, but just as nutty. What are you? The Spotless Avenger? Whyn't you go find work in a comic book? Ruffi is a sad sorry little creep who can't walk past a mirror without stopping and smiling at himself."

"Okay. Maybe, if I find him, maybe I'll call you."

There was a sudden twist of pain on his face, a spasm of one arm. He smiled again. "Don't take too long. Go get Briney."

I found her in the kitchen. She hurried to him. "A bad one, kid," he said. She trotted out of the room and came back with a hypo kit. She flipped his robe open, turned him to expose a wasted haunch and shot him, scrubbed the place with cotton dipped in alcohol.

Willy said apologetically, "It's spread to places where it hurts. Listen. McGee. You've got everything. Don't piss your life away because you got some kind of blues. Honest to God, I never started to live until I found out I was dying. You promise you'll come get Briney?" His voice was getting slurred. She was where he could not see her, bobbing her head violently at me, frowning.

"Who am I to turn down something like that?"

"Atta boy. That's using the old . . ." And the next inhalation was a snore.

She walked over to a chair and dropped into it, crossed her arms, lowered her chin to her chest. I saw one tear fall to her lap. She raised her head and gave me a sweet sad smile. She spoke softly. "He was really glad to see you. I'm glad you came. I hope you'll come back soon. Please. He is not all that glad to see some of the other people who visit him. Some of them are very weird. Some of them, I have to leave the room while they talk. Thanks for telling him you'd come after me."

"A pretty strange offer."

"He's a funny old guy. He thinks I'm some dumb little kid he has to find a foster home for. Stuff is an old buddy of his. Stuff heard he was very depressed and he'd have to have around-the-clock nursing or go into a nursing home to die. So he sent me like a present. Only what he did was give me round-trip airfare and ten thousand dollars to come cheer Willy up, make him feel part of life again. It took a little while but I nudged him out of it. He can accept dying now. We talk about it. He's beginning to think of it as some kind of an adventure. A trip. He hates the needle because it takes him out of it, takes away some of what he has left. He hates to sleep at night. He talks to me about the old days. He hasn't got anybody else in the world. That must really be hell on wheels, to have nobody at all. He says he wasted his whole life and if he gets another life to live, it'll be different."

"I've never heard of a better present."

She shrugged. "So you do what you can. I gave him Demerol, so he'll be out four hours. Do come back."

She took me to the door. I looked back at her and said, "People are always giving you presents and then taking them back."

She winked at me. "Ain't it hell?"

17

When I walked into the lounge of the *Busted Flush* my phone was ringing.

Millis said, "Trav? My God, I bet I've called you thirty times. A friend of mine is here and he would like you to talk to him."

"Put him on."

"No. He wants you to come here."

"Who is he?"

"He goes sailing in the mornings."

"Oh. Well, sure. Give me a half hour."

When she let me into the duplex, the sea through the great windows was a soft shade of gray and there were streaks of rose and pink in the eastern sky, the afterglow of the unseen sunset behind us. They had not yet turned on the lights. Jornalero struggled up from a deep chair to shake my hand. He seemed to have lost the flavor of confidence and authority. His voice was softer, subdued. Millis brought drinks and turned on a low lamp on the table between our chairs. Our chairs were at right angles to each other. The light winked on the ice in his drink as he raised it to his lips. It left his face in shadow. Millis sat off to my left in darkness, sat yoga-fashion on a low square table surfaced in squares of ornamental tile. I had the feeling that she sat off to the side like that when Jornalero was keeping her, when he had asked men to come to the place he rented for her, to talk their business in safety.

"Was it what you hoped would happen?" he asked.

"I didn't know what would happen."

"A craziness," he said. "Madness. Hatred. I have lost valued friends. Friends of many years. I've sent my wife far away, just in case. There isn't any meaning to it anymore. Tit for tat. That's all it is. You kill my friend, I kill your friend, you kill me, my brother kills you. Did you know it would be like this, McGee, when you told me about Ruffino's boy?"

"I didn't. Browder did."

"Who is Browder?"

"An undercover agent with the DEA. He hoped it would be like this. He's dead."

"Why would anybody hope for this? Fathers and sons. Husbands."

"He said that if you shake the tree, the ripe fruit falls out. He told me the law can't touch you, Mr. Jornalero. He said you might possibly be indicted for violating laws about foreign currency exchange, but probably never convicted in any way that would stick."

"Then he is the one who told you about the mules?"

"That's right."

"I wondered. That was a long time ago. I am three and four times removed from any of that. I am a legitimate businessman."

"But you launder the cash."

He didn't answer directly. He seemed to be looking off into the distance, into the final fading streak of rose. "Sometimes it comes in cardboard boxes," he said. "Thirty and forty at a time. Supermarket boxes. Lux soap. Shredded wheat. Grapefruit juice. Sealed with silver duct tape. Fives, tens, twenties, fifties, hundreds. Just thrown in and packed down and they had no idea how much was there. They take my word. My word is always good. I've got two girls who do nothing but sort it, count it and band it. They won't have much to do for a while. Not for very long, though. Then it will start flowing again. It has to come somewhere. It has to come to a safe place."

"Three percent?" I asked.

He sighed. "Three to some. Four to others." He turned toward me and his tone changed. "My damned fool countrymen did a number on Tom Beccali last night."

"Who is he?"

"A prominent area businessman. Like me. Like Ruffino. I told them enough was enough. It's over. Forget it. But they thought the scales were out of balance. He won't be missed for some time. He travels a great deal. He is at the bottom of the ocean. The police don't know that, and the news people don't know it, but *they* know it. And I'm the logical response. Millis said I have to have your permission."

"For what?"

"He wants to be my house guest for a few days, maybe longer."

"I have no say in the matter. It's up to you."

"It was the only place I could think of," he said.

"Why my permission?" I asked Millis.

"Arturo used the wrong word," she said. "I meant more like advice. Could it be a bad idea?"

"Who knows you're here?" I asked him.

"No one outside this room. And two men downstairs."

"But there are people who know you two used to be friends?"

"Yes. Quite a few."

She broke in. "But the security here is good. I can tell anybody I'm alone here. He'll stay out of sight. What do you think, Travis?"

"It's up to you. But don't the security people downstairs know his name?"

"I used a different name."

She stirred uneasily. "Fortez," she said. "One hell of a shock."

He leaned toward me, putting his empty glass down. "Mr. McGee, even if I had known it would all go this far, I still would have had to pass along your information about young Ruffi. There were some doubts about it for a time. But not after his friend Bobby Dermon was . . . interrogated. They flew down to the Keys in a float plane Ruffi borrowed from a friend. They both boarded that boat. The man who'd made the buy had hidden the money and the product and he tried to negotiate a better deal. They tied him up and questioned him. Dermon kept the women from trying to leave. Once they found the money and the shipment, they raped the women. Ruffi killed both the women. Dermon suffocated the man by jamming the money into his mouth. Her uncle in Lima now has the full story. I wanted to talk to you to tell you nobody wants you dead, not anymore."

"How about Ruffi?"

"He will be found. Sooner or later. There is a reward. A big one. And so the interest is high. He is the rabbit in the forest with ten thousand wolves."

"Nothing that happens is going to resurrect Billy Ingraham," I said.

"Or many, many others," Jornalero said.

"But Billy was an innocent bystander," I told him.

"Innocent people and guilty people are killed every day. Stray bullets in small wars. Fog on the Interstates. If innocence could keep us alive, my friend, we'd all be saints."

"I'm sure Billy would be very comforted to hear that, Jornalero, especially from the lips of a man who's made it big in the world's dirtiest business, an unctuous, well-dressed, high-living son of a bitch who may have even convinced himself he isn't doing anything rotten. All you do is make all the rest of it possible by keeping it profitable."

"Trav!" Millis said sharply.

"I do a lot of good in the world," Arturo said. "The rest of it is a small favor for old friends."

I grinned at him. "I know. Somebody has to do it. Right? Now your hide is at risk too, Artie. I hope they find you."

"Goddamn it!" Millis said. "Who are you to get so Christly? From stuff Billy told me about you . . ."

"I never told you I was perfect. Have a happy reunion, kids."

After I was back aboard my refuge, drinking by a single low light, with Edye singing along with the Tres Panchos in the background, I mourned the sappiness of my exit lines. I had used old Arturo to get myself off the hook, and then took some swings at him. Somewhere there are intelligent and highly skilled design engineers working the bugs out of ever more deadly weapons—lasers to blind armies, multiple multiple warheads, flames that stick to flesh and can't be extinguished, heat beams to fry the crews inside their tanks. And they pack up the printouts and turn off the computers and have a knock with the guys on the way home to the kiddies. Somebody has to do it. Right?

Night and gin and music—the right setting for peeling off

the thin clinging layers of bullshit and finding one's way down closer to the essential self. I had let loose on Jornalero because I had been disturbed by the feeling of the relationship between him and Millis. A residual fondness, a product of years shared. And that of course could be peeled back to reveal a dissatisfaction with myself for having sought out sex with her. That first time was by her invitation. From then on by my design. The proceedings had been very skillful, orgasms noteworthy, pleasure intense. But I had not gotten one millimeter past the surface gloss of those tilted green eyes. Though our actions had elicited a wide range of sounds and responses from her, from little yelps to earthy groans, she was just about as real to me as would have been one of those blow-up pneumatic ladies Japanese sailors tote aboard for the long freighter trips and stow in little satchels under the bunk until needed. They now make them with microprocessors, little motors, long-life batteries and voice boxes. Crever people.

So, as Edye sings of her *corazón*, peel back another leaf. I had wanted the curiously impersonal relationship with Millis because I did not want to set up any new emotional debts or obligations. I wanted no involvement in any significant dimensions. I wanted Millis as a receptacle.

So, recharge the glass with more ice and Boodles, change the tape and go back and peer under the next leaf. Why no emotional involvement? Because there was nothing left in the inventory. Nothing left to give. I had said "forever" too many times to too many people. I had spent my stock. I was bankrupt.

With the next leaf pulled back I discovered that the bankruptcy was what was souring the look of my world. That led me back to Willy Nucci's concern and advice.

But, for God's sake, you can't suddenly spring up and clap your hands and say, "Hey, what a wonderful world!" Piss and vinegar can't be summoned on command. The muted colors of a muted life will not suddenly brighten because you think it a good idea they should. What could I look forward to otherwise? To a winding down? To becoming a sour, peevish old bastard, too stubborn to admit loneliness. Long ago I had been unable to commit myself totally when I should have. And later, when I wanted to, the timing was tragic. But as Jornalero had pointed out, the bad things happen to the innocent and to the guilty without reference to their desires or merit.

The answer, of course, would be under the next leaf. So I peeled it back and there it was. Nothing! Just a little hole in the middle, protected by all the folded leaves of self-deception. McGee, the empty vessel. The orifice had at one time been packed full of juice and dreams. Promises. Now there was a little dust at the bottom of it. Some webs across it. It is to moan, beat the breast, tear the hair. I had no smart retort, nothing witty to say to myself. I was ten thousand times better off than Willy Nucci physically. But in spirit, he was laps ahead.

So I pulled myself away from the dubious pleasures of introspection and self-analysis. Think about Ruffino Marino the Second. A smart-ass. Vain. Tricky. Violent. What would he be thinking now? I could assume he had sense enough to be terrified. They had gotten into the old man's fortress and slit his fat throat in bed as he slept. He had awakened, dying, unable to make a sound, able to thrash a little but not enough to awaken his wife.

He would probably know Bobby Dermon was gone too. To run and to hide takes the motivation of terror. To run and hide well takes money. Lots of it. Assume he was able to grab it before he started running.

Okay, even though he couldn't act, he probably thought of himself as an actor. Out of his vanity he would think his face would be recognized anywhere. I got out the publicity shot of him and studied it. Take off most of that glossy black hair, down to a boot camp cut. Dye it pale blonde. Dye the brows too. Pad out those flat cheeks with some cotton behind the side teeth. Glasses with gold rims. New ID, Nordic name, fake address, a history easy to memorize. To trace somebody, you have to know their habits, their tastes. In time they slip up. A man cannot change himself into somebody else. When there is no great urge to find a man, he can stay lost. No problem there. The countryside is full of men with new identities.

I decided it would be stupid romanticism to believe for an instant that I could find him. I believed also that young Marino did not have the discipline or control to get lost and stay lost. He couldn't let himself fade into the woodwork. Too much ego. Too much restlessness and recklessness.

I was startled by the bong of someone stepping on the mat on the aft deck next to the small gangplank. When there was no knock at my door, I took the little Airweight from its temporary resting place in the back of the yellow couch, wedged into the springs and padding behind an inconspicuous slit in the fabric, and went to the door, staying well off to one side as I flicked the switch for the outside light. I looked out cautiously and saw nothing.

After five minutes of listening and waiting, I went forward, up into the bow, released the hatch, lifted it a few inches and listened, then folded it back silently, eeled out and squatted in half darkness. Nothing. Nothing on the side decks or up on the sun deck. Nothing on the bow or stern.

I went down through the bow hatch, dogged it from below and went back through the lounge to turn out the aft deck light. Then it occurred to me that maybe someone had left a note.

It was not exactly a note. It was three more pipe-cleaner cats arranged in a row at the edge of the mat. A black one, a white one and a gray one. If it was some kind of kid trick, the point eluded me. Now I had five of the beasts. Again there was the tiny tug at memory. It was like trying to remember the name of a place you had visited long ago. All I knew was that if I could retrieve the memory, it would be saddening somehow. I had not liked that place.

I picked them up to flip them into the trash tin, then changed my mind and brought them in. I locked the door, turned out the light and put the cats with their prior visitors —the two colorful ones—on a shelf with a raised lip near my bed. I put them in the order of delivery. The red one shortly after New Year's Day, the blue one a week later. And now, on the thirtieth, in order—black, gray, white. A code of some kind? R-B-B-G-W. Someone was trying to tell me something, but the message wasn't clear. Cat, kitten, feline, tomcat, puss, pussycat. Nothing there to remind me of anything except a woman I had known once, who died long ago.

The last day of January was warm and gentle, with a breeze from the southwest moving the kind of air that makes the snowbirds get off the airplanes and say, "Ah!" I walked to the hotel and bought a morning paper to go with a stunted breakfast of juice and coffee. Nothing about any Tom Beccali. The murders looked ordinary. A Haitian had drowned his crippled sister in a bathtub. A drunk passed out in his own driveway and his wife ran over him with a Ford station wagon—seven or eight times. A naked secretarial trainee had shoved an ice pick into her supervisor. A crazy had burst into the bus terminal at a full gallop, firing at random blacks with a .22 target pistol, killed one, slightly wounded four. A thirteen-year-old girl had shot a fourteen-year-old boy to death in a dispute about whose turn it was to ride a bicycle. Everyday stuff—the kind of thing you read about in every urban paper in the land. Minor characters in the play buying lifetime regret. People scuffling around, trying to make sense out of the mismatched parts of their lives.

I walked over to see Meyer, but he was out and the *Veblen* was locked up. The chairs had been taken in off the cockpit deck, so it looked as if he would be gone a while. And he hadn't even mentioned going anywhere. So I had not been mentioning where I was going lately. The hell with him. The hell with everybody on every vessel in the whole damn yacht basin and every other yacht basin and boat dock within a forty-mile radius.

When I got back there was a man up on my sun deck. He looked down at me over the stern rail and smiled a merry smile. "Welcome aboard," he said. He was a brown man with a lantern jaw, blue eyes, dingy teeth. He wore a white shirt open to the belly to show a good rippling of the kind of chest muscles you get from weights. He had three gold strands around his neck. His ears stood straight out like Mortimer Snerd's. He had on blue shorts and running shoes. He had a brown purse on a long narrow shoulder strap. He had a pale brown brush cut and bushy sideburns that came down past his ears. I guessed they were to draw attention from the ears, but instead they seemed to highlight them. When I climbed up to the sun deck and saw him at closer range I could see how the weights had built his arm and leg muscles. He stood about five ten, a very solid five ten.

"And you would be . . ."

"Let me get a look at you. I been interested in you."

"That's nice. I can't think of anything I want to buy today. What are you selling? Muscle building?"

He kept his smile. "Hey, that's pretty good. My hobby is the old bod. Treat it right and it treats you right. Where can we talk?"

"Right here."

"McGee, let's at least get a little bit under cover. Like over there where you steer this thing. Suppose somebody took a shot at me and hit you instead, after all you've been through."

"Who are you?"

"I'm the Foreman, pal. I'm the Capataz." And as he passed me on the way toward the wheel, he whacked me on the arm. He sat in the pilot seat and left the copilot seat to me. He swiveled around toward me.

"You sent those three clowns after me?" I asked.

"Listen, Rick, Louie and Dean are not the very best in the world, but they're pretty good. I mean, they were pretty good. You did a hell of a job on Sullivan. The bone guy says it was a twisting impact, and the legs were turning as you went over them. So all he could do was freeze both knee joints. Rick is going to walk like one of those electric people, you know."

"Like a robot."

"That's it."

"He happened to get in the way."

"You see a robot coming, duck. He wants you so bad he can taste it. You don't need to worry about Dean Matan. He got taken out in the troubles."

"Why did you come here?"

Still smiling, he said, "There aren't too many places left I can go, you want to know the truth. A lot of things are over for good. Over and done. Browder was a plant. It didn't take too long to figure that out. But what he turned in didn't do much damage. They just change the routes around a little, zig instead of zag. They lose a little that's coming in, and they lose a little in transshipment. But there you are. For the little guys like me, it's nothing much, right? But the boss men, they've gone crazy. There they were, tucked back out of sight, no way to pin a thing on any of them, and they go nuts. I don't know what it is. Why should it make so much difference that Ruffi the actor killed the Reyes kid? Maybe it's because there's been too much money for too long. Or things have been easy for too long. What we got here, you'd think it was Jews and Palestinians. All of a sudden everybody hates everybody. My boss ends up in the back of a car, fried. I get orders to take out the boss of the people who took my boss out, so I did. Now they are working their way down the list. So I hang around, my head is going to roll. I got warned day before yesterday. What is it, something in the air down here? I can't even get to my safety-deposit box. I've got a little over forty dollars. Think of that! Cappy, who had it all made. Who'd believe it?"

"Why did you come here? What do you want with me?"

He didn't seem to hear the question. "The big hassle is over. Annoyed the shit out of the politicians and the developers. Tourism is down already, and all of a sudden all over the country there's news pictures of dead bodies. It has to hurt. So the pressure is on to stop it, but it won't stop it. I mean, it will be a lot more quiet. But it will keep happening for a while. You have to get the scales dead even. After that happens the money machine gets cranked up to full speed again, and the payoffs get made and the product comes in and gets shipped out, and dollars get turned into pesos and sent south. The coke base will come in by ship and they'll keep cooking it into white lady out in those garages in the suburbs, and the money will roll." He turned to look directly at me. "And I need twenty thousand dollars. I think six months will clear things up. I've got a place I can go. When I can come back and get to my box, I'll pay you back thirty."

"I don't have that kind of cash money."

"I think you do."

"If I did, why would I give it to you?"

"It would be a loan, like I told you."

"Absolutely no way."

"You haven't heard about the sweetener. As a kind of bonus, I'll give you young Ruffi. You can sell him to the Latinos. I can't get close enough to them to make a deal without getting myself hurt."

"How would I go about getting close?"

"I can give you a name. You could come out of this in real good shape. Invest twenty and you get back thirty from me plus what you can sell him for."

"How do I know Ruffi will be where you say he'll be? How do I know you'll ever come back?"

"You go through this world looking for guarantees, McGee, you'll live small."

"Where is he?"

"Money in hand, and I tell you."

"Half the money in hand until I see him."

He thought it over for a slow ten count and then said, "Let's give it a shot."

18

I had been planning on turning the rental Buick in after breakfast. But Cappy said he would not ride in that crazy Rolls pickup of mine. He said Dean had told him about it. He said it was too conspicuous. He took a pair of very dark sunglasses out of his purse and put them on and asked me if I had a hat he could use. He said he had lost his in the night, running down an alley. I found him an old white canvas fishing hat with a Sherlock Holmes shape. He pulled it well down on his head.

"Button up the shirt," I said, "and take off the jewelry."

"I never b . . . Oh, hell yes. It's hard to keep from being stupid."

After I got him into the car, I said I had forgotten to get the key to my box. I knew he would stay put. He got edgy whenever he was out in the open. I got the ten in hundreds, divided the pack into two parts and inserted them into the two flat black packets that Velcro neatly just below my knees.

I drove to the branch bank near the marina where I have

a safety-deposit box. I left him in the car in the lot and after the girl helped me unlock the little door, I carried my box into one of their little phone-booth rooms. I have it only because there are a few little items I would not care to have sunk or burned. Pictures of my mother and father and brother, all long gone. Birth certificate. Army discharge. Some yellowed clippings of my brief prowess as a tight end before they spoiled my knees. One theater ribbon, one Purple Heart, one Silver Star with citation for Sergeant McGee. A smiling photograph of Gretel Howard, another of Puss Killian, a few—a very few—letters, a copy of my will, which Meyer keeps telling me should not be in a safety-deposit box. I took the brown envelope in which the will had been, and put the hundred hundreds into it, a stack not an inch thick.

When I got back to the car he looked asleep with his hand over his eyes, but when I opened the door on my side, the blued muzzle of an automatic pistol flicked up and stared at me across his thigh. Then it was gone and he straightened up and said, "Sorry, pal. I thought I saw visitors. Got it?"

"Put away the gun."

"Sure."

"Here it is. Count it."

He held it well below the dash, below the level of his knees. He took two bills out at random, bent forward and examined them very carefully. He sighed, smiled, put them back in the envelope and slid the envelope into the zippered pocket on the back of the brown leather shoulder bag.

"Keep much in the box?"

"Millions," I said. "Untold millions." I've never kept money in the box. Money is expendable. It can always be replaced, one way or another.

"My problem was keeping too much in the box and not enough around loose. But who'd think things would get so jammed up I'm like on some kind of a list?"

"Where to?"

"What we've got to do is get a look at him. You, not me. So you know it's him. We have to do it without making him jumpy, or he'll run, God knows where. It isn't going to be easy. He's maybe up to twenty or thirty lines a day. That's how he got into all this. That stuff makes you think you can do anything and get away with it. He's using enough to make him very hard to figure, but not enough to make him easy to take. Years ago he used to be not too bad of a little kid. But they gave him the moon and the stars. The oldest kid, the favorite."

"Where to?"

"We're going to have to work out something. I won't tell you where, but I'll tell you what. What you've got is an asphalt two-lane road running along the side of a canal. No trees growing close to the canal. Then you've got a wooden bridge that is kind of a hump that crosses the canal. The canal is maybe fifteen feet wide, I don't know how deep. There's a one-story frame house on the other side of the plank bridge, set back twenty or thirty feet. It's got an aluminum carport on one side, big enough for one car. In back of the cottage and on either side is like jungle. Maybe there's a way back through there. I never tried. At night there's a big bright barn light fastened to the front of the house, lights up the whole place. It's got electric and a telephone."

"How do you know so much about it?"

"I stayed there waiting for a man to come home. He was doing ten to life in Raiford and they let him out in a little over six. That was last year. I don't want to get into all the whys and wherefores. Put it this way. It was the kind of scene you have to do it yourself and not put somebody else on it. So I was there with his wife and kid, waiting. It took him four days to get home. She was scared out of her wits he'd be too much for me. She hated the bastard. We kept the kid out of school. The kid had her orders—the minute he arrives, she shuts herself in her room. It went quick and easy and the woman and me, we dragged him way back into the saw grass and water and palmetto and slid him into a gator pond and put cement blocks on him to hold him down. Then we let the kid out and they hugged each other and they both cried, but they weren't crying for old Daddy. They were crying for happy."

"Ruffi's there now?"

"He lets her go shopping while he stays with the kid. She's eleven years old. The woman hasn't dared try anything. I left her my phone number last year. Nice woman. She phoned me from the supermarket ten miles down the road, asked for help. She said he was starting to mess with her kid. I said I'd try, but I didn't tell her that right at that point in time I was trying to figure some way of getting out of my place without getting myself killed. It was staked out very tight. That was yesterday."

"How did she know his name?"

"She didn't. I asked her what he looks like. She told me and said he came in a white Mercedes convertible and it is in her carport with tarps hiding it. It's Ruffi."

"So why don't you go take care of him and pick up his cash?"

"First, because I happen to know he got out without hardly any. It cost him what he was carrying to bribe his way out. Second, I don't know if I could take him. It's hard to tell what a nutcake will do next. And Ruffi is quick and tricky. And he's the one sent me there last year, so he knew the layout."

"So why don't you make a phone call and sell the information?"

"The people that want Ruffi don't buy information from dead people. I'm on the list, so I'm dead. There's some others on the list too, running like hell, or holed up someplace."

"Why did you come to me?"

"Jesus H. Christ, McGee! I happened to find out you told Art Jornalero about Ruffi cutting throats down there in the Keys, and that's what started the whole shit storm. I heard you want him. How should I know? Maybe he killed friends of yours. People living around on boats, the kind of rent you have to pay at places like Pier 66 and Bahia Mar, you have to have some money. I knew where to find you from when they told me you should have an accident."

"What kind?"

"Dean was in charge. He was going to work something out."

"What's the woman's name?"

"Irina Casak. The kid is Angie. The RFD box is out by the road next to the bridge. It says Casak on it in red paint."

"What name does she know you by?"

"Good question. Maybe the way you took my guys out, it wasn't all dumb luck. She knew me as Ben Smith."

"What kind of car does she have?"

"Last year it was a yellow Volkswagen bug, pretty beat up. Maybe she's got the same one now. I don't know. Do you know him by sight?"

"From a publicity still. I wouldn't forget the eyelashes."

"So what we got now, McGee, I take you there and we have to figure out some way you get a look at him without stampeding him. You're satisfied, we come back and you loan me the other ten and I give you the name you can sell him to. You'll have to work out your own arrangements to keep from getting screwed on the payoff. Done right, you'll end up smelling like roses."

So we went to take a look. It took an hour and forty minutes to get there, first south and then west. A lonely road on the edge of the Glades. Lumpy asphalt running string-

"Little old black-and-white RCA."

When I told him the plan, he didn't like it at all. The second time around he thought better of it. The third time I told him, he made minor changes. I would turn around after I came across the bridge and park heading out, and I would leave the Buick keys in the ignition. He assured me before I phoned her that there was just the one telephone.

"Hello?" she said, her voice soft and hesitant.

"Irina, this is a friend of Ben Smith. I want to help you. Is the man there?"

"Yes."

"Can he hear you?"

"I don't think so."

"You tell him you ordered a color TV from K-Mart and it has just come in and they are coming out to deliver it in an hour."

"But I . . ."

"You ordered it two months ago. I'm bringing it out."

I heard a man's voice in the background. "What's going on."

She turned to him and said, "The K-Mart is sending out my new color TV."

"Tell them you don't want it."

"But I ordered it . . ."

He came on the line. "She changed her mind."

"It's all paid for, Mr. Casak. I'm the manager of the television and electronics department here at K-Mart and I have to come out that way on personal business and I thought I could kill two birds with one stone instead of having Mrs. Casak come in here to get it. It's our best table model, guaranteed parts and labor for six months. A really beautiful reception even in fringe areas like you have out there."

"Well . . . okay. Bring it out. Leave it on the front porch."

I had counted on boredom to sway him. He was used to a

straight through wetlands past wooded hammocks wher
white birds sat on bare trees like Christmas doodads, thin
white bird thoughts.

He told me when to start slowing. We cruised pas
bridge and the mailbox at a sedate thirty-five. I saw a ye
beetle pulled halfway into the carport on the left side of
frame house. The house was gray with green trim, and I
a glimpse of a broken rocking chair on the shallow porch,
springs in the side yard, a swing made of a tire.

"Same car as before, parked in front of his," Cappy said

Two miles down the road I found a shell road off to
right. It went about fifty feet before it went underwate
pulled in and turned off the motor. I rolled my window do
and heard ten billion bugs saying it was a nice warm day.

"We can't risk going by more than one more time," I s;
"I didn't know there's no neighbors at all. Who would h;
a reason for stopping there?"

"Mailman, meter reader. Look, maybe the easy thing to
is you take my word he's in there, and sell him."

It was momentarily tempting. The shabby house in t
swampy setting had an ominous look. And I didn't want
sell Ruffi to the people who would take him out too quickly
wanted to sell him to the law, for ten cents' worth of satisfa
tion. I wanted to untie the knot in my necktie. I wanted Ru
to make some ineffectual attempts to maintain his ego and I
vanity in jail.

We had passed the supermarket and shopping plaza to
miles back, the other side of a village. So I headed back the
as soon as I found out Cappy could remember Irina Casak
phone number.

The plaza was anchored by a big K-Mart. As I sat broo
ing in the car, Cappy began to get impatient with m
"What's going on?"

"Deep thought. She have television?"

wider world. I didn't know what his plans were, but I imagined he wanted to stay right there until the trail was cold, and then go whizzing away in his little white car.

I took back the cash from Cappy to buy the set, $439 plus tax or $460.95 with tax. The clerk gave me a cash receipt form and a claim slip to present at Customer Services near the loading dock. Cappy grumbled about giving up the money. He said there was no way I was going to get into the house.

I found a place to pull off the road on the way back. The big cardboard carton was in the Buick trunk. An inch bigger and the trunk wouldn't have closed. I opened the carton and got the set out, then took it out of the clear plastic that sheathed it. I put Cappy's flat little .32 automatic in the plastic sack where it would be close to my right hand when I reached down into the carton and lifted the set out, with the screen facing away from me. Cappy didn't like that part either. I had made certain there was a full clip and the safety was off. I had fired once into the woods to see how it felt. It had a nasty, flat, cracking sound. He said it was a spare, all he could pick up when he left in a hurry, and he didn't like it either. He said it was Czech, and badly made.

I set off again with Cappy on the floor in back. I rumbled over the private plank bridge, turned around in the yard and parked with the front wheels inches from the bridge. I got out, whistling, and walked around to the trunk and opened it. Whistling is disarming. It can't be done with a dry mouth. I had to gnaw at the inside of my cheek to get enough spit to whistle.

I lifted the carton out and carried it to the porch, put it down beside the front door and knocked. I knocked again and again. "Oh, Mrs. Casak! Mrs. Casak?" I called, and thumped the door.

"Go away!" yelled Ruffino Marino, Junior.

"She has to sign the deliver slip."

"Sign it yourself, dummy!"

"But I can't do that. Mrs. Casak has to sign."

The door opened just enough for her to slip out. "Just sign right here," I said cheerfully, putting the cash receipts on the carton and handing her a ballpoint. I pocketed the receipt and dipped and lifted the set in its plastic sack out of the carton. "Will you get the manual and guarantee out of the carton, please, Mrs. Casak? Thank you. Now we have to make sure there's nothing wrong with the set. It wasn't checked at the store. It's better to check them out at the customer's home. Open up, please."

She was terrified. She was shaking. But she turned the knob and pushed the door open. I carried the set in. I caught a glimpse of Ruffi in the doorway to the kitchen. "You dumb bitch!" he yelled as he moved back out of sight. I had seen only that his hair was tousled and he had blue beard shadow on his jaws. Up until that instant I hadn't been certain Cappy was pulling some kind of elaborate scam.

I ignored him. I had her move the black-and-white set off the low table it was on. I put the new set on the floor, reached down into the plastic bag and lifted the set out, with my fingertips holding the automatic pistol against the underside of the set. I put the set so far to the front of the low table I was able to ease the weapon out from under it and leave it on a couple of inches of table behind the color set.

Chatting merrily about what a good set it was, I plugged it in and I took the aerial leads off the black-and-white set and fastened them to the new one. When I turned it on I got a splendid picture on Channel 5, and I quickly jiggered one of the back side controls until I started the picture rolling slowly. And then, of course, I was very concerned.

"I can't imagine why this is happening, Mrs. Casak. I'm very sorry about this. I don't understand it."

She stood near me, breathing through her open mouth,

almost panting with nervousness. Her breath was sour. She was a flat-faced pallid woman with a wide flat nose and so much dark discoloration around her eyes she made me think of a raccoon. The cotton dress, sweaty, revealed a ripe, big-breasted, serviceable body. Her face was twisted with alarm. Her fists were clenched.

So I couldn't depend on her to play her part in the original scenario. I fixed the horizontal hold and got the good picture back. I motioned her to back away from me. I yelled, "Mr. Casak! Hey, Mr. Casak. Will you please come see if these color values are okay? Mr. Casak!"

He had to know I had seen him in the kitchen doorway. And he had to know that if I had recognized him, I probably wouldn't be hollering for him.

He came into the living room, and glanced at the screen. "It's okay, dummy. Get the hell out!"

I said, "I can make an adjustment in the back here to give it slightly less vivid color values."

As my right hand closed on the grip of the pistol, I sensed movement out of the corner of my eye and knew before I turned that he was too close.

19

When I turned he was on the inside, clubbing my wrist away with a sharp and powerful swing of his left forearm. Before I could bring it back, he dropped away and kicked me on the point of the right elbow. Red-hot wires ran up into my shoulder and down to my fingertips, and the arm went slack, half numbed. The gun fell and skidded across the frayed grass rug. When he pounced toward it, bending to pick it up, I took one long stride and drop-kicked him in the stomach, lifting him clear of the floor.

Instead of quieting him, it galvanized him. He started bounding around like a big rubber ball, yelling sounds without words. I was in a small room with a crazy person. In hospital wards and precinct stations it takes six people to subdue one crazy. Six trained people. He came at me and drove me back against the wall, hit me a good one high on the left side of the head, and I went over, taking a tall cabinet with a glass door with me. When he spun to lunge for the gun, I dived forward and caught an ankle, hugged the foot to my chest and spun with it. He went down and turned with the foot, kicked me on top of the head with the free foot and tore loose. By then I had a glimpse of Irina holding the gun in both hands.

I yelled to her to throw it out the window. They were double-hung windows, the bottom sash up, screening across the bottom. As he reached for her she spun and flicked it through both layers of glass, out past the porch and into the dirt yard.

Roaring, he came back at me, swinging good punches. I could lift the numbed arm. I took the blows on my forearms and upper arms, protecting my head. It was like being hit with round rocks. When he saw what was happening, he came right down through the middle with an overhand right that hit the shelf of my jaw and knocked my mouth wide. My knees went loose and white rockets sailed behind my eyes. I bicycled backward and only the wall kept me from going down. I hit it hard enough to shake the house. Just as my head was beginning to clear I saw him coming at me again, and this time he launched himself into the air in some kind of strange scissor kick, coming at me feet first. I slid sideways along the wall, and with my good left arm operating well, I snatched at the heel of the lower of the two feet and whipped it as high as I could. The first thing that hit the floor was the back of his head. He rolled slowly up onto his hands and knees, shaking his head. Once again the dropkick. He came down on his back, rolled up, and as he came halfway up, I chopped him hard with the edge of my left hand, a diagonal blow just under the ear. He melted down onto the floor, eyes unfocused. And then he began to climb back to his feet, in slow motion. He was like some mythical monster that can't be killed, blinking slowly, like a lizard.

As I was reaching to chop at him again, Cappy pushed by me, and with a wide swing laid the flat side of the automatic against the side of Ruffi's curly head. It made a crisp, sickening sound. Ruffi lay down so hard his head bounced. There was a nearby scream and a plump young girl came running in to drop to her knees beside him. She had a fatty face, long straight brown hair, lipstick, mascara, little wide-apart breasts the size of baking-powder biscuits under a tight pink T-shirt. She wore short white shorts. "You kilt him!" she sobbed. "You shits kilt him!"

"Shut up, Angie," said her mother in a tired voice.

"Don't get too close to him," I told Cappy. "He'll play possum."

"Not for a while, he won't."

"Something to tie him up with, Mrs. Casak?"

She took me into the kitchen and opened a large low drawer. It was full of odds and ends of string, tape, rope, chain, screwdrivers. As I was selecting some rope, I noticed two little tubes of Miracle Glue, still in the store pack that can only be opened by gorillas. It would be easier and quicker.

I took the Miracle Glue into the living room. I nipped the tip off one tube and divided it evenly between the palms of his slack hands. Then I pulled his shirt high, crossed his arms and pressed the hands against the sides of his torso, against the hairless skin just above belt level. I rubbed them around a little bit, then pressed them hard against his body. In a few moments when I released his hands, they stayed right there. I used the second tube on the inside of one thigh, after pulling his shorts high, spreading it from just above the knee to halfway to the groin. I pressed the thighs together and in a few moments they clung.

He coughed and rolled his head from side to side and then opened his eyes.

When he couldn't move his hands or his upper legs he frowned and muttered, "What's going on?"

"Miracle Glue has a hundred household uses," I told him.

"Hey, Roof," Cappy said.

He turned his head to see Cappy. "Getting a nice bonus, you freak?"

"Get away from him! Get away!" a child-voice said from the other doorway, which I assumed led to back bedrooms. The voice trembled. She held a Ruger long-barrel .22 target pistol in two fat tan hands.

"Atta girl!" Ruffi said. "At's my lover girl. Shoot them, sweetie. Shoot 'em all and we'll go away together and I'll show you the whole world. Shoot the big bastard first."

Cappy dropped to his knees and socketed the blued muzzle of his pistol in Ruffi's left ear. He grinned at the child. "It better be me first, pumpkin. My finger will probably twitch, though, and it'll come right out that other ear."

Irina walked slowly toward her daughter, saying in a singsong voice, "Shoot your mommy, dear. Go ahead, Angie. Shoot your mommy."

The girl began crying. "But I love him and he loves me."

Irina reached and took the target pistol out of the girl's sagging hands. "He doesn't love you, honey. He can't love no eleven-year-old fat dumb kid. The only thing he loves is that thing that sticks out of the front of him. He stuck it into me a dozen times by promising if I let him he'd leave you alone. Then he got tired of me. So he started sticking it into you. He'd stick it into a gator if she'd lie quiet. And I know what I'm going to do to him so nobody else has to put up with him."

She handed me the target pistol and as she did so her back was to Ruffi. She gave me a wink that screwed up the entire left side of her face. Some people can't move the eyelid alone. It has to be half the face. I knew it meant she wanted to have her way. She went out into the kitchen and came back with poultry shears. They were slightly rusty but they looked able to cut through tough skin and chicken bone.

She knelt beside him and unzipped his shorts and reached in and pulled him out.

"Mom!" the child yelled. "Oh, Mom, no!"

Ruffi raised his head and looked down. "No, Irina, please." He raised his knees and tried to scooch backward. She followed right along, moving sideways on her knees until his head reached the wall and he could move no further. He was circumcised and the glans was so bloodless with his fright it was a pallid lavender. She opened the shears and laid the penis between the blades.

He groaned, his face contorted, ashen.

"Want you to remember this, Ruffi or Roof or whatever they call you. Anytime the rest of your life you get a chance to stick this thing into anybody or anything, you're going to remember how steel feels and it won't get hard."

She gave it a little pinch with the shears for emphasis, then tucked it back into his shorts and zipped him up. She grunted to her feet. Ruffi was trembling, his eyes leaking.

Cappy had put the gun away, probably back into his shoulder bag. He went over and put his arm around Irina. She turned toward him, rested her forehead on his shoulder. "Thanks," she said in a low voice. "Thanks for helping me one more time."

He patted her. "We gone sell this cat to the Peruvians. Won't bother you again."

In a husky voice, Ruffi said, "Cappy, I can make you a good deal. More than you can peddle me for. I know where you can get to one hundred thousand dollars. I can't get to it, but you can. It'll be a better deal for you."

Cappy said to me, "You think of any reason we have to keep listening to all that shit?"

"None whatsoever."

Cappy picked up the two tubes of glue, discarded one, squatted next to Ruffi and put one hand on Ruffi's forehead to hold him still and dribbled the final bit of glue along his lips. He tossed the tube aside and then pinched the lips together, smiling up at me. He did too good a job. He left Ruffi all pooched out, looking as if he were about to kiss or whistle. Ruffi's eyebrows went high and his cheeks hollowed as he tried to pull his mouth open.

"It's gone nice and quiet around here," Cappy said.

"Mmmm gh mmm mm," Ruffi said.

"I want to look around," Cappy said. He went into the back of the house. The television was still on, the sound off. A woman who looked like an expensive hooker was apparently yelling bad things into the face of a man who looked like a hairdresser. They were both overdressed and standing in what could have been the bedroom of the departed Shah of Iran. So it was an afternoon soap, and I felt the hollowness of no lunch yet. My jaw creaked. I had sore bruises on both arms. My head ached.

"What about the TV?" Irina asked.

"Enjoy."

She turned the sound up. Mother and daughter moved closer, watching and listening. Cappy came out of the back of the house carrying a tan leather duffel bag and a jar with a screw-top lid.

"These clothes will fit, and what I got here is maybe eleven or twelve ounces of prime white lady."

"Leave me some!" Angie yelled. "You leave me some."

Her mother stood up and Angie never saw the hard palm coming. It smacked her on the side of the face, spun her halfway around and dropped her onto her hands and knees. Angie scrambled to her feet and went bellering into her bedroom and slammed the door.

"Will she testify?" I asked Irina.

"Would that be a good idea?"

"I think so. He killed a couple of girls on a boat last year. Raped them and cut one's throat and cracked the other one's skull. I don't think they'll ever nail him for it. The only witness is dead. They can get him for this."

"What charges?"

"Statutory rape. Corrupting the morals of a minor child."

The woman nodded. "She'll testify. By God, she'll testify! He's been here a week yesterday. I had to phone her in sick at school. He walked in on us like he owned the place."

Cappy came in from outside. "McGee, I don't think I'll go back in with you for that other ten. On the same ratio when I pay off, you get fifteen. Wait a minute. You took five hundred back, so you'll get . . . fourteen thousand two hundred fifty."

"What are you going to do?"

"The big genius there with his mouth stuck together, he had the title and registration in the side pocket of that Mercedes out there. It shows no paper out on it. It's got a little over four thousand miles on it, and give me half hour I can sign his name better than he can. And I got a contact on Route 19 a little north of Clearwater. I can get thirty minimum for it in cash in ten minutes. I go back in with you, I'm taking an extra chance. I head west from here. How about you come out with me, Irina, and move that little junker of yours out of the way."

He picked up the duffel bag, nodded to me and said, "See you around."

"Hold it. You're forgetting something."

He snapped his fingers. The three of us went out. He led me away from Irina and said, "What you do, you go to the magazine stand in the lobby of the Contessa over on the Beach and you find a girl works there name of Alice. She's got little half glasses. You tell her you want to see Lopez. She'll say she doesn't know any Lopez. You tell her the Capataz told you to ask her. Wait until there's no tourists around. Okay? Try for fifty. What the hell. See you around. You got good moves, McGee."

He put the top up on the Mercedes. I moved the Buick back out of the way. He gunned the white car a few times, then put it in gear and went rumbling over the hump bridge, turned west, waved, and was soon a high-pitched whine in the invisible distance.

I went back into the house with Irina. Ruffino had managed to work himself up into a sitting position, back against the wall, dark eyes glaring at us over the pursed mouth. She went to the ruins of the toppled cabinet and picked a small white bowl, unbroken, out of the shards of other treasured things. She put it on top of the new television set.

I asked her permission to use the phone, and looked up the number for the county sheriff. It had been a few years. I wondered if Wes was still there. A lot of them leave. The top slot is political, and the pressure seeps down through the ranks. When the communications clerk answered, I asked if Deputy Wesley Davenport still worked for the department.

"Yes, sir, Captain Davenport is here today. Is this a personal call."

"Yes," I lied. She gave me a different number to call.

"Cap'n Davenport," he said.

"Wes, this is McGee. Travis McGee."

"You kilt somebody again, pardner?"

"I've managed to hold back."

"Builds character. What have you got?"

"Last time I talked to you those twin daughters of yours were pretty small. How are they doing and how old are they?"

"They are just fine little old gals. Going on eleven."

"You know where the Casak house is?"

"Rings a little bell. Hang on. Sure. Hugo Casak, armed

robbery. Put him away and he's been out well over a year now. But he never reported in, so right now he's on the list for violation of parole. He lived out there on that damn little lonesome swamp road that goes nowhere. Okay. I can find the house. So?"

"I'm calling from the house. I want to ask you to do things a certain way."

"For old times' sake, I suppose."

"Congratulations on making captain."

"Well, thanks heaps. What have you got?"

"I've got a guy here hiding from the Miami fireworks."

"Looks to me like they all went nuts over there."

"They did indeed. This one has a big coke habit. And he's right here looking at me. Before you come out here, you stop off and buy a big bottle of nail-polish remover."

"Of what!"

"I've got him glued together with Miracle Glue. Mouth, hands and legs. Second thought. Let's try it another way. He can move his legs from the knees down, so maybe we better walk him to your car and you get him into a cell before you unglue him. He's strong and quick. I outweigh him maybe fifty pounds but he nearly took me. He kicks."

"Okay, champ. What am I arresting him for?"

"The only people here when he came in on them were Mrs. Casak and Angie, her eleven-year-old daughter. He's been here over a week and he got the kid on coke and taught her to enjoy screwing."

The silence was so long I finally said, "Wes?"

"Okay. I was just thinking it through." His voice had grown heavy and tired. "Can I get statements?"

"Guaran-damn-teed, Wes."

"But there's more, isn't there? Knowing you."

"Remember the rape killings aboard the *Lazidays* down off Big Torch last October?"

etting too old for this kind of boyish shit? Have you lost
ore than a half step getting to second?"

f-delusion is one of the essentials of life. I told myself
y bruises and abrasions were not the result of a fading
ue, but rather the result of a mental lapse. I had
stimated young Marino. And that gave him an edge he
deserve. I wondered if he had enjoyed a restful night.
hen I stepped out onto the fantail I found another pipe-
r cat on the mat looking up to me. With quick and
ected anger, I stomped it flat. Then I sighed and picked
bent it back into shape, took it back in and stood it in
tion on the shelf with the earlier arrivals.

ent to the hotel alone and for breakfast I had *USA*
, double fresh orange juice, three eggs scrambled with
and onion, crisp bacon, home fries, whole-wheat toast
o pots of coffee. The exercise improved the right elbow.
hen I went back aboard my home I went up onto the
ck and came upon the seventh cat, a purple one, star-
me from the flat place atop the instrument panel. I sat
pilot seat, the cool wind on my face, and looked at the
ing. Somebody was going to elaborate trouble to have a
it of fun. If they were sending a message, they had
ten to include the code. Maybe somewhere in the world
vas some other McGee who'd find the pipe-cleaner cats
ehensible and delicious and hilarious.

Saturday morning when I approached my blue truck
to head for Miami, I found a brown pipe-cleaner cat
windshield with one paw under the wiper so it could
at me. I put it in the ashtray.

the Contessa, I browsed the newsstand paperbacks
he girl was free. She had half glasses, no makeup,
t mouse-colored hair.

r?"

"Surely do."

"There were two of them did it. This is one of them. The
other is in the foundation of a new condo. Nobody will ever
make this one I got here for it. Never."

"So?"

"Wes, I want him held as John Doe. Maybe his prints are
on file. Send the wrong classification. Anything. Also, this
little shit is very big on publicity. He loves his picture in the
paper."

"Will the mother and the girl talk it up? If they do, there's
nothing I can do on this end."

"They won't say a word. She'll keep the kid out of school
for a while longer."

I looked over at Irina and she nodded agreement.

"Then okay, McGee. You got my provisional promise to
bury the son of a bitch. But first I have to come check it out.
You stay there?"

"Right here."

By the time Wes arrived I felt better for having had two
of Mrs. Casak's oversized fried-egg sandwiches and a quart of
milk.

Wes and I shook hands, surveying each other. He was
heavier and he had less hair. He told me I was leaner and had
less hair.

He had a bottle of nail-polish remover. He squatted heavily beside Ruffino and scrubbed the man's mouth roughly
with a rag he got from Mrs. Casak.

After Ruffi had run out of breath, Wes turned to me, face
a mask of imitation surprise, and said, "You hear that? You
ever hear a dirtier mouth? My, my! Right now I got me a tank
full of weight lifters. They're motorcycle queens down from
Houston, tattooed all over butterflies and spring flowers.

Guess I'll put this John Doe in with them. They'll take to those eyelashes."

He went in and had a closed-door session with Angie. He came out looking sour and angry. After we got Ruffino Marino into the back seat of the county sedan, he took me over to the side and said, "I know an assistant state's attorney that can take this on without making waves. Maybe he can work out a plea. He goes into state prison as a child molester, he won't last through the first year. Too many doing time up there got kids of their own. There's still something I don't know. Right?"

"Wes, the people looking for him, I'm going to tell them where he is."

"Look, I don't want any wild men trying to bust him out of our store."

"That's not their style."

"That name he was yelling, that's his real name?"

"Except in the movies. In his one dud movie. Then it was Mark Hardin, Florida's answer to Rocky one, two, three, four, five and so forth."

"I'll tell the weight lifters he's a movie star."

"You really going to put him in with them?"

He stared bleakly at me. "How much choice did that kid in there have? How much choice did the girls on the boat have? You always do fine up to a point, McGee, and then you get a little bit mushy at the edges."

20

On Friday, the first day of February, it
to get out of bed I decided Miami Beach
day. My worst knee kept threatening t
elbow was agony. There were big dark
and shoulders. I could not recall how I
on the back of my head.

This was no morning for a shower.
by inch, into the imperial bathtub, i
could stand it. I soaked there for a long
off on the biggest towel I own, I too
dug into the Ace bandage box and fo
well on the knee, and used a strip
elbow.

I checked the morning and found
chill, so I put on an old sky-blue wo
wool socks and the gray running sho
the mirror and said aloud, "Tell me th

"I want to talk to Lopez."

"Lopez? I don't know any Lopez."

"Aren't you Alice?"

"Yes. Yes, my name is Alice."

"The Capataz said to tell you I want to talk to Lopez."

Her eyes changed. "Just a moment, sir." She helped a new customer who'd come in, took his money for a racing form. She came back to me. "Go out to the pool bar and wait."

"How long?"

"Just wait. That's all I know."

After an hour I went back to the newsstand and she told me to go back and keep on waiting. It was past noon when a man sat down beside me. He sighed as he climbed onto the padded stool. He was short and fat and he sounded as if he had emphysema. Each inhalation had a throaty little snore at the end of it. He wore a Palm Beach suit and a white straw hat. His nose and cheeks were tinted purple by tiny broken veins.

"What I got to tell you, friend, no choice in the matter. I got to tell you right now there's absolutely no way Cappy can make a deal."

"I think he knows that."

"What he should do, he should get out of town."

"That's what he's done."

"He could stay like a year someplace and keep his head down, then put out some feelers. Stick his big toe in the water."

"That's the way he has it figured out."

After a thoughtful silence the man swiveled his head on his quarter inch of heavy neck and stared at me. "Then what the fuck you want with me?"

"Before Cappy left he said you might want to make an offer for young Ruffi."

"Shush!" he said. "Jesus Christ, hush your mouth." He looked around. "Let's move over to that farthest-away table."

It was in the shade of tall, broad-leafed plantings—elephant ears, rubber plants, a juvenile banyan, a white iron table with a glass top, four iron chairs. In spite of the chill in the air, the pool people were warm and happy. The pool Cubans had laced the canvas wind shields in place. Executive types who had recently acquired a tan were parading around in a distinctive way. You can always pick them out. They have to hold their bellies in. To do this properly, they have to tense their muscles and square their shoulders. This makes them hold their arms out from their sides, slightly bent. They cannot swing the arms naturally, and so they walk slowly. If they were turkeys, the tail feathers would be spread. The young girls look beyond them and through them and never see them at all. Sad world.

Lopez put his drink down, took off his hat and wiped his brow with a dingy handkerchief. "With Cappy, people know he was a hired hand, all right? So when the blood cools down it can come back to live and let live. But young Marino, he went against everything. No class at all. Who are you?"

"McGee."

He tilted his head. "Like they were trying to set you up for the Reyes girl?"

"Like that. Yes."

"It was you found out Ruffi did it?"

"I didn't find out. But I passed the news along."

"And you started up a feud that got a hell of a lot of good men killed."

"Instead of standing and saluting and letting them kill me like they killed an innocent friend of mine, Billy Ingraham."

"That was sloppy and dumb, that Ingraham thing."

"And all you people are good God-fearing, law-abiding businessmen."

"You've got no call to get smart-ass, McGee."

"I know that. I know that. I just want to sell him."

"Alive or dead?"

"Alive."

"Where?"

"Where he'll stay for a while. One hundred thousand."

"For that little punk kid?"

"For that little punk kid."

"I can't get approval for that kind of money, even if I was sure you got him."

"That kind of money wouldn't half fill one of those corn-flakes boxes that get shipped to Art Jornalero."

He nodded slowly. "You get around pretty good."

"Maybe I can fly to Lima and sell him down there."

"Maybe you try to do that, they wouldn't set up any kind of exchange that would be safe for you to make."

"What are you offering?"

"Frankly, I think it might be closer to fifty than a hundred."

"I've had a hundred worth of grief from this."

"Look, what can I say? I'll do my best."

"How do you want to work it?"

"If we come up with a figure makes us both happy, we pick a third party everybody can trust."

"Such as?"

We ran through several names before we came to one we could both agree on. Hillary Muldoon of Muldoon and Grimes, specialists in labor law. On Monday, the fourth, the agreed figure was sixty thousand. On Tuesday afternoon, the fifth, Lopez and I met with Muldoon, a narrow, stooped bald man with one eye that looked off to the left. The money was counted. I objected to his fee coming out of my end. We compromised. I would come up with half the fee, provided the reward money was granted. Fifty-seven thousand, net.

So I opened the envelope Wes had given me and handed them the full-face and profile mug shots and the Xerox copy of the arrest report, including the charges filed.

After they studied it, Lopez said, "Hillary, I don't like this a damn. He's in some damn little boondocks slam. This McGee doesn't have him. The law does."

"You understand I can't know why you want him, Lopez, but I do understand that he is awaiting trial and as such he can be released on bail. He could be released in the custody of whoever makes bail. I would say that, in effect, Mr. McGee has lived up to his end of the bargain. Fifty-seven thousand to Mr. McGee."

We shook hands and I left with the money and hastened to the nearest branch post office and sent it to myself by registered mail.

I got home to find, in the last light of day, an orange cat on the mat. And so, with a pattern roughly predictable, I made preparations for bed, cut all the lights, put on dark slacks and turtleneck, eased out the forward hatch, crept around the side deck and settled down in the deep shadows, my back against the bulkhead, a navy-blue blanket over me. I could see the mat in the angle of dock light, five feet away. Got nothing but an almost sleepless night. No cat. No intruder.

At noon Millis phoned me, her voice remote, lifeless. "Travis? Arturo died."

"What happened?"

"I don't know. I was up early working in the garden. So many things died in the cold. When he didn't get up I looked in on him. And he was just there dead. Maybe his heart. I don't know. Nobody got in here. Nobody did it. He was so very depressed. Did you know he was sixty-eight? He was so proud of not looking that old."

"Is he still there?"

"Oh no. I phoned some people, and finally they sent an ambulance and took him down like he was sick. With a mask on his face, oxygen or something, so he wouldn't look dead. People are dying around me, Travis. I hate it so. They said I did the right thing. They'll keep me out of it. Roger Carp kept me out of that other thing. I had to appear, you know. But the indictment said person or persons unknown and they sent a copy of the grand jury minutes and the medical records to France."

"I'm glad you had no trouble."

"I'm getting out of everything, aren't I? I haven't even gone to Billy's grave."

"Do you think you should?"

"I don't know. What we talked about, it's still open. If you want. Not the same ship or the same cruise. We can find one we think we'll like. If you want."

"Your enthusiasm is fantastic."

"Don't lean on me like that. I'm not up to it today. I'll be here for a couple of weeks. Call me. Whatever you say, I'm going anyway."

She hung up before I could say goodbye.

I tried not to think about Millis all day. It worked half the time. I didn't answer the phone. It rang twice. I couldn't think of anyone I wanted to have a conversation with.

That night I was out under my dark blue blanket by nine-thirty, all lights out aboard. February has a cheerless sound about it. Halfway to Valentine's day. Five days to old Abe's birthday. The winter wind whips around the ancient images of the homeplace, sleet whisk-brooming the kitchen windows.

Tipsy boatmen went past, guffawing their way back to their floating nightcaps. ". . . let Marie take the wheel and she had it hard aground in ten minutes . . ." "You remember

Charlie. He found three bales of it floating off Naples and he got them aboard. Took it home and dried it out and he's got enough there to keep the whole yacht club airborne until the year two thousand." ". . . should have had it surveyed, damn it. Dry rot down all one side of the transom."

And some sour harmony, ending when somebody used a bullhorn to tell them to knock it off, people were sleeping.

Slow hours. And then a swiftness of slender femininity, half seen in the glow from the distant dock lights. Creak of my small gangplank. She had learned not to step on the mat. She kneels, hair a-dangle, leans far forward to put the pipe-cleaner cat on the door-side edge of the mat. I gather myself. Lunge and snap my hand down onto slender wrist. Yelp of fright and dismay. Then some real trouble when I dragged her aboard. Impression of tallness. She was all hard knees, elbows, fists. She butted and kicked and thrashed, and almost got away once, until finally I caught her hand in a come-along grip, her hand bent down and under, her elbow snug against my biceps.

"Ow!" she yelled. "Hey, ow! You're breaking it."

"Shut up or I will."

It settled her down. She made whimpering sounds, but she had become docile enough for me to fish out my keys and unlock the door and escort her into the lounge, turning on the lights as we entered. I shoved her into the middle of the lounge and she spun around, glaring at me, massaging her wrist. Just a kid, sixteen or seventeen. A reddish blonde kid, red with new burn over old tan, a kid wearing a short-sleeved white cotton turtleneck and one of those skirts, in pink, that are cut like long shorts, surely the ugliest garment woman-kind has ever chosen to wear. But if anybody could ever look good in them, this one could. Tall girl. Good bones.

"You're brutal. You know that? Really brutal!"

"Okay," I said wearily. "I'm brutal. What's all this with the cats, kid?"

In response I got a wide humorless grin. "Got to you, hah?"

"It has begun to annoy me. Puzzle me. That's all."

She stared at me. "You're serious? You're not having me on?"

"Kid, when somebody starts invading my privacy with pipe-cleaner cats, I would like to know what's going on. That's all."

She stared at me. "My God, you're even more opaque than I thought. You're an animal!"

"Okay. The animal is asking you to sit down and the animal will buy you a Coke. Maybe you can stop emoting and make sense. What are you kids taking lately? It has warped your little head."

She hesitated and then sat on the edge of the yellow couch. "Thank you, I don't want a Coke. And I don't take anything. Aside from getting a little woozy on wine a couple of times. You sit down too. Are you ready for a name?"

"I'm Travis McGee."

"I *know* that! Oh, *don't* I know that. I've made a study of your life and times, Mr. McGee. I can't think of anything more pathetic than an aging boat bum—beach bum—who won't or can't admit it or face it. You are a figure of fun, Mr. McGee. Your dear friends around here are misfits or burnouts, and I don't think there's one of them who gives a damn about you. You're a womanizer, and you make a living off squalid little adventures of one kind or another. You have that dumb-looking truck and this dumb-looking houseboat and nobody who cares if you live or die."

"Kid, you've got a good delivery and a pretty fair vocabulary."

"Stop *patronizing* me!"

"What's with the multicolored cats, kid?"

"My name is Jean Killian." It was almost shouted, like some kind of war cry.

And then I knew why she had reminded me of someone. I felt the tears behind my eyes. I got up and walked over toward her and she got up, tall, to face me. In a rusty, shaky old voice I said, "You're her kid sister."

Eyes so pale in her sun-dark face they looked like the silver of old rare coins, stared into mine. The strength of her emotions had narrowed her eyes. I could not remember any-one ever looking at me with such venomous concentration. There was hate in there. Contempt. But she spoke softly. "No, you stupid jerk. I'm Puss's daughter. And, God help me, I'm your bastard child. Look at me! People around here have asked me if I'm related to you. To him? I said. Hell no!"

I really looked at her. The shoulders and the long arms. The level mouth, shape of the jaw, the high cheekbones, tex-ture of the hair, with my coarseness and Puss's auburn.

"That's . . . what the cats were all about?"

"If you had any kind of conscience at all, Father dear, it would have hit you. Puss. Pussycat. But she didn't even mean enough to you so you'd get the connection." She sat down again and put her hands over her face. "A rotten pointless idea."

"Why should I have a bad conscience about Puss?"

"Perhaps for men like you it is standard procedure. But I think it is cruel and wicked for a man to live with a woman and then, when she becomes ill and pregnant, he kicks her off his dumb houseboat and looks for a new lady."

"Puss told you that?"

"My mother lived just long enough to have me, and she died the day afterward. Her sister brought me up. Her sister, my Aunt Velma, told me all about you and where and how life. I seemed to hear the click as each slide fell into place. Everything familiar had assumed a different shape, sharper outlines, purer kind of color. It seemed very much to me like the strangeness which happens after you have spent weeks in a hospital, when you come back out again into the world, seeing everything fresh—a stop light, a brown dog, a yellow bus. Something has changed the world and washed it clean.

I paced the lounge and paced the sun deck half the night, thinking about her, wondering if she would be there. I knew she had to be there. If Puss and I had given her anything at all, it would be a sense of fairness.

When the hard winds of change blow through your life, they blow away a lot of structures you thought permanent, exposing what you had thought was trivia, buried and forgotten. The sweet soft taste of the side of the throat of Puss Killian. The rough and husky edge of her voice as her laughter stopped. The small things are lasting things.

you live, and I've been planning this for three years. I wanted to make you feel so guilty you'd kill yourself. But you d-didn't even know what the c-cats meant."

"How old are you?"

"Seventeen in April. What's that got to do with anything?"

I moved over to the chair by the built-in desk, put my foot up on it, rested my forearms on my knee and studied her. She sat on the yellow couch, out on the edge of it, fists clenched, returning my inspection, meeting my gaze, showing me her contempt, her hate.

"I had the feeling there was something wrong with Puss. But I never realized she was sick."

"Or pregnant. Sure. You just never realized."

"Do you want me to try to tell you a little bit about this, kid, or do you want to step on everything I say?"

"There's nothing you can say."

"Do you want to know how I met her?"

"Not particularly, Mr. McGee."

I sighed. "Kid, I just wish you . . ."

"Stop calling me kid!"

"Okay. Jean, then. I was running on the beach one morning. Puss had stepped on a sea urchin in shallow water. She came hobbling and hopping ashore, in obvious trouble. Okay, so I got the spines out and brought her over here and got her heel fixed up. She was . . . a lot of fun."

"Lots of fun, huh? A great sport, huh?"

"Merry is the word. A big random redhead who believed the world was mad. A loving person. Her mind and her speech went off at funny tangents. It made some people irritable. Not me."

"Oh, no. Certainly not you!"

"Kid. Jean. I am talking about your mother and you never got to know her. Maybe you want to know a little bit about her."

"Not from you!"

"She was with me for a few months. She stayed aboard this houseboat with me. I was involved in something at the time. A friend of mine had been killed. Tush Bannon. Some people wanted his land. In the process of finding out who killed him and why, some other people got killed and got badly hurt. Puss was especially good with Janine, Tush's widow. Sometimes she would . . . go off somewhere inside herself, out of touch. It seemed odd. Meyer—he's my best friend—"

"I know."

"He noticed it too. We talked about it and we decided it was probably something about her divorce."

"What divorce? She was never divorced."

"So I found out."

She stood up. "What's the point of all this? You'd lie to me. You lied to her. You'd lie to anybody, wouldn't you? After I watched you walk by me on the beach, I knew you're my father. I was hoping you weren't. I can't make you sorry because you haven't got any conscience at all. And that is giving me some pretty wonderful thoughts about my heredity, Dad. Sorry I went to all the trouble. You aren't even worth that much. You are so smooth and plausible, you make me sick. You worked a scam on her, but it won't work on me."

"Hate is poison, Jean."

"It nourishes me."

"I have a farewell letter from your mother."

"So?"

"Do you hate her so much you don't even want to read it?"

"I never said I hated her!"

"What is your opinion of her?"

"Okay, I guess she wasn't very smart about people. Why should I tell you my opinion of her?"

"I want to know why you are afraid to read her letter t me."

"Afraid? Bullshit! Let me see it."

"It's one of the few things in my life worth keeping ir safety-deposit box."

"I bet."

"The bank is closed. It will open tomorrow morning ten. I don't want you to think I have any possible way tricking you. I had no idea you existed, so I couldn't faked a letter in expectation you'd show up someday." I w the name and address of the bank on a slip of paper. " me there at ten in the morning."

"I don't want to meet you anywhere ever."

I took the chance. "Okay. Then don't bother. I'll be in case you change your mind. In case you decide it mig nice to know something more about your mother than yo It'll be a better check on your heredity, kid. Now ge Tomorrow you might grow up a little, and when you do I'll want to talk to you. But not now, not the way y now. Good night."

I matched her flat and level stare until she spun and had detected no uncertainty in her. I felt that may gamble had failed and I had lost her. I went out slow saw her, far down the pier, walking swiftly under th lights.

I wanted to tell Meyer, but not yet. Not now. want to tell anybody while I was still trying to com what had happened to me. I saw the cat she had bee to leave. It had been flattened in our little fracas. I ened it out, went in and put it with the others.

I could recall every plane and texture of her fa the timbre of her voice, the style of her movemen sweetly excruciating detail. Some strange mechanis head was projecting color slides of all the familiar pa

21

Friday came in with a hard winter rain and a steady wind. I awoke with the conviction I would never see her again. She was half real and half imagined. I was too restless to have anything but coffee, too edgy to keep my attention on any small manufactured boat chore. Wind tilted and creaked the houseboat again and again.

Finally I put on foul-weather gear, a complete set, with hood, in that electric orange-red of the gloves and flags they wave at you at road construction sites. It is useful when anyone falls overboard in heavy weather, to become the only dot of color in a steep gray surging world.

I started walking so early I was at the bank by nine-fifteen, and I knew that if I tried to just stand there and wait, I would be maniacal by ten o'clock. So I went striding past the bank and kept walking for a measured twenty-three minutes. A mile and something. Turned on the mark and came back. But got to the bank at five of ten. Had I found shelter in the entrance I wouldn't be able to see her coming. So I stood out in the rain. It made such a deafening clatter against the crisp plastic of the hood I could not hear the traffic sounds. I kept turning my head like a man at a tennis match, because I did not know from which direction she would arrive.

Ten o'clock. Five after. Ten after. And I knew it had been a bad gamble. From the two of us she would have gotten an unforgiving stubbornness, stronger than the sense of fair play. The rain was heavier. It bounced high off the asphalt, an eight-inch curtain fringe of lonely silver rain. I could stand there until it ended and nothing would change.

She came moments later at a hard run, with a transparent raincoat over sweater and jeans, her hair tucked into a shower cap. Her face looked set and pallid, her lips almost colorless. We went in and stood over at one side, dripping on their giant rug. I pushed my hood back and she pulled her shower cap off and shook her hair out.

"So we play your game, Mr. McGee, whatever it is."

"I was beginning to think you wouldn't show."

"I nearly didn't."

"Where are you staying?"

"What's that got to do with anything?"

"I guess it was social conversation."

"Don't waste it on me."

So she walked with me back to the vault area, where I signed the card and gave the tall black attendant my key. She buzzed the gate open and we followed her back to the aisle where my box was. I pulled it out and took it to one of the little rooms where people clip their coupons, and closed the door. There were two chairs in front of the counter top, a lamp with a green shade, scissors on a chain.

Before I opened the box I took off the rain jacket and pushed my sleeves up. I showed her my hands were empty, then opened the box lid and reached in and took out the letters, took Puss's from the thin stack and handed it to her. Then I told her to wait a moment. I took some other things out of the box and said, as I showed them to her, "This is a picture of your paternal grandfather standing beside his automobile long ago. It is an Essex. This is a picture of your paternal grandmother sitting on the steps of a vacation cottage on a lake you never heard of. This is your uncle, who died young. And this is a picture of your mother."

She had been feigning indifference until I showed her Puss's picture. She took it from me and read the inscription aloud, "Chocolate peanut butter love." She looked at me in question.

"A private joke."

"She was lovely, really lovely!"

"Now if you wouldn't mind reading the letter aloud? Careful unfolding it. The paper has cracked in a couple of places."

"Why should I read it aloud?"

"Because your voice quality is a lot like hers."

She shrugged, unfolded it, began reading.

Old dear darling, I said one time that I would write it down to get it straight for you, and so I have and even have the eerie idea you might be able to read all the words between the words. The name was right. I lied about that. But the town wasn't, and Chicago isn't the town either. And there was no divorce. And I love Paul very dearly and have all along, and love you too, but not quite as much. That lousy Meyer and his lousy Law. Get a pretty girl to kiss Old Ugly and tell him he was absolutely right. You see, my dear, about six months before you met me on the beach with that living pincushion stuck into the sole of my foot, they took a little monster out of my head, maybe as big as an English walnut almost, and with three stumpy little legs like a spider. Half a spider. And the men in white dug around in my head to try to find every little morsel of the beast, because he turned out to be the bad kind. So . . . I got over confusions and got my memory all straightened out again, and my hair grew back, and I pinned an old buddy of mine to the wall of his office and he leveled because he has known me long enough to know I have enough sawdust to keep me solid. His guess was one chance out of fifty. No treatments possible. Just go off and get checked every so often, bright lights in the eyes, stand and touch the tip of your nose with your fingertip while keeping the eyes closed. That stuff. And pens drawing lines on little electric charts. I could accept it, my dear, because life is very iffy and I have busied up my years in good ways. But I could not accept the kind of life that went with the waiting. Dear as Paul is, he is a sentimental kraut type, and we had the awareness of the damned time bomb every waking moment. So life became like a practice funeral, with too many of our friends knowing it, and everybody trying to be so bloody sweet and compassionate during a long farewell party. I began to think that if I lucked out, I'd be letting them down. So I finally told Paul that if it was the end of my life, it was getting terribly damned dreary and full of violin music, and I am a random jolly type who does not care to be stared at by people with their eyes filling with tears. So I cashed in the bonds for the education of the children I'll never have, and I came a-hunting and I found you. Was I too eager to clamber into the sack? Too greedy to fill every day with as much life as would fit into it? Dar-

ling, I am the grasshopper sort, and so are you, and, bless you, there were dozens of times every day I would completely forget to sort of listen to what might be happening inside my redheaded skull. Be glad you jollied and romped the redheaded lady as she was coming around the clubhouse turn, heading for the tape. She loved it. And you. And how good we were together, in a way that was not a disloyalty to Paul! He is one of the dogged and steadfast ones. Can you imagine being married, dear, to Janine, great as she is, and having her know you could be fatally ill? She would mother you out of your mind until you ran. As I ran. But there was the little nagging feeling I was having it all too good. I kept telling myself, Hell, girl, you deserve it. And then hairy old Meyer and his damned Law about the hard thing to do is the right thing to do. I suppose you have been wondering about me and maybe hating me a little. I had to run from you exactly when I did and how I did, or I couldn't have left at all. You see, the dying have a special obligation too, my dear. To keep it from being too selfish. I was depriving Paul of his chance of being with me, because it is all he is going to have of me . . . all he did have of me, and I was forgetting that I had to leave him enough to last him long enough to get him past the worst of it at least. The darling has not done the interrogation bit, and if he thinks or doesn't think there was a man in the scene, I couldn't really say. You would like each other. Anyway, the female of the species is the eternal matchmaker, and I have written the longest letter of my life to Janine, all full of girl talk, and about living and dying, and I have, I hope, conned her into spinning a big fancy pack of lies about the Strange Vacation of Puss Killian, because I am leaving her name and address with

*Paul, saying that she could tell him how I was and what
happened among people who didn't know. It is a devi-
ous plot, mostly because they would work well. He is a
research chemist, and perhaps the kindest man alive.
Anyway, last week all of a sudden the pupil of my big
gorgeous left eye got twice as big as it should, and they
have been checking and testing and giving me glassy
smiles, and I am mailing this en route to the place where
they are going to open a trapdoor and take another
look. So they may clap the lid back on and say the hell
with it. Or they may go in there and, without meaning
to, speed me on my journey, or they may turn me into
a vegetable, or they may manage to turn me back into
me for another time, shorter or longer. But from the
talk around the store, the odds on that last deal make
the old odds seem like a sure thing bet. Do you understand now? I'm scared. Of course I'm scared. It's real
black out there and it lasts a long time. But I have no
remorses, no regrets, because I left when I had to, and
Meyer got me back in good season. Don't do any
brooding, because if I can try to be a grownup, you
ought to be able to take a stab at it. Here's what you
do, Trav my darling. Find yourself a gaudy random
gorgeous grasshopper wench, and lay aboard the Plym-
outh and the provisions, and go fun-timing and sun-
timing up and down the lovely bays. Find one of good
appetite and no thought of it being for keeps, and romp
the lassie sweetly and completely, and now and again,
when she is asleep and you are awake, and your arms
are around her and you are sleeping like spoons, with
her head tucked under your ugly chin, pretend it
is . . .*

Puss, who loved you.

At first it had been a mechanical reading, but then she slowed. The words had almost too much meaning for her to handle. And for me to handle. I had closed my eyes for a little while pretending it was Puss. But that was too much for me, and I had to watch Jean as she read, watch the slow tears, listen to the breaking voice.

Without looking at me she folded it and put it back in the box and said, "Can we get out of here? Can we walk?"

We walked. She had the same good long stride Puss bequeathed her. We walked back to the beach, where the hard rain had pocked all the footprints out of the sand above high mean tide. The wind-driven waves curled and smacked. Kids were out there, vague in the rain curtain, surfing. Some G-stringed joggers passed us. No talk. I knew she would talk when she was ready.

Finally we sat on one of the small fat fences that keep the parked cars off the beach. The rain was easing.

"They did a caesarian in the eighth month when they knew she was slipping away. She was too far gone for labor. She died the next day. I . . . I just didn't *know* all this!"

"She must have told her sister something about how she . . . about how it was like between us."

She thought that over, frowning. "Maybe she did. I guess she probably did. Maybe she told her husband too. From what Velma said, he was really great to my mother after she came back. But he couldn't handle having me. The arithmetic was all wrong. Child of unknown person. He fixed it with Velma to raise me with her batch. Look, I love Velma and all my half brothers and sisters. She didn't treat me differently at all. Not in any way. She's great. He sent money all the years, what he thought was fair. More as prices went up. I've never met him. I think he's a fine person. I can understand him not wanting me as a kid. I wasn't his kid."

"I never knew she was pregnant. I never knew she was dying."

"I know that now, McGee. I thought you knew all that stuff. I thought you just didn't want to be involved. Let me tell you something I wish they'd never told me. No. Cross that out. I'm glad Velma told me. Puss hurt a lot. Some of the stuff they wanted to give her for pain would have hurt the baby inside her. Me. So she stiffed it out alone. For my sake. Loved me."

She bent over, face against her knees. She made a small sound of grief, lost in the surf crashing and hissing.

Carefully, gently, I put my hand on her shoulder. "Maybe Velma lied about me because she didn't want to lose you. She didn't want you to get some kind of romantic image of your beach-bum father and come looking for me, ever. She know you're here?"

She straightened and looked at me with reddened eyes. "Oh, no. She thinks I'm visiting a girlfriend in Santa Barbara."

"Where is home?"

"Youngstown, Ohio. I graduated high school last June."

"You graduated *from* high school."

She gave me a crooked, tear-stained smile. "Old Dad takes over the grammar, huh?"

"Takes over whatever he can take over. Whatever you'll let him take over. Have you been working?"

"At a Charming Shoppe. It's a chain. I worked through Christmas and quit. Look, can I have a copy of that letter? To keep?"

"Why not? We'll walk back and get a copy made at the bank."

She looked at me, her head tilted, her expression puzzled. "You know. I feel as if I've just gotten over being sick, sick a long time. I used to dream about you dying. You were always fat and bald."

you live, and I've been planning this for three years. I wanted to make you feel so guilty you'd kill yourself. But you d-didn't even know what the c-cats meant."

"How old are you?"

"Seventeen in April. What's that got to do with anything?"

I moved over to the chair by the built-in desk, put my foot up on it, rested my forearms on my knee and studied her. She sat on the yellow couch, out on the edge of it, fists clenched, returning my inspection, meeting my gaze, showing me her contempt, her hate.

"I had the feeling there was something wrong with Puss. But I never realized she was sick."

"Or pregnant. Sure. You just never realized."

"Do you want me to try to tell you a little bit about this, kid, or do you want to step on everything I say?"

"There's nothing you can say."

"Do you want to know how I met her?"

"Not particularly, Mr. McGee."

I sighed. "Kid, I just wish you . . ."

"Stop calling me kid!"

"Okay. Jean, then. I was running on the beach one morning. Puss had stepped on a sea urchin in shallow water. She came hobbling and hopping ashore, in obvious trouble. Okay, so I got the spines out and brought her over here and got her heel fixed up. She was . . . a lot of fun."

"Lots of fun, huh? A great sport, huh?"

"Merry is the word. A big random redhead who believed the world was mad. A loving person. Her mind and her speech went off at funny tangents. It made some people irritable. Not me."

"Oh, no. Certainly not you!"

"Kid. Jean. I am talking about your mother and you never got to know her. Maybe you want to know a little bit about her."

"Not from you!"

"She was with me for a few months. She stayed aboard this houseboat with me. I was involved in something at the time. A friend of mine had been killed. Tush Bannon. Some people wanted his land. In the process of finding out who killed him and why, some other people got killed and got badly hurt. Puss was especially good with Janine, Tush's widow. Sometimes she would . . . go off somewhere inside herself, out of touch. It seemed odd. Meyer—he's my best friend—"

"I know."

"He noticed it too. We talked about it and we decided it was probably something about her divorce."

"What divorce? She was never divorced."

"So I found out."

She stood up. "What's the point of all this? You'd lie to me. You lied to her. You'd lie to anybody, wouldn't you? After I watched you walk by me on the beach, I knew you're my father. I was hoping you weren't. I can't make you sorry because you haven't got any conscience at all. And that is giving me some pretty wonderful thoughts about my heredity, Dad. Sorry I went to all the trouble. You aren't even worth that much. You are so smooth and plausible, you make me sick. You worked a scam on her, but it won't work on me."

"Hate is poison, Jean."

"It nourishes me."

"I have a farewell letter from your mother."

"So?"

"Do you hate her so much you don't even want to read it?"

"I never said I hated her!"

"What is your opinion of her?"

"Okay, I guess she wasn't very smart about people. Why should I tell you my opinion of her?"

"I want to know why you are afraid to read her letter to me."

"Afraid? Bullshit! Let me see it."

"It's one of the few things in my life worth keeping in a safety-deposit box."

"I bet."

"The bank is closed. It will open tomorrow morning at ten. I don't want you to think I have any possible way of tricking you. I had no idea you existed, so I couldn't have faked a letter in expectation you'd show up someday." I wrote the name and address of the bank on a slip of paper. "Meet me there at ten in the morning."

"I don't want to meet you anywhere ever."

I took the chance. "Okay. Then don't bother. I'll be there in case you change your mind. In case you decide it might be nice to know something more about your mother than you do. It'll be a better check on your heredity, kid. Now get out. Tomorrow you might grow up a little, and when you do, then I'll want to talk to you. But not now, not the way you are now. Good night."

I matched her flat and level stare until she spun and left. I had detected no uncertainty in her. I felt that maybe the gamble had failed and I had lost her. I went out slowly and saw her, far down the pier, walking swiftly under the dock lights.

I wanted to tell Meyer, but not yet. Not now. I didn't want to tell anybody while I was still trying to comprehend what had happened to me. I saw the cat she had been trying to leave. It had been flattened in our little fracas. I straightened it out, went in and put it with the others.

I could recall every plane and texture of her face, recall the timbre of her voice, the style of her movements—all in sweetly excruciating detail. Some strange mechanism in my head was projecting color slides of all the familiar parts of my life. I seemed to hear the click as each slide fell into place. Everything familiar had assumed a different shape, sharper outlines, purer kind of color. It seemed very much to me like the strangeness which happens after you have spent weeks in a hospital, when you come back out again into the world, seeing everything fresh—a stop light, a brown dog, a yellow bus. Something has changed the world and washed it clean.

I paced the lounge and paced the sun deck half the night, thinking about her, wondering if she would be there. I knew she had to be there. If Puss and I had given her anything at all, it would be a sense of fairness.

When the hard winds of change blow through your life, they blow away a lot of structures you thought permanent, exposing what you had thought was trivia, buried and forgotten. The sweet soft taste of the side of the throat of Puss Killian. The rough and husky edge of her voice as her laughter stopped. The small things are lasting things.

21

Friday came in with a hard winter rain and a steady wind. I awoke with the conviction I would never see her again. She was half real and half imagined. I was too restless to have anything but coffee, too edgy to keep my attention on any small manufactured boat chore. Wind tilted and creaked the houseboat again and again.

Finally I put on foul-weather gear, a complete set, with hood, in that electric orange-red of the gloves and flags they wave at you at road construction sites. It is useful when anyone falls overboard in heavy weather, to become the only dot of color in a steep gray surging world.

I started walking so early I was at the bank by nine-fifteen, and I knew that if I tried to just stand there and wait, I would be maniacal by ten o'clock. So I went striding past the bank and kept walking for a measured twenty-three minutes. A mile and something. Turned on the mark and came back. But got to the bank at five of ten. Had I found shelter in the entrance I wouldn't be able to see her coming. So I stood out in the rain. It made such a deafening clatter against the crisp plastic of the hood I could not hear the traffic sounds. I kept turning my head like a man at a tennis match, because I did not know from which direction she would arrive.

Ten o'clock. Five after. Ten after. And I knew it had been a bad gamble. From the two of us she would have gotten an unforgiving stubbornness, stronger than the sense of fair play. The rain was heavier. It bounced high off the asphalt, an eight-inch curtain fringe of lonely silver rain. I could stand there until it ended and nothing would change.

She came moments later at a hard run, with a transparent raincoat over sweater and jeans, her hair tucked into a shower cap. Her face looked set and pallid, her lips almost colorless. We went in and stood over at one side, dripping on their giant rug. I pushed my hood back and she pulled her shower cap off and shook her hair out.

"So we play your game, Mr. McGee, whatever it is."

"I was beginning to think you wouldn't show."

"I nearly didn't."

"Where are you staying?"

"What's that got to do with anything?"

"I guess it was social conversation."

"Don't waste it on me."

So she walked with me back to the vault area, where I signed the card and gave the tall black attendant my key. She buzzed the gate open and we followed her back to the aisle where my box was. I pulled it out and took it to one of the little rooms where people clip their coupons, and closed the door. There were two chairs in front of the counter top, a lamp with a green shade, scissors on a chain.

Before I opened the box I took off the rain jacket and pushed my sleeves up. I showed her my hands were empty, then opened the box lid and reached in and took out the letters, took Puss's from the thin stack and handed it to her. Then I told her to wait a moment. I took some other things out of the box and said, as I showed them to her, "This is a picture of your paternal grandfather standing beside his automobile long ago. It is an Essex. This is a picture of your paternal grandmother sitting on the steps of a vacation cottage on a lake you never heard of. This is your uncle, who died young. And this is a picture of your mother."

She had been feigning indifference until I showed her Puss's picture. She took it from me and read the inscription aloud, "Chocolate peanut butter love." She looked at me in question.

"A private joke."

"She was lovely, really lovely!"

"Now if you wouldn't mind reading the letter aloud? Careful unfolding it. The paper has cracked in a couple of places."

"Why should I read it aloud?"

"Because your voice quality is a lot like hers."

She shrugged, unfolded it, began reading.

Old dear darling, I said one time that I would write it down to get it straight for you, and so I have and even have the eerie idea you might be able to read all the words between the words. The name was right. I lied about that. But the town wasn't, and Chicago isn't the town either. And there was no divorce. And I love Paul very dearly and have all along, and love you too, but not quite as much. That lousy Meyer and his lousy Law. Get a pretty girl to kiss Old Ugly and tell him he was absolutely right. You see, my dear, about six months before you met me on the beach with that living pincushion stuck into the sole of my foot, they took a little monster out of my head, maybe as big as an English walnut almost, and with three stumpy little legs like a spider. Half a spider. And the men in white dug around in my head to try to find every little morsel of the beast, because he turned out to be the bad kind. So . . . I got over confusions and got my memory all straightened out again, and my hair grew back, and I pinned an old buddy of mine to the wall of his office and he leveled because he has known me long enough to know I have enough sawdust to keep me solid. His guess was one chance out of fifty. No treatments possible. Just go off and get checked every so often, bright lights in the eyes, stand and touch the tip of your nose with your fingertip while keeping the eyes closed. That stuff. And pens drawing lines on little electric charts. I could accept it, my dear, because life is very iffy and I have busied up my years in good ways. But I could not accept the kind of life that went with the waiting. Dear as Paul is, he is a sentimental kraut type, and we had the awareness of the damned time bomb every waking moment. So life became like a practice funeral, with too many of our friends knowing it, and everybody trying to be so bloody sweet and compassionate during a long farewell party. I began to think that if I lucked out, I'd be letting them down. So I finally told Paul that if it was the end of my life, it was getting terribly damned dreary and full of violin music, and I am a random jolly type who does not care to be stared at by people with their eyes filling with tears. So I cashed in the bonds for the education of the children I'll never have, and I came a-hunting and I found you. Was I too eager to clamber into the sack? Too greedy to fill every day with as much life as would fit into it? Dar-

ling, I am the grasshopper sort, and so are you, and, bless you, there were dozens of times every day I would completely forget to sort of listen to what might be happening inside my redheaded skull. Be glad you jollied and romped the redheaded lady as she was coming around the clubhouse turn, heading for the tape. She loved it. And you. And how good we were together, in a way that was not a disloyalty to Paul! He is one of the dogged and steadfast ones. Can you imagine being married, dear, to Janine, great as she is, and having her know you could be fatally ill? She would mother you out of your mind until you ran. As I ran. But there was the little nagging feeling I was having it all too good. I kept telling myself, Hell, girl, you deserve it. And then hairy old Meyer and his damned Law about the hard thing to do is the right thing to do. I suppose you have been wondering about me and maybe hating me a little. I had to run from you exactly when I did and how I did, or I couldn't have left at all. You see, the dying have a special obligation too, my dear. To keep it from being too selfish. I was depriving Paul of his chance of being with me, because it is all he is going to have of me . . . all he did have of me, and I was forgetting that I had to leave him enough to last him long enough to get him past the worst of it at least. The darling has not done the interrogation bit, and if he thinks or doesn't think there was a man in the scene, I couldn't really say. You would like each other. Anyway, the female of the species is the eternal matchmaker, and I have written the longest letter of my life to Janine, all full of girl talk, and about living and dying, and I have, I hope, conned her into spinning a big fancy pack of lies about the Strange Vacation of Puss Killian, because I am leaving her name and address with

*Paul, saying that she could tell him how I was and what
happened among people who didn't know. It is a devi-
ous plot, mostly because they would work well. He is a
research chemist, and perhaps the kindest man alive.
Anyway, last week all of a sudden the pupil of my big
gorgeous left eye got twice as big as it should, and they
have been checking and testing and giving me glassy
smiles, and I am mailing this en route to the place where
they are going to open a trapdoor and take another
look. So they may clap the lid back on and say the hell
with it. Or they may go in there and, without meaning
to, speed me on my journey, or they may turn me into
a vegetable, or they may manage to turn me back into
me for another time, shorter or longer. But from the
talk around the store, the odds on that last deal make
the old odds seem like a sure thing bet. Do you understand now? I'm scared. Of course I'm scared. It's real
black out there and it lasts a long time. But I have no
remorses, no regrets, because I left when I had to, and
Meyer got me back in good season. Don't do any
brooding, because if I can try to be a grownup, you
ought to be able to take a stab at it. Here's what you
do, Trav my darling. Find yourself a gaudy random
gorgeous grasshopper wench, and lay aboard the Plym-
outh and the provisions, and go fun-timing and sun-
timing up and down the lovely bays. Find one of good
appetite and no thought of it being for keeps, and romp
the lassie sweetly and completely, and now and again,
when she is asleep and you are awake, and your arms
are around her and you are sleeping like spoons, with
her head tucked under your ugly chin, pretend it
is . . .*

Puss, who loved you.

At first it had been a mechanical reading, but then she slowed. The words had almost too much meaning for her to handle. And for me to handle. I had closed my eyes for a little while pretending it was Puss. But that was too much for me, and I had to watch Jean as she read, watch the slow tears, listen to the breaking voice.

Without looking at me she folded it and put it back in the box and said, "Can we get out of here? Can we walk?"

We walked. She had the same good long stride Puss bequeathed her. We walked back to the beach, where the hard rain had pocked all the footprints out of the sand above high mean tide. The wind-driven waves curled and smacked. Kids were out there, vague in the rain curtain, surfing. Some G-stringed joggers passed us. No talk. I knew she would talk when she was ready.

Finally we sat on one of the small fat fences that keep the parked cars off the beach. The rain was easing.

"They did a caesarian in the eighth month when they knew she was slipping away. She was too far gone for labor. She died the next day. I . . . I just didn't *know* all this!"

"She must have told her sister something about how she . . . about how it was like between us."

She thought that over, frowning. "Maybe she did. I guess she probably did. Maybe she told her husband too. From what Velma said, he was really great to my mother after she came back. But he couldn't handle having me. The arithmetic was all wrong. Child of unknown person. He fixed it with Velma to raise me with her batch. Look, I love Velma and all my half brothers and sisters. She didn't treat me differently at all. Not in any way. She's great. He sent money all the years, what he thought was fair. More as prices went up. I've never met him. I think he's a fine person. I can understand him not wanting me as a kid. I wasn't his kid."

"I never knew she was pregnant. I never knew she was dying."

"I know that now, McGee. I thought you knew all that stuff. I thought you just didn't want to be involved. Let me tell you something I wish they'd never told me. No. Cross that out. I'm glad Velma told me. Puss hurt a lot. Some of the stuff they wanted to give her for pain would have hurt the baby inside her. Me. So she stiffed it out alone. For my sake. Loved me."

She bent over, face against her knees. She made a small sound of grief, lost in the surf crashing and hissing.

Carefully, gently, I put my hand on her shoulder. "Maybe Velma lied about me because she didn't want to lose you. She didn't want you to get some kind of romantic image of your beach-bum father and come looking for me, ever. She know you're here?"

She straightened and looked at me with reddened eyes. "Oh, no. She thinks I'm visiting a girlfriend in Santa Barbara."

"Where is home?"

"Youngstown, Ohio. I graduated high school last June."

"You graduated *from* high school."

She gave me a crooked, tear-stained smile. "Old Dad takes over the grammar, huh?"

"Takes over whatever he can take over. Whatever you'll let him take over. Have you been working?"

"At a Charming Shoppe. It's a chain. I worked through Christmas and quit. Look, can I have a copy of that letter? To keep?"

"Why not? We'll walk back and get a copy made at the bank."

She looked at me, her head tilted, her expression puzzled. "You know. I feel as if I've just gotten over being sick, sick a long time. I used to dream about you dying. You were always fat and bald."

"At times I have a fat bald disposition. Look, Jean. It's just the same for me. That strange feeling."

"How can it mean anything much to you? You never knew I was alive even."

I reached for her and she put her hands in mine. "I don't know if I can say this. It means more than I can say. It turns my life upside down. It changes a lot of things I thought I was. It's some kind of a door opening for me. We've got lots of plans to make."

"I said rotten things to you last night."

"And enough of them were true."

"No. Now I know what you're really like. Puss is telling me in that letter what you're like. She didn't know she was telling her daughter anything, but she was."

And we walked back slowly, talking all the way. There was a lifetime of good talk ahead of us. There was another feeling I had about myself more difficult to grasp. In the last few years I had been ever more uncomfortably aware that one day, somewhere, I would take one last breath and a great iron door would slam shut, leaving me in darkness on the wrong side of life. But now there was a window in that door. A promise of light. A way to continue.

It is May, early May, a lovely time of year in Florida. We have taken the *Busted Flush* north up the Waterway to a place where it opens into a broad bay. I have dropped the hooks at a calm anchorage well away from the channel and far enough from the mangrove coast to let the south breeze keep the spring bugs away.

We brought aboard pungent cauldrons of Meyer's Special Incomparable Chili, and enough icy beer to make the chili less lethal. How many of us are there? Twenty? Thirty? Let's say a lot. Jim Ames and Betsy. The Thorners, Teneros,

Arthur and Chook Wilkinson, the Mick and Carlie Hooper, Junebug, Lew, Roxy, Sue Sampson, Sandy, Johnny Dow, Briney, Frank and Gretch Payne, Miguel, the Marchmans, Marilee, Sam Dandie with two nieces, and a leavening of beach folks, and two dogs and a cat, dutifully ignoring one another.

We are here, and there is music and there are bad jokes, and so we are all a little bit longer in the tooth and have seen life go up, down and sideways without any rhyme or reason anyone can determine. We laugh at tired old jokes because they are old and tired and familiar, and it is good to laugh.

I am prone on a large sun pad on the bow, beside that incomparable bikinied, sun-lush figure of Briney, who'd been on loan to Willy Nucci until he breathed his last.

I am staring at four small freckles on the outside top of her left shoulder, four inches from my nose. Connect the dots and find the farmer's cat. The freckles are brown against gold, and there is a fuzz of tiny white peach hairs, almost too fine to be visible.

"What are all these people doing in our home, sweetheart?" she asks drowsily.

"We invited them all, every one."

"Oh?" she says. "That's nice."

"Figuring on staying a while?"

"Too long already, love. Gotta get back out to the big surf, ride the dark blue tunnel under the big white curl. Don't let it get you. Bam, you're out. Hey, two more weeks, then gone. No regrets."

Somebody brings us two cold beers. Briney rolls up onto an elbow and drinks with her eyes closed. I lift my beer and say, "To Willy."

She grins and says, "To the Nooch."

In a little while she is asleep, beer half gone. I study the amount of tan on her smooth broad back and I peer at the angle of the sun and decide she's in no danger of burning. In a momentary flash of panic I believe the gaudy boat, the noisy people, everything is dead and gone, imagined long ago and forgotten. It passes.

I get up and go ambling back through the folk. A great day. I find Meyer up on the sun deck leaning against the aft rail, alone for a change. He is now Uncle Meyer, a dispensation from my daughter Jean which pleased him immensely.

We talk about Jean, about her latest letter. "You two get talked out before she left?" he asks.

"There's a couple of years of talk to make up," I say. "We'll have time. You get a chance to look over the trust agreement Frank sent you?"

"Good work," he says. "As a trustee I can vote to invade the principal in case of emergency. Sound."

"She got one hell of a score on her college boards."

"Three times you've told me, Travis."

"And she's a horse bum. Imagine that? A horse bum from Youngstown who is going to go to a school of veterinary medicine eventually. Imagine me, fathering a horse bum from Youngstown?"

"Travis, she is handsome. She is tough and good and staunch."

I look at him. It strikes me that he has not been surly or hostile at any time. Lately I have been bringing out the worst in people. No more.

He seems to know what I am thinking. "How much went into the trust?" he asks.

"Everything!" I say.

He stares in consternation. "Everything? Everything?"

"Well, I saved out about four hundred bucks, and so I've got to scramble around and find some salvage work real soon."

He puts his hand on my arm, beams at me and says, "Welcome to the world."

A NOTE ON THE TYPE

This book was set on the Linotype in Janson, a recutting made directly from type cast from matrices long thought to have been made by the Dutchman Anton Janson, who was a practicing type founder in Leipzig during the years 1668–87. However, it has been conclusively demonstrated that these types are actually the work of Nicholas Kis (1650–1702), a Hungarian, who most probably learned his trade from the master Dutch type founder Dirk Voskens. The type is an excellent example of the influential and sturdy Dutch types that prevailed in England up to the time William Caslon developed his own incomparable designs from them.

Composed by Maryland Linotype Composition Co., Baltimore, Maryland

Printed and bound by Fairfield Graphics, Fairfield, Pennsylvania

Typography and binding design by Dorothy Schmiderer